AND MY SHOES
keep walking back to you

AND MY SHOES
keep walking back to you

A NOVEL

Kathi Kamen Goldmark

CHRONICLE BOOKS
SAN FRANCISCO

Page 320 constitutes a continuation of the copyright page.
All song lyrics copyright © individual authors.

"My Shoes Keep Walking Back to You" by Lee Ross and Bob Wills © 1956 (Renewed) Unichappell Music Inc. All rights reserved. Used by permission. Warner Bros. Publications U.S., Inc., Miami, FL 33014

This is a work of fiction. Names, places, characters, and incidents are products of the author's imagination or are used fictionally.

Library of Congress Cataloging-in-Publication Data available.

ISBN 0-8118-3495-6

Manufactured in the United States of America

Book and cover design by Benjamin Shaykin
Composition by Kristen Wurz
Typeset in Stempel Garamond, Cg Behemoth, Knockout, and Altast Greeting

Distributed in Canada by Raincoast Books
9050 Shaughnessy Street
Vancouver, British Columbia V6P 6E5

10 9 8 7 6 5 4 3 2 1

Chronicle Books LLC
85 Second Street
San Francisco, California 94105
www.chroniclebooks.com

I must say that I don't care,
hold my head up in the air
Tell my friends I'm glad that you don't call
But when the day is through,
my heartaches start anew
And that's when I miss you most of all
My arms keep reaching for you,
my eyes keep searching for you
My lips keep calling for you,
and my shoes keep walking back to you

—LEE ROSS and BOB WILLS

Part One

≈ 1993 ≈

Chapter

1

THE LAST TIME I STOOD ON HOT ASPHALT AND breathed diesel fumes and french fry grease, I was wearing torn cutoffs and an extra-large George Thorogood and the Destroyers T-shirt. And even though I knew better, I was flirting with the rhythm guitar player over the rim of a Styrofoam cup, on our last pit stop just before rolling into Nashville.

I was one of three backup singers on Cindi-Lu Bender's Magnolia Heart tour, living the lyrics to all my favorite road songs. Each night, I got dressed up, stood onstage, and sang gentle *oohs* and *aahs* behind America's biggest country music star, backed by a kick-ass band and the world's best road crew.

It was part of the show to have a blonde, a brunette, and a redhead on background vocals. Kathleen was the tall, cool blonde; Amy the petite, dark-eyed brunette; and me, Sarah Jean, all curves and curls, flaming red, with a little help from Clairol's Auburn Rain mixed with henna. In the teasing way of bandmates, the guys often told us that combined, the three of us boasted the physical attributes of a "perfect ten"—Kathleen's long beautiful legs, Amy's cute little butt, and my impressive cleavage, all terrifically showcased in our one-size-too-small stage costumes.

Our band bus was a deluxe Silver Eagle with cigarette burns in the Naugahyde upholstery and *Magnolia Heart* painted on the outside in huge purple letters next to Cindi-Lu's dimpled bouffant smile. (She wasn't smiling when she discovered that the bus and the album and the tour were supposed to be called "Magnolia *Hart*," the title of the original song by Nashville hitmeister K. N. Right. But it was cheaper to leave the misspelling, and after a while her fans just thought Cindi-Lu was being clever and subtle.) We stopped often enough that the dysfunctional toilet didn't really bother anyone. The broken radio was a nuisance since it would have been fun to hear ourselves promoted on local radio stations, but we had a boom box and great tapes, mostly vintage country and soul. We also had air-conditioning, a TV, bunk beds, a microwave, and a VCR, so we weren't exactly roughing it. That last day, I'd been on tour for almost a year, a proud and seasoned road warrior. And I was smart enough to know there was absolutely nothing wrong with my life.

I even liked Cindi-Lu, the two times I met her. That might sound strange since I was in her band, but she didn't travel with the rest of us and never used the shared dressing rooms or backstage hospitality areas. I don't know what it's like in other country superstars' road bands, but in ours there wasn't much fraternizing with the help. Unless we were actually onstage together, she kept to herself.

During the show, Cindi-Lu treated us like girlfriends, as though we'd known one another since grade-school jump-rope games, and it just happened to be her turn that night to be lead singer. The way she teased and played with us, you really would think we were the best of friends. In fact, much was made in the press of our onstage chemistry, an ironic testament to the acting abilities of our star. She was a dynamic performer, adored by her fans. Her set was tightly arranged and rehearsed, down to the apparently spontaneous moment when she tried to play Buddy's pedal steel guitar and broke a fingernail. For me, a bar band veteran coming off years of gigs during which literally anything could happen, including a '67 Chevrolet driving clear through the wall of a nightclub, this took a little getting used to. But our sound guys made sure we got plenty of vocal mix in the monitors, and the parts were simple, so it was easy to relax and sound fine.

We lived for that hour every night when we entered "the zone"—a kind of magical altered state we'd slip into when our performance was on, where we felt totally connected to one another and to the audience, not to mention deep mysteries of the universe. I can't describe it very well, except to say there was no question about whether we were in or out of the zone, and the three of us seemed to hit it together. When we were there, our ears were wide open and our harmonies and movements shimmered. It was as close as we ever got to church.

To be part of an act that thousands of people yelled and stomped and wept for every night, even as a backup singer, was an unbelievable experience. We'd stand in the wings sweaty and grinning before the encore, hearing the hungry sounds of a crowd that couldn't get enough of her—of us—and wait a dramatic moment before running back out onstage. The shouts would turn into one huge rafter-shattering scream while the achingly lonely acoustic guitar introduction to "Magnolia Heart" began. We'd lock into our gorgeous three-part harmony as Cindi-Lu walked to the edge of the stage, one single "tear" ever so slightly smudging her mascara. She'd bow her head, then look up, bright eyes moist and shining, and sing the shit out of that song. We always finished with something up-tempo, the only variable in the entire set. Then the show would end, she'd disappear with her manager, Cal Hooper, and we wouldn't see her again until the next city.

Cal was his own very special piece of work. A brilliant Nashville barracuda, he wasn't exactly what you'd call good with people. You could tell he had once been quite handsome, and he dressed as though he were still a cute young stud, spangled shirts stretched across sagging belly. Perpetually red-faced, sweaty, and upset about something, he kept a professional distance from the band and concentrated on Cindi-Lu, with one notable exception. Cal had a weakness for peppermint schnapps, and overindulged every month or so, resulting in a peculiar fixation on oral sex. He'd start pounding on all of our doors, usually very late at night, demanding blow jobs. I have to say it wasn't exactly pleasant or flattering to be the chosen target—we all learned to use the double security locks and ignore his drunken, pathetic requests. Luckily, when Cal wasn't drinking schnapps we had very little contact with him. The musical director rehearsed us and the tour manager filled us in on the schedule and other details, and they were great guys.

That last night my heart might have known something was going to happen, but unfortunately my head wasn't clued in. The hotel bar was closed by the time we got back from the show, and everyone ended up in my room, ready for a party.

I'd developed a system, over many months on the road, for making any hotel room feel like home in five minutes. A couple of glittery scarves thrown over the bedside lamps, a little zebra pillow tossed on the synthetic beige quilted spread, my treasured leopard-print bathrobe draped over the back of a vinyl chair, and a scented candle or two helped me feel a little less lonely in the endless parade of interchangeable rooms. Due to a registration desk snafu, I had been accidentally upgraded—this room was larger and sported a view of the park, as opposed to the parking lot. And it had a minibar. Pretty soon there were at least fifteen sweaty band and crew members sprawled on the bed, chairs, and floor, calling room service and fighting over the TV's remote control.

Sacks of fast-food takeout and a couple of bottles appeared. It's the truth that Wild Turkey on ice from the machine down the hall, in a hotel bathroom glass, can make you a very special kind of stupid. Soon we were strumming guitars, improvising dumb song lyrics to go with the late-night TV infomercials for exercise machines and psychic hotlines, and howling at the moon through my fifth-floor window.

"Drink your H_2O, honey, we don't want to wake up all puffy." Kathleen held out a glass of water, our preferred method of hangover prevention.

"Thanks!" I was drunk enough to wonder if I'd sounded sincere.

"Say," she asked slyly, "what do you think about the new rhythm guitar player?"

"Seems like a good picker. Why do you ask?" I wondered what my pal was getting at. It was unusual for her to ask my opinion before expressing her own.

"Well, he sure seems to be pickin' you," she said with an exaggerated wink.

"What are you talking about?"

"Oh, come on!" She nudged my shoulder. "Bobby Lee hasn't taken his eyes off you all night long."

"Kath, I think you're out of your mind."

"Girlfriend, you must be the only one who hasn't noticed. That boy's got a big old crush on you."

I felt my cheeks turning pink. "Don't be ridiculous. Bobby Lee is nice to everyone."

"Look at you, you're blushing. I think maybe you have a teensy little old crush on him, too," she said, then sauntered off with a glass of water for Amy.

It sounds dumb, but that was all I needed to hear. I suddenly couldn't take *my* eyes off *him*, Bobby Lee Crenshaw, the new guitar guy. But it also seemed crucial to get to Amy before Kathleen started a rumor that would spread through the band like wildfire. I sprinted across the room, nearly tripping over our bass player, and found Amy pulling things out of a greasy paper bag.

"Eat your vegetables, honey." She offered a fried onion ring, the closest thing to a vegetable that I'd seen in weeks.

"Uh, no thanks."

"Oh, come on, you need your fiber. Hey, Kath says you and the new guitar player are madly in love with each other and too stupid to realize it." Her mischievous smile glistened with smudged lipstick and onion ring grease.

"Well, we're not, at least I'm not," I said. "I mean, he's cute and nice and talented and everything, but even if I were, I wouldn't. You know, because of my rule." I thought that was a good enough explanation for the moment.

You see, I had a rule about not getting involved with members of the band, and, except for a couple of lapses early in my undistinguished musical career, I'd found this easier than you'd think. It probably had something to do with the fact that in a band on the road you've all seen each other look your worst and act your crankiest, so it feels way more like brothers and sisters after a while. It had been a long time since I'd had any kind of a boyfriend, even a stupid one-night stand, and I didn't think about it much. Being on tour was almost enough to keep me completely happy. But every now and then, as I saw the others pick up messages from home or reconnect with old lovers in different cities (or, sometimes, both), I wondered if I was missing out on some sort of wildly adventurous rock-and-roll sex life I was supposed to be having.

The truth was Bobby Lee and I had been flirting all day—all week, really. We'd been making an overly casual point of sitting near each other on the bus, hands touching slightly longer than necessary, and I sometimes caught him looking at me in a goofy way. He was definitely cute, with wavy auburn hair and gray eyes and a wonderful smile. I liked his sense of humor and the fact that he read books instead of always joining the other guys' endless card games and porn marathons. Something was happening between us that seemed crucial to ignore, at least as long as we were both on the Magnolia Heart band bus.

I was determined to stick to my not-getting-involved rule, but sometimes (not that this would be related in any way to the consumption of vats of Wild Turkey or anything) you're not in total control of your own feelings, you know? It can be instantaneous, like Cupid's arrow. That moment you're hit with the awareness of having a crush can be counted on to transform your evening, at the very least. But Cupid as a sweet little cherub is diabolically misleading—I've always pictured him more along the lines of Alfred E. Neuman with a cherry bomb, the Crush Bomb that can detonate at any moment. That was the night the Crush Bomb hit me.

Bobby Lee suddenly looked so good to me, he was practically glowing. Some internal adolescent radar-magnet in my brain was conscious of his whereabouts in the room every second. There he was, courteously handing a beer to Buddy's girlfriend, then laughing at one of Lester's stupid jokes. I wasn't paying attention to what Kathleen was saying to me; I was too busy tracking his movements, and when he dashed across the hall to his room to get his guitar, I literally stopped breathing till he came back. Then he casually draped his arm around Linda the wardrobe lady's shoulder, and I quietly decided to have her killed. When someone put one of my prized country compilation tapes on the boom box, he kicked off his shoes and with exaggerated politeness walked over and asked me to dance. It was my favorite country shuffle, "Pick Me Up on Your Way Down," by Ray Price. Musicians are terrible dancers as a rule; they spend too much time on the bandstand and not enough on the dance floor. But he was pretty good at the Texas two-step, and the others, laughing, took his lead and started dancing, too, crowding the tiny bit of available floor space. Even though there was barely room to move, we danced well together, and because there was barely room to move, we danced close. We'd all come directly from the show without a chance to shower, and his clothes and skin had absorbed the backstage smell of old beer, stale sweat, and burnt electrical wiring, an aroma I suddenly found intoxicating. I felt that tingly buzz touching his hand, so far gone I could barely look at him, afraid of giving myself away, and I realized I was going to have to be really careful. Either that or I was in for the adventure of a lifetime. How it played out seemed to be up to me.

The song ended, and Bobby Lee turned off the boom box and picked up his guitar. The room grew quiet as he strummed the changes to the Ernest Tubb classic "Waltz Across Texas" and started to sing, looking right at me. So what if we'd been dancing the two-step? I got the message loud and clear: "I could waltz across Texas with you." I've always been a sucker for corny country waltzes, and it was at that moment that I turned completely to jelly.

It was getting so warm I was melting into the floor, but I had to hide it, which was hard because of the way he was looking at me. I could have responded properly in private, but it's a whole other story in front of the entire band and crew. There was no way I could pretend I didn't know this guy was interested, and there was no way I could let him know I was interested back without inviting an avalanche of good-natured teasing for months to come. Kathleen would say I was blushing, but she has a tendency to exaggerate, and as the only married backup singer, she also has tendencies toward the odd vicarious romantic thrill. Pretending I felt flushed from whiskey and dancing and that was all, I grabbed the guitar right after he was done and answered with a silly, flirty version of "Mind Your Own Business," sending my favorite Hank Williams verse, the one about not fooling around at work, his way.

He looked genuinely embarrassed—better him than me, I told myself—but he joined in on the chorus with everyone else, and the fragile, breathless mood was broken.

They all finally left around three A.M. I was walking around turning off lights and brushing my teeth and trying to remember the lyrics to a new song, when I saw them.

His shoes. In my room. At three in the morning. Oh, shit.

And the powers of rationalization being, well, powerful, returning those shoes suddenly took on the most immediate and urgent importance. What would happen, I wondered, if the hotel caught fire and he burned to death because he was looking for his shoes instead of running for the fire escape? What if there was a tidal wave (unlikely in Nashville, but you can't predict such events) or a major earthquake? These things had been known to happen. The man needed his shoes. But given the mood of the last few hours, if I knocked on his door we'd probably start tearing each other's clothes off, and it might be really fun, but there was my famous rule.

I'd seen romances shake up the family dynamic of a band, and frankly it never seemed worth the risk, especially considering the horrible awkwardness of the next morning. Okay, it shouldn't really matter that you suddenly know what he looks like naked, or that he's heard that funny little noise you make without realizing it, or that you both have the same exact hangover and haven't slept and everyone else can tell. But what if we showed up in the hotel coffee shop the next morning and things got incredibly weird? He'd give me a different kind of smile, or maybe—oh no, he'd blush. Or worse, I would. I'd suddenly wonder if he'd think I was crowding him if I plunked myself down at his table, something I've done a dozen times before without a thought. I'd remember a particular moment and suddenly sort of feel him remembering, too, and I wouldn't know where to look. Then because I don't know how to just act normal, I'd end up making some smart-ass remark and see the shadow cross his eyes while he thought of an equally sarcastic comeback. Everyone would think we were not getting along except for Kathleen, who would already have figured everything out and decided it was pretty hilarious, and would maybe even start kicking my legs under the table, as likely as not to be see-through glass. Then the hotel buffet scrambled eggs would turn to paste in my mouth, and the coffee taste suddenly bitter. The worst part would be that we wouldn't feel comfortable flirting anymore.

And then at sound check there would be that one particular song we fell in love over, our eyes meeting at microphone level, pumped up, hot and sweaty from playing. But he'd probably have no awareness of its being our special song and would say something about not liking the chord changes on the bridge, or maybe that he's sick of it altogether. This would be enough to send me weeping to the dressing room, and pretty soon we'd really not be getting along. So it seemed best to avoid getting into this kind of predicament with Bobby Lee Crenshaw.

All this ran through my head as I gingerly picked up the shoes and put them down again. Then I did what any intelligent, confused, drunk, and horny person would do under the circumstances. I stripped down to my panties, sat on the floor, and made a list of everyone in the band and crew, and whether or not I would think twice about returning any of their shoes at three in the morning. I decided that, with the exception of Cindi-Lu and Cal Hooper, I would not hesitate to do so.

This did not help.

I placed the shoes in the middle of the coffee table and walked around them a few times, observing them from every angle, but they didn't express an opinion one way or the other. They were soft brown leather moccasins slightly worn at the heel, and looked like they'd be pretty comfortable anywhere. So I decided to call Amy for advice. She seemed to be the most level-headed and sincere of the three of us, and usually stayed up pretty late. The phone in her room rang three or four times.

"Mmmmmf?" she answered.

"Amy, sorry to wake you. It's Sarah Jean. Listen, if you left your shoes in my room and I just found them, would you want me to bring them back now so you wouldn't have to worry about where they ended up in the morning?"

"Mmmmmf!" she exclaimed, and hung up. I took that as a yes.

Kathleen's answer was pretty much the same as Amy's.

Convinced at last that it was perfectly appropriate behavior, I grabbed my room key, threw on my sweaty old T-shirt, marched across the hall to his door, and knocked.

Well, in the time it had taken me to figure out what I would actually do, he had fallen asleep. And when he stumbled to the door (oh my God! He was wearing . . . the bedspread. Wrapped around his otherwise totally naked body), I held out the shoes as though they were some kind of poison, and made the most fabulously provocative and witty remark I could think of:

"You left your shoes in my room."

"Uh . . . um . . . I was sleeping. Thanks. Want to come in for a minute?"

The next thing I knew, the bedspread was on the floor, we were all tangled up and sweaty, his tongue burning in my mouth, long fingers hot between my legs, and it felt, for just that minute, like coming home.

Chapter
2

IT OCCURRED TO ME IN THE ELEVATOR THE NEXT
morning to agonize over the whole incident, but frankly, I
was feeling too good. Besides, I decided to be way more worried about the next night's gig. We were playing at the Grand Ole
Opry, where the stage is set up in a peculiar way. The audience is
out front as usual, but the really important people—friends, family, record executives, etc.—sit in bleacher seats behind the band,
actually very close up, on the stage. Stuff that normally doesn't
show—a pinned hem, a ripped seam, a butt flabby from months
on a tour bus with too little exercise and too much greasy food—
would be obvious to the most influential and critical observers. At
the Grand Ole Opry, you literally have to watch your back.

Despite the previous night's excesses, Amy, Kathleen, and I
had all been dieting madly in preparation. This was going to be
Cindi-Lu's first Opry appearance since I'd been on the tour and
my first, ever. Another reason, I reminded myself, why it had
been especially stupid to get drunk and stay up all night, though
considering everything, I could have felt a whole lot worse.

This was also an important gig because it was the day that
nominees were to be announced for the upcoming Patsy Awards,

and Cindi-Lu was counting on her fifth Country Legend nomination. The Patsies are held annually in Nashville to honor the memory of the late, great Patsy Cline, and Country Legend is the last award presented, the equivalent of the Motion Picture Academy's Best Picture. If my employer won, she'd be the first ever to take home that particular prize five years in a row. According to Cal, the nomination and the award were in the bag, but even so, he had booked a practice studio for the day and the entire entourage was pretty tense. A van was waiting to take us to rehearsal.

My heart lurched as the elevator doors opened and I saw Bobby Lee standing in the lobby. But he just winked and smiled and handed me a steaming cup of coffee and a room service rose, and it was, well, it was okay; I was relieved that I didn't have too much time to feel awkward.

A hotel employee approached. "Excuse me, you're Sarah Jean Pixlie, aren't you?"

"Yes, I am."

"I have a message for you from Mr. Calbert Hooper. He said to catch you before you leave. He needs to see you right away, in Miss Bender's suite. That's Room 1228."

That was weird. I shrugged, told Bobby Lee I'd catch up with them all later. Hoping Cal hadn't gotten into the schnapps early, I headed upstairs to whatever unpleasantness awaited.

Cal looked even more stressed than usual as he drummed his fingers on the table, his polyester shirt already soaked with sweat. I sat down, sipping my coffee, and waited for him to say something.

"Sarah Jean, thanks for coming up. There's something I need to talk to you about, and it's pretty fucking important." He called down to the front desk, asked them to put a "Do not disturb" on the phone, and started pacing around the room.

"You know, this isn't easy for me. Everyone likes you, and for a chick singer you've always acted like a pro. But stabbing Cindi-Lu in the back like this, well, I'm sure you understand that she is extremely upset."

I didn't know what he was talking about, and it didn't help that I was still a bit dazed and moony from the night before. I tried hard to concentrate on what Cal was saying but kept drifting back to memories of sweet moments with Bobby Lee. Then the thought hit: Bobby Lee, of course! Cindi-Lu must have some sort of a romantic thing going with him. But how did she find out about last night? I had left his room less than an hour before, with barely enough time to throw on a pair of jeans and get downstairs, and Cindi-Lu was known to require her beauty sleep. I didn't get it.

"Cal, gosh, I don't know what to say. I didn't realize . . ." I stammered.

"You didn't realize? Excuse me, sweetheart, but don't you think that's a little naive? Couldn't you have asked Cindi-Lu if she wanted first crack? After all, this is her show."

I couldn't believe it. I had to run everything by Cindi-Lu via Cal? It didn't seem possible that I was the first person on the tour to sleep with someone else in the band, or that management could possibly care one way or the other.

"Look, I didn't know you expected me to check with Cindi—"

"Wake up, Sugar. You know Cindi-Lu comes first. It's just not right to run in behind her back and grab something she's always wanted for herself. The last thing we need is for the star to get upset before this show. Didn't you think of that?"

"What? I'm sorry Cal, but listen. I work hard and I'd do anything within reason, but what I do on my own time is none of your business, and I don't see why I have to ask Miss Country Legend Fancy-Pants first. Speaking of which, it takes two, so why isn't Bobby Lee here if she's so upset about it?"

"What does Bobby Lee have to do with this?" Cal was fuming.

"Well, of course, I mean, I couldn't exactly do it by myself, could I?"

"It was our impression that that's exactly what you did. We had no idea you were involving other band members. This is even worse!"

"Hey, Cal, this doesn't make any sense. Why is it such a great big deal all of a sudden? I don't remember anything in my contract that says Cindi-Lu gets first crack at my lovers."

I got up to leave, planning an indignant door-slamming exit, when Cal started laughing his signature high-pitched whinnying giggle.

"Oh, baby, you're funny," he gasped. I really wasn't in the mood for joking around, especially the kind where someone is laughing his head off at me.

"Okay, want to tell me what this is all about? I'd really appreciate it. Why am I here?"

"Honey, Cindi-Lu doesn't care who you fuck. You can blow the whole band in the hotel lobby if you want to. This is about your song—the little ditty that's been all over the Young Country radio airwaves lately—and your Patsy nomination for Newcomer of the Year."

"My what?"

His voice grew quiet and ice-cold.

"You heard me, Sarah Jean. And don't try the innocent routine with me; it won't work. Have your bags packed in an hour.
We've booked you a flight home. You're fired."

PEOPLE NOT IN THE MUSIC BUSINESS MIGHT WONDER HOW
in the world someone could record a song that was getting
national radio airplay, receive a nomination for the Newcomer of
the Year Patsy, and not know about it. Living in that little road
cocoon keeps you isolated and oblivious to the outside world.
When you're on tour, you're in a different city almost every
night. You get up, get on the bus, get to wherever you're going in
time for sound check, food, and maybe a nap, do the show, get on
the bus, and do the whole thing again. You can easily go days
without reading a newspaper or talking to anyone who isn't on
the tour. That was one of the things I loved about road life; there
was only one important thing to do every day, the show, and
everything else was taken care of. All the stuff that had been going
on with Bobby Lee—the flirting and finally the wild night—had
put me in a goofy state. I realized that I hadn't turned on a C&W
station or read a magazine in weeks, hadn't returned the few messages that had managed to reach me, and was apparently missing
all the excitement of watching my song climb the charts. I was too
busy making goo-goo eyes at a rhythm guitar player.

So here's what had happened. Right before being hired for
the Magnolia Heart tour, I'd recorded a songwriter demo in San
Francisco. The guy who engineered the session liked one of my
songs so much that he played it for another client, a producer
looping a low-budget film in post-production across the hall. It

turned out they were on deadline, desperate for one more tune for the sound track, and mine fit the bill. I signed some papers and forgot all about it once I got caught up in life on the road with Cindi-Lu. I never imagined that the movie would become a surprise hit, the sound-track album one of the biggest-selling records of the year. My song, "Heartaches for a Guy," was getting the kind of radio airplay that can inspire a Patsy nomination. And to make matters worse, according to Cal in his final farewell speech, delivered in a menacing whisper as I was stumbling out the door, Newcomer was the one and only Patsy that Cindi-Lu Bender had never claimed . . . and never could.

All I wanted was to keep from crying until I got back to my room. It was so unfair. I would have loved to let Cindi-Lu record "Heartaches for a Guy," which would have made it a guaranteed hit. But it wasn't that easy to get a song to Cindi-Lu. Friends of friends were constantly slipping demos into my pockets at after-show parties, convinced I could get her to listen and maybe record them. Since we hardly ever saw her except onstage, getting anything to her required considerable effort, and after a while everyone stopped trying. Besides, the sound track was a done deal when I got hired for the tour, and nobody had expected it to do much of anything.

Add getting fired with a hangover, no sleep, and a heart pried open by a night of spectacular sex—it was too much. I collapsed on my bed, a sobbing puddle of runny mascara and unromantic snot. I had just a couple of hours to pack, pick up my last check, and get to the airport, but I couldn't move. The phone rang and rang, but the receiver looked too heavy to pick up. I was sure it would be Kathleen or Amy calling to find out where I was, and I couldn't tell them what had happened without totally losing it.

I didn't want anyone to feel disloyal for running back to rehearsal after hearing I'd been fired. They'd know soon enough, and by then I'd be gone.

Finally finding enough strength to get up and wash my face, I threw some random stuff into my suitcase, left an extravagant ten-dollar tip for the maid, and made my plane by minutes.

It wasn't until turbulence thirty-thousand feet over the Rockies jolted me awake from a restless nap that it hit me— Newcomer of the Year! Holy shit! What if I actually won? Suddenly I couldn't stop laughing, couldn't sit still. Unfortunately, I was in the window seat on a very full plane, next to a handsome older woman in a polyester pantsuit, the kind who spends her spare time doing volunteer work and chuckling over the "Laughs and Gaffes" column in *Reader's Digest.* Her helmet of steel-gray hair was streaked and carefully styled, and didn't move along with the rest of her head. Next to her, on the aisle, a portly man in a business suit tapped away on a small portable computer, oblivious to both of us.

"Are you all right, dear?" asked the woman.

"You know what? I think I am," was my enthusiastic reply.

"That's nice, dear," she replied, and went back to her magazine.

"I mean, yeah. I'm all right. I'm more than all right. I just got fired from the best job I ever had because of some really good news. What do you think of that?"

"That's very nice, dear." The woman sighed quietly, carefully folded down the corner of the page she was reading, and closed her magazine. "Would you like to tell me about it?"

That's how Marge from Omaha, a lifelong good listener on her way to a national meeting of the Presbyterian Women's

Association, got to hear my entire life story: how despite country music credentials that were questionable at best, I'd ended up with a Patsy nomination and a hit record. I started with my mother, who might have been the only East Coast Jewish woman in the rural Oklahoma town where she'd ended up teaching music and drama after a stint in the Peace Corps, and how she met my dad, a fiddle and mandolin virtuoso from Beaumont, Texas, when he came to her school on Career Day between gigs as one of the twin fiddles in the Tex Wilder Swing City Playboys. They fell in love, started their own touring band, and eventually moved west to settle in Lake County, the isolated Northern California community where I grew up. Small-town life was boring for a restless, music-loving teenager, and I successfully begged my parents to let me move in with my aunt Perle in New York so I could go to high school with "real" people. I started my first New York rock band when I was about fifteen. My mom helped me buy a secondhand PA on one of her frequent bagel-fix visits (apparently it's impossible to get a decent bagel west of the Hudson River), and I never looked back. I've been in one band or another ever since.

"My dad said I was a 'good little team player,' and I guess I was," I told Marge. I had to hold back tears as I told her about the year I'd just spent on tour, singing harmony with my two best friends, and how much I'd miss the magical way our voices blended.

"Good for you, dear," she said. "I wish I could say the same about some of the gals in our church choir. Why, you wouldn't believe the bickering over solos, and the shrieking of sopranos trying to outdo each other, getting louder and louder. They could learn a thing or two from you, bless their hearts."

She had just described what my family called "chick-singeritis," the unfortunate disease that tends to attack young female vocalists who, thinking they are the center of the universe, don't understand teamwork, vocal blend, or the concept that the whole can be more than the sum of its parts. My hippie parents might have neglected things like chicken pox vaccines and open school night, but I had been inoculated early and often against this particular disease, information that Marge apparently found delightful. As we straightened our seat backs and tray tables and the crew prepared the aircraft for landing, she patted my arm.

"What a charming young woman you are," she declared. "I simply must ask you something. I once saw Cindi-Lu Bender on a TV show with Billy Ray Cyrus. Have you ever met him in person?"

I told her I had seen him from the wings of the stage but we'd never actually met.

"Oh, that's too bad," she replied. "He's not much of a singer, but I'd sure love to pinch that cute little ass." Marge from Omaha winked, collected her belongings, and with her elegant hairdo and ramrod-straight posture, walked off the plane.

THIS WAS THE FIRST TIME IN MY LIFE I'D EVER BEEN fired, and I didn't even have my own home to go to. I'd given up a cute little San Francisco sublet and arranged to get calls and mail forwarded to my folks. That seemed easier than having to constantly check voice mail, or worry about what was happening to my stuff. So my parents' address was my official home as far as Cindi-Lu's business people were concerned, and they'd been so eager to get rid of me before I had a chance to talk to anyone that they'd booked a flight to San Francisco without asking if I'd prefer New York. As far as I knew, no one was expecting me. I figured I'd rent a car and make the three-hour drive up north by myself. It would give me a chance to catch up with local news and music, and maybe—deliciously—hear my song on the radio for the first time ever. I needed a little time to think things over quietly before entering the warm, chaotic embrace of my family.

Which is why I almost walked right past Aunt Perle, waiting for me with a bouquet of wilting roses, at SFO.

"Sarah Jean Pixlie! Who do you think you are, young lady, ignoring your old auntie?" she shrieked, jumping up and down in her hot-pink Reeboks.

A relentless New Yorker, Aunt Perle had been a semipro athlete in her youth, then quit sports to help her husband, my uncle Eddy, run his contracting business. After Eddy died tragically in a Little Italy restaurant shooting, she sold the business and went back to school to study Chinese herbal medicine and nutrition. She worked part-time as a yoga instructor at a New Age center, hosted an Internet conference on holistic health, and maintained her *Living Well—Naturally* Web site and newsletter. Her self-published book on Mexican wild yam cream sold steadily, supporting her idiosyncratic life.

"Perle, what are you doing in San Francisco? How did you know I was coming? What's this?" She was thrusting a smudged copy of *USA Today* toward me.

MAN BASHING — C&W TREND OR NOVELTY? NEWCOMER OF THE YEAR NOMINEE SARAH JEAN PIXLIE SINGS ABOUT HEARTACHES FOR A GUY

The story included the lyrics to my entire song:

There was no cream for your coffee,
　and a wrinkle in your shirt
After everything you ate last night your stomach really hurt
Your buddies canceled bowling, didn't even tell you why
Well, that's a lot of heartaches for a guy

The mosquito in your bedroom nearly kept you up all night
And the TV cable conked out during Foreman's latest fight
And she made your Sunday breakfast over easy 'stead of fried
Well, that's a lot of heartaches for a guy

Poor guy, just don't see eye to eye
Didn't anyone ever tell you life is hard and then you die?
Oh my, you're doing the best you can
Better bite the bullet and take it like a man

Your woman wouldn't treat you right because she was
  all bent
Out of shape about some trivia like the children and
  the rent
And the Giants lost the game last night,
  just makes you want to cry
Well, that's a lot of heartaches for a guy

Apparently, *USA Today* had heard the news before I had!
The article went on to say that radio stations were getting a record
number of requests to play "Heartaches for a Guy," mostly from
disgruntled married women, that an established male country
artist was about to release an answer song, and that I could not be
reached for comment. There was even a snappy quote from a
spokesman for Cindi-Lu Bender, five-time Country Legend
nominee, saying that although she was sure the song was meant to
be amusing, she wished that men and women could stop sniping
at each other and just get along for once. She also wished me the
best of luck in my solo career, and said she'd miss me and would
be rooting for me to win the Patsy. What a total bunch of crap.

My resourceful auntie had read the story, figured out that I
was leaving the Magnolia Heart tour, and called Cindi-Lu's management office in Nashville to get my flight information.

I HADN'T BEEN HOME IN ALMOST A YEAR. OF COURSE, THE band got occasional time off and most everyone went home, but most everyone's home was Memphis or Nashville. It didn't make sense for me to waste two days just traveling, especially since Lake County isn't near any major airports. I usually spent my free time in New York, visiting friends or staying with Aunt Perle.

On our way up Highway 101, Aunt Perle filled me in on the latest family gossip. She was visiting for a few months while her old SoHo loft was being renovated, keeping busy teaching vegan cooking and yoga classes at one of the small spiritual communes up in the hills. This particular group, the Bhalahdis, supported themselves with a thriving appliance-repair business, and Perle felt appreciated and well paid. The Dewdrop Inn, my parents' night-club, was doing fine. They were auditioning drummers this week because Pete Rawley, long-time family friend and the house band's drummer, had broken his arm in a Laundromat accident.

Pete was a sweetheart and a good player, but wound up being the butt of the drummer jokes that Aunt Perle and my mom gleefully pulled off the Internet and e-mailed to each other. (How do you get a drummer off your doorstep? Pay for the pizza.)

"So, Sarah Jean," my aunt said, "there are some things you should know before we get home. The phone's been ringing off the hook, darling. Everyone in the world wants an interview with my niece. *Entertainment Tonight* wants to come to the club with a TV crew. A *People* photographer has been lurking, claims he just wants to be a fly on the wall for a day or two. You're gonna walk into the Photo Op from Hell, sweetie, and if you don't mind my saying so, you look like shit."

"Hey," I replied indignantly, "it's been a pretty action-packed twenty-four hours—no time to freshen my lipstick."

Aunt Perle had the perfect solution. We stopped at a shopping mall in Marin County for lunch, then hit the Lancôme department at Nordstrom. For the price of a Velvet Midnight mascara, I got a full makeover and the life story of the young cosmetician behind the counter. Then we slammed into the men's department, where we bought an extra-large black T-shirt to replace what I suddenly realized with horror was still the stinky old George Thorogood and the Destroyers shirt I'd worn when I crossed the hall last night. With my jeans and boots, a little makeup and the new shirt, I could at least sort of pass for a Newcomer of the Year even if I didn't exactly feel like one.

As a special treat, we made one more stop, at the Hopland Brewery for an ice-cold local beer. Well, I had a beer. Aunt Perle had one of her special concoctions, something she called a "bio-beer," consisting of a nonalcoholic brew and some horrid-smelling green powder. Feeling refreshed and ready for anything, we took the turnoff for the road over the mountain, the last leg on my trip home.

Once a fashionable resort area, Lake County named its towns after elegant European retreats-by-the-sea. It's a shock for first-time visitors to see road signs pointing the way to Nice and Lucerne. As the Lake Tahoe area became more popular with the social set, Lakeport and the neighboring towns became more year-round, blue-collar communities. A huge Colonial-style house with manicured lawns, the private residence of a retired doctor, might sit right next to a dirt lot on which a rusty trailer boasts signs advertising itself as "Fred's Resort," offering a boat dock and cable TV. We passed California stucco houses, New England brick houses, suburban ranch houses, RV parks, Indian casinos, and everything else you could imagine, all jumbled together in comfortable proximity. The main attraction is Clear Lake, sparkling and welcoming in the afternoon sun despite rumors of dangerously high levels of mercury and other pollutants. Majestic Mount Konocti and the neighboring mountains keep the area protected or isolated, depending on how you look at it. That's Lake County for you: more than its share of unemployment and the highest percentage of parolees in the entire state of California, alongside a large population of fun-loving working folks, and an assortment of old hippies, survivalists, and true believers maintaining religious communities up in the hills. This peculiar mix of people was one of the reasons my parents had been able to turn their little honky-tonk into a successful business and get themselves off the road.

We turned off Main Street and there it was: the rambling old roadhouse I called home. Perle honked the horn as we pulled into the long gravel driveway that led around back to the kitchen door.

Next thing I knew, a mass of shrieking red curls came flying at the car, and I was smothered by my mom, Alice Cohen Pixlie. Like everyone else, I've always called her Allie, her official stage name. In her fifties, shorter and more athletically built than me, and incredibly young looking—people often assumed she was my sister. Allie has always been a bit dreamy and vague, the type who can remember who was playing at the Whiskey A Go-Go on June 23, 1972, and what she wore to the show, but shows up late for an appointment because she forgot to iron her blouse and couldn't find the car keys. In fact, she can *never* find her car keys! The only time I've ever seen her completely focused is when she's onstage; otherwise she seems forgetful and distant—quiet until she comes out with some dramatic and heartfelt observation that lets you know she hasn't missed a thing. No one in the world loves harder or cares more; it's just that the pesky details of day-to-day life seem to mystify her. My aunt Perle, older by four years, is exactly the opposite: practical and bossy and always in control. The two of them together are a riot.

I saw them in the afternoon light: two short, slim women with wide smiles—Perle with her close-cropped, no-nonsense New York haircut in a natural-fiber drawstring getup and hot-pink Reeboks, and Allie with cascading auburn curls and bare feet, wearing cutoff jeans and a wrinkled lace blouse she'd accidentally put on inside out. They were doing a goofy secret handshake they'd invented as children, laughing, clearly thrilled that I was home.

"Where's Dad?" I asked, looking around for my father, Johnny Pixlie, leader of the Dewdrop Drifters, the club's house band.

"Oh, he's off playing at some music festival or other in Texas—or is it Oklahoma? You know—summers." Allie waved her hand dismissively, figuring that was all the explanation required after twenty-seven years of marriage to a fiddle legend. "He'll be back in a week or so, I think."

The next few hours were a blur. There was indeed some local press around, asking polite questions about country music and man-bashing. I soon got the hang of the sound bite. No, I do not really hate men. Yes, I'm still on good terms with my great pal Cindi-Lu Bender, and I wish her the best in the Patsy Awards. No, I don't know who's going to replace me on the Magnolia Heart tour, but I'm sure that whoever it is will do a fine job. No, I don't expect to win Newcomer of the Year, of course not, what with all that great talent out there, but it's a pleasure to be nominated. As for the male country star's answer song, well, he certainly must be suffering from a heavy dose of PMS envy. I smiled for the cameras, and finally everyone left and we went inside.

The Dewdrop Inn hasn't changed much since its glory days as a country music showcase club in the fifties. Back then, every major act on the county fair circuit played there. Autographed photos of Ernest Tubb, Patsy Cline, Johnny Cash, and their peers line the walls, along with the stuffed moose heads and cowboy-and-Indian murals left by the original owners. There's an enormous dance floor surrounded by booths and tables, a large open kitchen, and a long bar. Sparkling amber liquor bottles are lined up on a shelf under a large mirror, backlit as though on an altar, the liquid sacraments of fun.

The place had fallen into shabby disrepair before my folks bought it, and they had to do a lot of renovating to bring the building up to code, but in the interest of preserving what they felt was a historic monument to honky-tonk, they left the decor pretty much the way they found it. They added a mesquite grill for tourists and a jam night for local musicians. Johnny and Allie Pixlie were tired of traveling and wanted a place where they could keep playing without being on the road. Their band was great in the old country-swing style, and the locals and summer boating crowd loved the place. They turned Thursday nights over to me, and I put together a little blues-rock band, *Raisin D'etra and the Raisinettes*, that appealed to a younger crowd, sometimes giving up my regular night to a touring act.

My absolutely favorite feature is the Ball of Love, a standard-issue revolving *Saturday Night Fever* disco ball suspended over the middle of the dance floor. But our Ball of Love is controlled by a switch on the floor of the bandstand; one of the great treats at the Dewdrop is stomping on that switch with the toe of your leather boot right on the downbeat of the first song. The room is suddenly transformed from dingy tavern into dazzling palace of romance. People meet, dance, and fall in love under that crystal ball. They also pout and punch each other out on occasion. The house rule is that the Ball of Love is turned on only while the band is playing, and the privilege of stomping on that switch belongs to the bandleader.

The bar and restaurant became our living room and kitchen years ago. A long picnic table separating the kitchen from the edge of the dance floor serves as our official gathering spot— off limits to customers, reserved for band members and family. Upstairs, where my family sleeps, are about a dozen bedrooms left over from a short Picturesque Country Inn period, and there's always a friend or relative staying in one of the extra rooms. The Dewdrop is no longer a hotel because my dad said it would be unfair to charge people money to stay above a noisy club with live music playing till 2 A.M., but I think the real reason is that my mother needs to take in strays. She's housed pregnant teenagers, itinerant musicians down on their luck, government officials from Borneo and other old Peace Corps buddies, an entire high-school pep squad, and a psychic medium who put her in touch with my great-grandma Clara. She meets these people everywhere, they tell her their stories, and the next thing you know, they're staying in one of the upstairs rooms, kept clean and ready at all times. Growing up, I called our home the Dewdrop Dorm. I got used to it, even grew to enjoy it. My dad put up with it; Allie can't live without it. She makes a pot of jasmine tea and sits and listens and gives advice straight from her heart, which usually amounts to suggesting they get themselves a little band together and play music. She really thinks that the world's problems would be solved if everyone could be in a band.

WHEN I ARRIVED WITH AUNT PERLE, THE ONLY OTHER visitors were Pete Rawley, the injured drummer, and Lloyd, the pedal steel player, who was between apartments. I felt lucky that there was a room for me.

"Come on, Sarah Jean, I'll put you in the Pink Room," Allie yelled over her shoulder as I followed her up the stairs.

It was called the Pink Room because my old Pepto-Bismol–colored comforter, loved since childhood, was draped across the canopied four-poster bed and covered with a lifetime accumulation of dolls and stuffed animals. Seeing my old toys was comforting and tender and sad, all at the same time. I decided it might be a good time to wallow in nostalgia.

"Do you still have my box of diaries and yearbooks and stuff?" I asked.

"In the back of the hall closet, I think. You know Saro Rogers down at the library was doing a town history, and I almost gave her that box," Allie confessed, "but I thought better of it. Seemed like it might be kind of private."

"I'm not even sure what's in there, but I don't think I want it turning up at the library."

"Well, then it's a good thing I didn't give it to her, isn't it?" She sat down next to me on the bed and gently held my hand. "Listen, I want to say this without everyone else around, okay? Whatever happened out there, well, we're so proud of you. In all the years I spent on the road playing music, I never got to go on a big-time tour. I never had a fancy bus or wrote a song that got on the radio, and if anyone knows how hard it is to pull that off, Dad and I do. We want you to stay as long as you need to."

"Thanks." I was trying really hard not to cry.

"I don't know what the Patsy committee told you," she continued.

"I haven't talked to them yet; I guess I'm supposed to call."

"Well, it's always been my understanding that the Newcomer nominees have to show up and perform at the show to be eligible to win. Did you know that?"

"No! I was thinking I could just call it in, have Kathleen or someone accept for me if I won. How in the world can I get it together to perform in Nashville in six weeks?"

"Oh, sweetie, if you need help pulling a band together for the Patsy show, all you have to do is ask. We have the best band in the world right downstairs."

"Thanks," I sighed, "but it might be easier to just give it up. This whole thing feels so weird. I don't think I want to go to the Patsies, let alone perform. I'd have to see Cindi-Lu there, and she and Cal hate me, and it might just be too hard. Let me think it over."

She was shocked in the way other mothers would be if you told them you were dropping out of medical school to become a crack dealer, but she took it well. She brushed my cheek with her hand and closed the bedroom door, leaving me feeling quiet for the first time since—well, since I'd knocked on Bobby Lee's door at four in the morning in Nashville, holding his shoes. It seemed like a long time ago.

Chapter

4

I SLEPT STRAIGHT THROUGH TO THE NEXT AFTERNOON, restlessly dreaming about Cindi-Lu Bender and drooling on my pillowcase. I was startled awake by my mother's voice, yelling to me from downstairs.

"Hey, kiddo—I know you're tired, but I need your help with something!" I'm sure all mothers yell upstairs for help; only mine would call for help auditioning drummers. Since it looked like I was going to be home for a while, hearing the backbeat through the floor of my room every night, it was in my interest to participate.

"Hold on," I yelled back. "Give me a minute."

I rummaged through my bag and found clean boxer shorts and a Magnolia Heart crew T-shirt, ran a brush through the top layer of my tangled hair, and joined the perpetual party downstairs.

The drummer was tall and lanky with waist-length blond hair, and looked like he'd be more comfortable in a mosh pit. He seemed about my age, with a couple of well-placed tattoos and thick chains attached to various parts of his leather outfit.

"Hi, honey, this is Greg Carson." Allie looked tired. She hated auditioning musicians because it meant she might have to say no to someone. But she was in charge and she had a club to fill. Greg smiled, showing off the results of expensive suburban orthodonture. He was adorable.

The Dewdrop Drifters, all lifelong friends of my parents and honorary uncles of mine, assembled on the bandstand. These are the best pickers in the county and the best people in the universe, as far as I'm concerned. In addition to Pete Rawley, the band consisted of Lee Franklin on bass, Lloyd Sanders on pedal steel, and Hoagy Guitarmichael, whose real nice-boy-from-New-York name hadn't been used in so long that no one remembered what it was, on lead guitar. Hoagy had gone to high school with Allie and Perle in New York—our family has seen him through two divorces, innumerable heartbreaks, letdowns, gambling debts, legal hassles, and an IRS audit—and he lived with us on and off between girlfriends. His guitar playing was versatile and tasteful, more than good enough for any road band on the planet, but he seemed to like his steady gig at the Dewdrop. With Allie on rhythm guitar, Dad on fiddle and mandolin, and whatever old road dog buddy of theirs was passing through, the band smoked. These guys had been playing in bars since before Greg was born, and it was hard for me to imagine him fitting in. But when Hoagy counted off "Lonely Weekends," Greg fell right in and nailed the Memphis beat. I saw Lee exchange a surprised wink with Hoagy and nod—their not-so-secret code for *Not bad, let's see what this wanker can really do!* They ran Greg through a sappy country waltz, a cowboy two-step, a Zydeco two-step, a Chuck Berry tune, a slow ballad, and a blues shuffle. He played flawlessly; I couldn't help being impressed.

"Hey!" Lee's voice blasted into the house PA. "That Sarah Jean Pixlie out there? Come on up and do a song with us, how about it?"

As I ran toward the bandstand, Lee announced, "Put your hands together, folks, for America's new country music sweetheart, man-bashin' Sarah Jean," to thunderous applause from Allie, Aunt Perle, and the kitchen staff.

There was one thing they hadn't thought of to throw at Greg, so I grabbed the live mic and yelled, "Okay guys, surf beat. Greg starts, everyone else wait for me. One-two, one-two-three-four."

I counted off a Dovels classic, kicked on the Ball of Love, and Greg was right in the pocket. The guys laughed their heads off, but they came in right and sang along on "You Can't Sit Down," and by the time we were done everyone was sweating, the cook was dancing, and the band had a new drummer.

"Shit," I heard Lee whisper to Hoagy, "that kid's so good, I bet he coulda been a musician."

I VISITED WITH HOAGY, LEE, PETE, AND LLOYD, LOUNGING at the family table while Allie worked out the business part of her arrangement with Greg. They were crazy with excitement over my Patsy nomination, rolled their eyes over the way I'd been treated by Cal and Cindi-Lu. It turned out that Lee had been in Cindi-Lu's touring band for a short time and was able to provide a plausible, if weak, explanation for their behavior.

"She's a princess," he explained. "Comes from country music royalty. Her pa and uncle were both members of the famous West Virginia Benders, who invented a new style of bluegrass fiddle-playing your daddy could show you if he were here. In fact, your granddaddy and her pa were once the twin fiddles in a band back in Oklahoma. When Cindi-Lu burst onto the scene, fresh out of high school, with that voice and pedigree—why, she achieved

Legend status so quickly that there was no time for her to be a Newcomer."

"But why take it out on me?" I whined.

"All the other country divas have a Newcomer Patsy, and Cindi-Lu is a competitive woman. She keeps track of who has what, and she tends to hold a grudge." Lee shrugged. "She's a star. It doesn't have to make sense."

The guys caught me up on their lives: divorces, kids, recording sessions, and fishing triumphs. They were all talking a mile a minute except for Lloyd, who seemed particularly quiet and distracted as he thumbed through the local weekly, marking pages with a red pen.

"What's with Uncle Lloyd?" I asked.

"Who, him? He's always like that. He's a steel player. Those guys never talk much; they disappear into the basement for a couple of years and come out making the most beautiful sounds in creation. Don't worry about him."

"Huh?" said Lloyd.

"Hey, let's see what you're reading that's more interesting than my country-western hit single!"

He blushed deep scarlet as I grabbed the paper out of his hands. It was open to the personals page. One ad in particular was circled three times in red: *SWF, 34: Bright, pretty, slender, nice, would like to meet an interesting, intelligent, considerate man with whom to enjoy movies, theater, restaurants, friendship, romance.*

The other guys tore the paper out of my hands with whoops. Poor Lloyd. He was in for tons of loving shit for a very long time to come.

I looked around the table at my favorite bunch of lowlife musicians: Pete, our huge, bearded Bubba in a baseball cap; Lee, short and wiry with close-cropped graying hair; Lloyd, quiet, balding beanpole; and Hoagy with his dark curls, round face and big, wide smile. I made an instant decision: They were so incredibly proud of me, so supportive, and such good players in every sense of the word, I decided right then and there to go for the Patsy. It was an honor and there was nothing to feel guilty about. I would bring the Dewdrop Drifters to Nashville to perform at the show, I would wear my best country-sweetheart spangles and my biggest smile, and I would win or not win, but I had to stop feeling bad about Cindi-Lu and Cal and all their bullshit.

I gave everyone a kiss and ran upstairs to the phone. There was suddenly a ton of stuff to do.

Chapter
5

THE INEVITABLE AND IMMEDIATE RESULT OF GREG'S hiring was the Perle and Allie Marathon Gossip Huddle, as my dad used to call it. The two sisters would spend many hours figuring out where Greg came from, what made him tick, where his life was headed, and which poor, unsuspecting local girl they could fix him up with. Bigger, stronger, and older men had succumbed to Allie and Perle's attentive efforts; once they decided to fix a guy's life, he might as well just roll over and let them.

I felt a little sorry for Greg, the night of his first gig with the Drifters. Perle had been staring at him from across the room for the entire evening, while making obvious "secret" gestures to Allie on the bandstand. Allie finally joined Perle for their ritual nightcap of herbal tea, alone at the family table in the empty club. I was on my way downstairs to say good night when I heard them talking.

"Well, what about Sarah Jean? Is she seeing anyone these days?" I heard Perle ask.

"No, Perle, she's totally wrong for Greg. For one thing, the kid's been on the road for a year, not to mention she has a record climbing the charts. No way she'd want to settle down with any-one right now. Anyway, Sarah Jean's always gone for the more corporate type, don't you think?"

I had? I stayed out of sight, listening.

"What do you mean, corporate type? You should have seen the boys she brought home to my apartment in New York—green hair, nose rings, the works. What about that boy Max in that band, you know, the Surgeons of Sound?"

"Perle, honey, Little Max and Sarah Jean have been pals since kindergarten. And besides, just because Max was into body piercing doesn't mean he didn't have a corporate heart. Do you know what he's doing now? Selling Hondas."

He *is?*

"Okay, but I think Greg is cute," Perle insisted. "And he's a nice boy, and the fellows in the band say he's a good drummer. Sarah Jean needs a good drummer."

Allie made the valid point that everyone needs a good drummer.

"Yeah, yeah, I'm just saying she could do a lot worse. My only concern is that it might be too late. What do you know about this Bobby Lee character?"

"Who?"

"Some young man on the tour." Perle sounded proud to know something about me that Allie hadn't heard yet. "Your daughter mentioned him in a very casual way, in that same sort of very casual way you used to talk about Johnny when you first met him—you know, pretending that he's just a good friend in case things don't work out. But she was all lit up. I'll bet you my Acme carrot juicer she's got a thing for Bobby Lee."

"A guy she met on the road? Come on, Perle."

I figured it was time to make my entrance when Freddie, the night janitor, accidentally hit a switch on the club's CD player, momentarily sending a most magnificent male voice through the house PA at ear-splitting volume. Perle jumped from her chair, spilling tea all over her sister.

"My God, Allie, what's that?" she shrieked.

Allie laughed. "George Jones's 'The Race Is On,' and I guess it is, with Sarah Jean home and a cute new drummer in the band."

"It scared me to death," Perle said. "Sorry I spilled this, but it's good for skin lesions when applied topically, you know. I guess I'm a little jumpier than usual."

"Let's call it a night, big sister. I'll take George Jones and go to bed."

Still out in the hall, I smiled to myself. Allie always did have good taste in men.

I DIDN'T HAVE MUCH TIME TO GET READY FOR THE PATSY show, considering the fact that I had no management, a borrowed band, and no gigs. I sort of had a record label, and I sort of didn't. A VP at Unicorn Entertainment, the company that had released the movie sound track, wanted to talk to me. There was a stack of messages from managers, A&R guys, musicians, and agents. There were a couple of sweet late-night phone calls from Kathleen and Amy, and a surprise parcel they sent, containing my beloved leopard bathrobe and some other things I'd left in my Nashville hotel room. There were even calls from my old pal Max, who was indeed selling Hondas and wondered if I wanted to buy one. But there wasn't a single word from Bobby Lee Crenshaw. I was a little too proud and sniffly to ask about him when the girls called, afraid I might give something—what?—away.

Greg went with me to the Honda dealership and made faces behind Little Max's back when my old buddy and former bandmate, who assumed I was suddenly rolling in megabucks, refused to show me anything but luxury cars way out of my price range, then hit me up for thousands of dollars to finance his band's new CD. I left sputtering with outrage and disbelief, but Greg helped me laugh the whole thing off and took me to a used-car lot owned by a friend of his family, where I got a terrific deal on a ten-year-old, fire-engine-red pickup truck.

In fact, Greg was helping me pull together all the loose ends for my show, often calling on the assistance of his "family friends." The guy was well connected and generous, a combination that was saving the day for me. When I asked why, he explained that his father worked in entertainment management down south and had some great connections as a result—no big deal, he was happy to help. Greg was also fun to be with and had a fascination with technological toys, including his state-of-the-art laptop computer with Internet access, which proved to be a tremendous advantage when it came to arranging travel.

Luckily, the one thing I'd been really conscientious about on tour was hotel and airline frequent-flyer miles. I had tons of them, just about enough to bring the band to Nashville and put everyone up for a few days if we doubled up on rooms. I also had almost all the money I'd earned on the road—there just hadn't been the time or opportunity to spend much.

It seemed the trick was going to be looking legitimate in the eyes of the Patsy organizers. Record labels pumped millions into advertising for these events, and I couldn't begin to afford full-page ads in the music trade publications. Unicorn Entertainment didn't seem to have a clue. They mostly released movie sound tracks, which meant they dealt with licensing and mechanical rights, not original material, and weren't used to a real, live performing artist. They hardly ever worked with country music or radio, either, and they seemed at least as surprised as I was by the sudden success of "Heartaches for a Guy." My gut feeling was that I should let them worry about distribution and marketing, and let Allie and Perle help with band logistics and other details.

"HEY, GIRLFRIEND, YOU READY YET?" GREG YELLED DOWN the stairs.

"Cool your jets, dude. I'm in the kitchen. Want a peanut-butter-and-banana sandwich?"

"No thanks. Didn't we have breakfast like an hour ago? Come on."

"I'm suddenly ravenous. Just wait a second, I'll bring it with me."

I'd been home almost two weeks, and we were heading down to the Bay Area to talk to some music business people, with a list of appointments and a longer list of things Perle wanted us to bring back to "the schticks" for her. Actually, it was hard work convincing both Allie and Perle that they didn't have to come with us. But Allie had booked an opening act that night, and it turned out she had to stick around.

"Sarah Jean!" Aunt Perle stood in the doorway in her bath-robe, barefoot, with chunks of green gunk all over her face and a container of freshly pressed wheat-grass juice in her hand.

"Yuck, what's that on your cheek?" I tried to wipe it off.

"Leave my face alone, young lady. It's my morning avocado facial. You should do this, too, if you want good skin into middle age." And she picked up an avocado peeling from the cutting board and tried to rub the inside of the skin on my face.

"Stop that," I protested, stepping aside. She missed, and ended up rubbing avocado gunk on the refrigerator door. "We're on our way out. What's up?"

"I can't believe you're eating that."

"What? It's a sandwich. I'm hungry. I'd make one for you, but we're running late—have to go."

"You're not going to eat bread and drive, are you?" she cried as she grabbed at my sandwich. She was fast, but I was faster. I held onto my offensive snack, yelled for Greg to follow, and ran outside, locking the doors of the truck before she could reach us.

Perle's impassioned lecture on wheat allergies and my road-life-compromised immune system was not going over well. Normally I would have at least felt a little guilty, but I was the kind of hungry where it was unwise to get between me and my sandwich. We tore out of the driveway just in time to avoid a wheat-grass shower as Perle lunged for the door handle.

OUR FIRST APPOINTMENT IN SAN FRANCISCO WAS WITH LOU Brady, an entertainment attorney who boasted Nashville connections and had negotiated deals for several well-known bands. He thought he could arrange for some paying gigs there after the Patsy show, and didn't seem to think it would be difficult to get Unicorn to pay our travel expenses—all it usually took was a couple of phone calls to the right VP. Lou seemed to know his stuff and sounded like he could save me some money. I didn't have a lot of time to comparison-shop, so I signed a management contract on the spot.

Walking from his Financial District office across Market Street, I noticed a distinct difference from the last time I'd wandered the busy downtown streets. It wasn't my imagination—people were looking at me in a peculiar way. Strangers caught my eye and smiled in recognition. It seemed ridiculous, but there it was, the unmistakable sign of my new celebrity status. I held my back straighter, meeting glances and returning smiles, delighting in my first taste of public recognition.

Our next stop was a SoMa recording studio, where I taped an interview for Sally Ruddy's *My Kind of Country* music show, syndicated on NPR. This was a thrill, since it had been my favorite radio show for years. Sally was delightful, full of gossip about the burgeoning roots music scene, excited about new Jimmy LaFave and Buddy Miller CDs she'd received in the morning mail, and certainly responsive to Greg's flirty hair tossing. She surprised us with an invitation to lunch at the trendy bistro down the street, and we accepted.

"Can we get a reservation on such short notice?" Greg wanted to know.

"No problem. It usually requires calling a week in advance, but I just pretended I was Sarah Jean, and got us in this morning."

"Wow, I never would have thought of that," was my stunned reply.

Other diners followed us with their eyes as we were seated, and once again it really did seem as though people recognized me.

"So," Sally asked, "how's Cindi-Lu taking this Newcomer of the Year nomination of yours? She has a reputation for giving some of the newcomers a hard time, you know."

That didn't surprise me, but I figured she'd already done her worst by having me fired. It seemed like the Cindi-Lu Bender machine had moved on, even going so far as to wish me luck in the national press.

So I could be charitable: "We're fine."

"That's good to hear. Maybe she's mellowing a bit in her old age. I can't wait to see you on the show. You are going to have an absolute blast." Then Sally shifted to her favorite subject, deconstructing the music she loved.

Last stop was KPFA in Berkeley, the Pacifica affiliate well known as the epicenter of admirable leftie politics and smug political correctness. An old buddy of Greg's who hosted a weekly radio show for Grateful Dead fans had invited us to join him on the air as guest deejays. We played all our favorites, from Hank Williams to Judas Priest, and it didn't take long to get the feeling that Deadheads all over the Bay Area were turning off their radios in droves.

"This last song is a very special treat. Sarah Jean has recently been nominated for a Patsy Award," our host announced as he cued up "Heartaches for a Guy" and leaned across the console, "and here's the tune that got her there."

We weren't even out of the first chorus when the phone lines lit up with calls from enraged male listeners, horrified at my pro-imperialist sexism (as one man put it) and KPFA's lack of ethics. Some women callers vehemently defended it, others accused me of bowing to cultural gender stereotypes, and the fight was on. I had been the good team player, Miss Congeniality, in every band I ever played in, and here I was outraging complete strangers and starting fights. So that's what it felt like to be famous.

Back in the truck heading home, lost in a fantasy that revolved around my new status, I was startled when Greg interrupted my thoughts.

"I've been meaning to ask you all day. What's that stuff on your face?"

"What stuff? What are you talking about?"

"That green gunk. At first I thought it was some kind of rash, but it seems to be moving around."

I checked the side-view mirror and realized with horror that Aunt Perle hadn't missed after all. I'd been cruising through my big day in San Francisco with a stripe of mashed avocado running down the length of my cheek, thinking people were looking at me because I was famous.

Okay, so maybe I wasn't really a big enough celebrity to turn heads on the street, but my name had gotten us a last-minute lunch reservation, and I *had* terrorized a few sensitive Berkeley men over the public airwaves. That surely counted for something.

WE RACED THE CLOCK AND PULLED INTO THE DEWDROP'S driveway ten minutes before downbeat. Greg ran upstairs to change while I checked in with Allie and Perle. I found them both in the kitchen leaning over Lloyd, whose long string-bean frame hunched over a yellow legal pad, his brow furrowed in concentration.

"No, no, no! Don't write that. You sound much too eager," Perle scolded.

"On the other hand, it never hurts for a man to be honest about his feelings," countered Allie.

"Sorry, Allie, but you're all wrong. If he wears his heart on his sleeve, she won't be interested. Believe me, I know about these things."

"Oh, excuse me, big sister, but exactly how did that come to be? As I recall, you were married to your high-school sweetheart for approximately eight hundred years."

"Look who's talking, big shot! Lloyd, take my word for it, you have to play a little hard to get here. She won't respond if you seem too anxious."

"But listen, don't play *too* hard to get, either. She might be a shy person. Make sure she knows you're interested."

Lloyd had chewed the top of his pen into an unrecognizable lump. He looked like he was about ready to lie down and die. I decided to come to the rescue.

"Hi, guys, we're back," I yelled from the doorway. "What are you all up to?"

"Hi, honey," Allie called back. "We're helping Lloyd answer a personal ad in the weekly."

"Aha! SWF 34, by any chance?"

Lloyd nodded glumly and handed me the letter. I read it carefully, twice.

"Look, it's not a bad letter," I reassured him. "Actually, it's pretty good. Allie's right, your personality does come through, but see? You misspelled a couple of words and your grammar's a little weird here. Tell you what; while you guys are playing your first set, I'll type it into Greg's laptop and run it through Spell Check. I'd hate to see you lose points for sloppiness—I mean, if you really want to make a good impression on SWF 34, that is."

Lloyd nodded gratefully and headed for the bandstand.

Chapter

6

GREG HAD MOVED INTO THE BEDROOM NEXT TO mine. I wasn't sure if Allie was just being her usual, hospitable self or if this was part of a scheme she and Aunt Perle were cooking up, but there he was in the glorified closet they called the Tonga Room because it was decorated with all the cheap souvenir treasures they'd picked up on trips to Hawaii.

"So, are my mom and her sister driving you crazy yet?" I asked. We were flopped on my bed, making phone calls to Nashville hotels, trying to find rooms for the band. Greg stretched and tossed back his mane of shimmering blond hair, a gesture I figured he'd fine-tuned during hours and hours in front of his bedroom mirror.

"Nah, I kinda like it, actually. They make me feel loved."

"Not smothered?"

"Not yet, anyway. It's cool to be part of a family again—it's been a really long time."

"Greg, can I ask you something?"

"Sure. Anything."

"How come you want this gig? Most rock drummers think country music is really boring."

"They're the stupid ones."

"Well, yeah, but how come you're so good?"

"Just 'cause I have long hair and wear leather doesn't mean I can't like country music, does it? Actually, Buddy Harmon is an old family friend, and got me started when I was a kid. Then I took lessons from Willie Cantu for a while, who used to play with Buck Owens. I loved my last band—I love playing really loud and hard. But the lead singer was my best friend, and I finally couldn't stand that someone that talented could care more about drugs than music. He almost OD'd in the men's room at the Cactus Club in San Jose. I got him to the hospital, made sure he wasn't dead, and headed north. I was having breakfast in a coffee shop in Santa Rosa, trying to figure out what to do next, when I saw your mom's ad in the weekly. I'm just happy to have a steady gig where no one is likely to throw up on me while I'm playing. Now can I ask you something?"

"Sure," I said.

"You know that those two maniac relatives of yours are trying to fix us up? Actually, I could think of worse ideas."

"Aw, shucks, Greg. You're so darn romantic."

He plopped his head in my lap, and I started stroking his long, beautiful hair. He kicked the door shut with his left boot and turned around to face me. He was so pretty, with delicate features and long eyelashes and the most amazing big blue eyes, I suddenly realized. He turned so that he was on top of me, and he felt so good in my arms, and we closed our eyes and kissed. And then I remembered my famous rule, which I seemed to be about to break for the second time in less than a month.

"Greg?"

"Hmm?"

"Hey. Stop nibbling my ear, take your hand out of my shirt, and think for a minute."

"You feel wonderful," he whispered. And I noticed he wasn't stopping.

I'd been mooning over Bobby Lee Crenshaw and feeling cranky about the fact that I hadn't heard from him. Having sex with Greg, whatever complications might result, could help me forget about Bobby Lee. Or at least it could defuse the sense of obsessive longing that was making me a little crazy, not to mention completely bored with myself. So I decided not to worry about my rule and go for it.

Greg's silky hair tickled my belly and nipples as he slowly undressed me, kissing my neck and lips and the inside of my knees. Then he stood up and took off his pants, and he was lean and golden, surprisingly well muscled, with a tan line low on his hips that I found sweetly touching for some reason. He sat down next to me on the bed and, with the tip of his finger, gently brushed a stray strand of hair off my forehead, murmuring, "So pretty."

I wish I could say that in the heat of that moment we had fantastic sex, but actually what happened was I totally lost it. That one tiny, tender gesture set me off somewhere way down deep and I started sobbing uncontrollably, pathetically, and unstoppably.

"Was it something I said?"

"No. I don't know. No, of course not," I wailed.

"Um, did I hurt you or anything?"

"No, no—I don't know what's wrong with me. It's just all so sad." And fresh tears appeared from nowhere.

"Look, I don't ever want to hurt you. Just tell me what I did, please!"

But I couldn't, because it didn't make any sense, and that was that.

Greg put his strong arms around me and let me cry for a while. Finally I calmed down enough to glance at the big round dressing-table mirror and wonder out loud how women who cry in movies manage to retain their dewy beauty while I, on the other hand, looked like a bunch of washed-up crap.

"How do you think I feel? I come on to a girl and she gets hysterical. I think maybe my pickup lines need a little work." He handed me a Kleenex, clearly expecting further explanation.

But I had nothing to say. "I'm so sorry. I guess I'm just not ready for this. I thought I wanted to, but—" And I started to cry again.

"Please stop crying. It's okay. You scared me, though."

I nodded.

"I have a great idea. Let's just be friends. We can hang out and go bowling and play music together and we don't have to wonder what each other looks like naked, 'cause we already know. And nobody has to cry or anything. What do you say?"

It sounded good to me. "Hey, Greg, I don't know what came over me. I'm sorry I acted like such an adolescent."

"Adolescent, huh? You're not up to adolescent yet, honey. But consider me your new pal. We don't have to have sex."

"It's a deal. Anyway, my mama always warned me about dating guys who are prettier than I am."

"Who said anything about dating?"

The pillow I threw at him missed and went sailing through my open bedroom window. We hesitated, staring at the open space. Something about the arc of the pillow disappearing over the windowsill struck me as incredibly funny. Giddy, laughing, relieved, and delighted to be friends, we salvaged our crumpled lists from under our clothes. Without bothering to get dressed, we began making more calls.

MAYBE I DIDN'T NEED CLOTHES TO HANG OUT WITH MY NEW buddy, but I was certainly going to need something smashing to wear to the Patsy show. Allie had vetoed throwing an outfit together out of old stage clothes. Instead, she hired Richie, costume designer and hair-and-makeup stylist for her community theater company, the Pillbox Players. As a result, I found myself spending way too many hours (luckily before the club opened for the day) standing in the middle of the dance floor in my underwear and swatches of fabric, listening to the never-ending Perle-and-Allie Boogie.

"You know, Perle," Allie said on the morning of his first visit, "I always thought I'd have a couple of years to enjoy not having teenage acne, before I started menopause. It's just not fair."

"Allie, you goose. Aren't you using your Mexican wild yam cream? You'll breeze right through, no hot flashes. And I've been telling you for years, lay off the café mochas and you won't get pimples."

"A life without mocha? Forget it. I'd rather have the pimples. I just can't believe this menopause thing is for real. I'm still working on my teen grooming tips. Sarah Jean, will you please stand up straight? Richie is trying to take your measurements!"

Richie bore an uncanny resemblance to rock-and-roll legend Little Richard and played it to the hilt. "Good golly, darling," he squealed. "Now turn to your left. Here's what I see . . ."

Richie's vision turned out to be lovely—a combination of black velvet, leather, and lace, trimmed with silver studs. It was pretty and definitely country, but just severe enough to be worn by America's newest country music man-basher. The rest of the band would wear black shirts and jeans, with rhinestone bolo ties. As I stood up straight and succumbed to Richie's tape measure, my mother and aunt continued their conversation.

"So," Perle wanted to know, "when is Johnny getting home, already? Didn't he say he'd be back this weekend?"

"Oh, right. I forgot to tell you. He's staying a couple of extra days to do some session work. It's working out fine, with Hoagy's friend subbing in the meantime, but I wish that man would remember to fill me in on his plans once in a while. I swear it's getting worse as he gets older."

I felt the need to come to my dad's defense.

"Hey, look who's talking. You never remember to tell him anything, either. He said you forgot to mention the last Pillbox Players production, and he missed it."

"Well, he didn't miss much, Missy." Richie glanced at Allie, who burst out laughing. "There was a little scheduling snafu, so *The Music Man* was staged on the fairgrounds right next to a Monster Truck Rally. The off-key soprano who got the lead was in the middle of 'Goodnight My Someone' when the inevitable happened. This huge green truck thing crashed right through the scenery and onto the stage. The truck got the standing ovation."

I wondered aloud how, with all the good singers in this area, a weak, off-key soprano ended up with the lead.

"Oh, the director thought she was cute, I suppose," Allie answered. "He's been trying to employ the casting couch for years, and every once in a while it actually works. Luckily no one was hurt, but the playhouse is still under reconstruction. There won't be any new productions for a while, which means poor Ira won't be getting laid. I'm staying out of his way, he's been awfully grumpy."

The phone rang. Hoping it was the call I was expecting from Unicorn about our travel budget, I ran to answer it.

"Hello, Dewdrop Inn."

"Hey, is that my little girl?" asked a deep, rough voice over long-distance wires.

"Dad! We were just talking about you. Where are you?"

"Damn, it feels very far away. You better catch me up, Buttercup." We talked about recent events, and although he had good things to say about my new manager, he scolded me for signing hastily. He was proud that I had decided to bring the Dewdrop Drifters to Nashville for the Patsy show, and he promised to send me some newspaper clippings he'd saved about my nomination.

"Why not just bring them with you? When are you coming home?"

"I'm not sure, Sugar. I need to talk to Allie. Put her on, will you?"

"Hey, Dad's on the phone!"

She took it in the office and closed the door, remaining there for a long time. Richie finished taking my measurements and agreed to come back later in the week for a fitting. Perle had a class to teach, and Greg decided to go rollerblading in the park. I went upstairs to work on a new song. I must have gotten lost in it, I guess. I still hadn't seen Allie, and it was already getting dark when Greg knocked on my door a few hours later.

"Hey, whatcha doing?" he asked.

"Just working on the next hit single, "My Baby Used to Hold Me (Now He's Putting Me On Hold)."

"How's it going?"

"It's not really finished yet, but here goes . . .

When we came to this city we were poor as we could be
I didn't have a thing but your precious love for me
We struggled hard, then suddenly you got that fancy job
You're making so much money now, but somehow I feel
  robbed—

"Now here comes the chorus:

My baby used to hold me, now he's putting me on hold
The lips that once were sweet and warm are turning cold
I thought our love would last as long as this ring of gold
My baby used to hold me, now he's putting me on hold

"I still have to write another verse, but then maybe at the end we'd do a fake dial tone with a pedal steel effect or something. What do you think?"

"I love it. It kind of reminds me of my parents, actually."

Greg never said much about his family, and this was a chance to find out. It took dozens of questions, but gradually he told me that his parents were freelance artistic types who had struggled for years in the Central Valley area until his father got into artist management and his mother inherited a thriving business in Bakersfield. He said they made a lot of money but were too busy to spend time together. I pictured them as yuppie executives in power suits, racing around Southern California freeways in BMWs, calling each other on cell phones.

"But enough about me," Greg said. "I almost forgot why I came up here. Allie wants to know if you can sub for her tonight. She says she's not feeling well and she's going to bed. That okay? First set starts in forty-five minutes."

"What's wrong?"

"Hell if I know. I came in from rollerblading and found a note. Her door's closed with a very definitive *Do Not Disturb* sign on it. I figure, she doesn't ask for much, and if that's what she wants, we should leave her alone."

"Screw that. She'd never do the same for you, and you know it. I'm going in to talk to her."

I ran down the hall to my parents' room. There was a huge crayoned *Do Not Disturb* fastened to the door with electrical tape. I opened the door anyway and tiptoed in.

My mother sat at her dressing table, staring blankly into the huge round mirror. The color had drained from her cheeks and she looked tired and sad.

"Hey, what's the matter?" I whispered.

"Sarah Jean, you're supposed to be getting ready for the gig. And please don't embarrass me by wearing those ugly sweats onstage, if you don't mind." Her voice shook, just a little.

"I won't. But you have to tell me what's wrong."

"I don't want to upset you before you play, sweetie. Please, we can talk in the morning."

"Nope. Sorry. I'm not leaving until you tell me what's happening. You're scaring me."

"All right, come over here."

I sat on the edge of the bed and leaned toward her.

She stroked my forehead and spoke in a soft voice. "Johnny's not coming home."

"Why? What happened?"

"I'm not sure. I was just remembering the day we brought you home from the hospital, how proud and excited he was. You'd think no one ever had a cute little baby girl before. We were living with Grandma then, 'cause really we were on the road all the time in those days, and she offered to help out. He couldn't wait to take you into the sleazy bars where we played and show you off—he loved dressing you up in tiny leather cowgirl booties and fringes. We were a happy little family. And now somehow twenty-six years have gone by and you're all grown up and starting to make a name for yourself. I don't know what happened to the time, and I guess while I wasn't looking, something happened to us. Johnny says he met someone who makes him feel like a real man, and he wants to stay with her for now. He wants me to send him some of his stuff, and he wants me to swallow the line that he feels guilty and it's nothing I've done and all that typical male midlife bullshit. I'm supposed to keep the business and the band going as though nothing has happened. Somehow he has this weird idea that it won't matter to me very much, that I'll understand. How the fuck am I supposed to understand?"

"Mom—"

"You must be really upset, kiddo. You haven't called me Mom since you were four years old. Now listen, I hate to drop this bombshell on you and kick you out, but I'm going to. Put on some decent clothes and get down there and sing. I need you to sub for me tonight, and I also need you to cover for me. No one can know what's happened yet, because a bunch of well-intentioned sympathy will push me over the edge. So go down there and somehow make it work, will you?"

And somehow I did.

I tuned my Strat and wrote a set list. I strummed and smiled and sang my songs. I joked around with the band and flirted with the regulars, just as though it was all okay.

Just as though my heart wasn't breaking in two.

MAYBE IT WAS A GOOD THING WE HAD THE PATSY show coming up, because it gave us all something to do besides worry about Allie. Perle spent a lot of time with her, freeing Greg and me to make arrangements without a lot of crazed intervention. Although I was still furious at Cal and Cindi-Lu, I felt thankful to them because the Magnolia Heart tour had given me a tough the-show-must-go-on professionalism that I hadn't had before, and needed badly. I was glad to give Allie and the people who had become her family something to focus on besides the fact that my father was being a jerk, a circumstance I was convinced would be temporary.

Any doubts I might have had about how the band would perform my original tunes were put to rest after the first rehearsal. Hoagy slid seamlessly into Dad's place as bandleader. It might have been tricky with another new drummer, but Greg was strong, and the Drifters made a game of trying to distract him, just to see what it would take to throw him off the groove. It simply couldn't be done. No matter what anyone said, did, or put in front of him, the guy played with flawless timing and concentration. They finally gave up, and one afternoon Hoagy presented Greg with a gift-wrapped box of printed business cards that read, *For the Correct Time Call... Greg Carson... Drums,* and included the club's phone number.

Although no one could distract Greg onstage, a major off-stage distraction was Lloyd's anxious mailbox stalking as he waited for a response from SWF 34. He went out to check the mailbox about forty times a day, every day, until finally a letter arrived, his name handwritten on the baby-blue envelope in perfect feminine penmanship. The note inside was short and polite, beautifully written on perfumed paper. She was a limousine driver from Ukiah, impressed enough with his letter to suggest that they meet. The two began a complicated round of phone tag, trying to come up with a mutually agreeable time and place. All the romantic buildup surrounding Lloyd was exciting and reminded me that I wanted a love interest of my own.

So I thought I'd try to go another round with Greg, since we were spending most of our time together anyway. He was cute, he was nice, he was totally responsive to my flirting—and he was *there.* It would be so convenient if we could become a couple, not to mention the fact that Allie would get a total kick out of having played a part, and she was a woman badly in need of some kicks.

On more than one occasion I marched cheerfully up the stairs, executing a seductive wiggle with Greg close behind, practically panting with lusty anticipation after hours of relentless flirting. The bedroom door slammed shut, a soft breeze parted the curtains, a candle was lit, and then the first soft kiss, the blouse unbuttoned, his callused hands caressing my face and hair. It was always a disaster. I'd be so completely in the mood, but the second he touched me with any kind of tenderness, I'd start weeping uncontrollably. Then we'd have that same old conversation where we'd agree to be friends, and end up in a ferocious naked pillow fight. After a couple of tries, we started going straight for the pillow fight without attempting sex. It seemed easier, and the "Let's just be friends" talk was getting old. We *knew* we were friends; it was the other stuff, our elusive chemistry, that was the issue.

During rare moments when the phone was free, I had a couple of unsettling conversations with my father, or as Allie called him, "Your-Father-the-Fucking-Dickhead-Who-Can't-Keep-His-Thing-in-His-Pants." For the first time since I was thirteen, we had trouble communicating, and I had the feeling he couldn't wait to hang up. But if I stretched my mind and my willingness to see things from his side to the limit, I could sort of understand the spell he was under. After all, I had nearly missed noticing my own entire chance at country music stardom, basically because of lust. It could happen.

"Yeah, but you weren't married for thirty years!" Greg protested when I tried to convince him that fiddle legend Johnny Pixlie might not be an entirely evil being. Greg was surprisingly old-fashioned for a guy with tattoos and a leather wardrobe.

But it was true that Allie wasn't doing very well. The sheer surprise of Dad's rejection had thrown her for a loop, and although she was furious, she couldn't help missing him a little, too. She looked exhausted most of the time, and her mood began to affect everyone else.

When I was little, if I sensed my mother was feeling blue, I'd make her a present. It might be a drawing or a photocopy of my head, or flowers, wet and grimy in my hand, picked in a neighbor's garden. For a while my gifts were Buggy Charms, fabulous bracelets I made by squishing garden ants between pieces of

Scotch tape, then stringing them up on fishing line from Dad's tackle box. Then later on I tried homemade perfume that ended up smelling like skunk cabbage, its primary ingredient. These gifts always got a laugh and they seemed to help. If there ever was a time to present Allie with a gift, this was it.

I worked hard on a song, which was supposed to be my grown-up version of skunk cabbage perfume and Buggy Charms. But it just didn't want to come out funny, no matter how hard I tried. I almost tossed the whole thing but decided to run it by Hoagy first, and he surprised me by loving it. We worked up an arrangement together and waited till the time felt right.

One night when the dinner rush was over and the crowd was mostly regulars, the band invited me to sit in. I counted off a medium-tempo waltz while warning the dancers of an impending "schmaltz attack." It was by far the saddest, corniest thing I'd ever written. I wasn't sure it would work, and my voice faltered as I started to sing.

Your shining eyes answered mine on the night that we met
A walk in the moonlight, a kiss we would never forget
The rose that you gave me is wrapped in pink ribbon and
     etched into my memory
It was the love of a lifetime, take it from me

We waltzed through the years and I'd say we lost track of
     the time
Living together since coffee and pie cost a dime
How did this happen, the house, car, and children, the dog
     sleeping under the tree?
The things you collect in a lifetime, take it from me

Flying through seasons, it seemed we were birds of
    a feather
Who could have ever predicted a change in the weather?

The soft summer breezes have turned into dark winter winds
You stutter and stammer and hardly know where to begin
You're standing there saying she's in the car waiting, and
    you really need to be free
It was the love of a lifetime—don't take it from me

I always wait for the moment when a song I've written becomes real, and sometimes it takes a while. Up to that point, the song is in process and subject to change. But when I see people singing quietly to themselves on the dance floor, I know my song is finished, grown up and left home. "Take It from Me," sappy as it was, was finished the first time out. I caught Allie's eye from across the bandstand; she toasted me with a shot of good whiskey, and smiled.

SITTING IN THE KITCHEN IN MY BATHROBE, MUNCHING on peanut butter crackers, I waited for Richie to stop by for my final costume fitting. When his car finally pulled up in the gravel driveway, I ran out to greet him.

"Oh, darling," he cried, kissing the air next to my cheeks, "you won't believe what I found for you in Ukiah!" He pulled out elbow-length gloves made of leopard-print velveteen, trimmed with long black fringe. "Are they perfect, Bunnymuffin, or what?"

"Richie, they're great. But I hate to break it to you—I can't play my guitar in those things."

"No problem, Sugar Doll. We'll just cut the fingers off, like so. And, oh my! I just thought of something—what color is your guitar?"

"It's right over there on the bandstand." I pointed to my beloved secondhand Stratocaster, on its guitar stand in the corner of the stage. "Robin's-egg blue, I think they call the color."

"Well, Pumpkin, it simply won't do. It just doesn't match."

"Richie, I never heard of anything so ridiculous. It's a musical instrument, not a fashion accessory."

"Missy, when I dress you up, everything you touch is a fashion accessory. Now really, *must* you play that horrid-looking thing?"

"Of course. It's a music show. That's the whole point."

"Well, now, there must be something I can do about this, but we don't have much time. I'll need to take that monstrous thing home with me. And where, oh where, will I find the right fabric? I don't have time for another trip to Ukiah. Wait! That bathrobe. Give it to me, and give me your guitar, young lady. Now!"

Allie and Greg entered the room in time to hear the end of our conversation, and to see Richie trying to strip my precious leopard robe—my road blanket, lamp shade, and stalwart tour companion—off my body.

"Mom! Richie's trying to steal my guitar and my bathrobe," I whined.

"If I were you I'd let him," Allie said, smiling. "Don't bother fighting Richie. You won't win."

I grumpily handed over the goods, but events continued to slide downhill with my dress fitting. Richie looked surprised when I slipped the luscious black velvet over my head.

"Cupcake, your measurements—did I make a mistake?" He frowned, looking at his notes. "I could have sworn . . . Have you gained weight?"

"No. Maybe a little," I answered defensively. "I've been really hungry lately."

"Hmmm, I guess I can let this out here, and . . . Yes, we can make it work, darling. But please, Babycakes, no more bonbons. You've got to watch that waistline until after the show. You know the camera adds ten pounds."

"Greg, do I look fat?"

"I think you look great, absolutely voluptuous."

That was all I needed to hear. I decided to starve myself until we got to Nashville.

AT LAST WE WERE READY. "HEARTACHES FOR A GUY" HAD been steadily climbing the country music charts, and Unicorn Entertainment had finally come up with a minimal travel budget and, miraculously, rooms at the Opryland Hotel. We even had a couple of gigs booked at the Nashville Palace the weekend after the show. I tried to get Allie and Perle to come with us—I wanted Allie to play in the band, and I knew Perle would make a world-class tour manager. Allie's excuse was that she needed to hold down the fort since the house band was going with me; she'd booked some experimental theater and music acts at the Dewdrop. But really, I think she couldn't stand the thought of being in Nashville without Dad. They knew a lot of musicians there, and I guess she didn't want to have to explain things or put up with the torture of their kindhearted sympathy. It pissed her off, too, because she hated to miss the fun. Aunt Perle opted to stay home with her, and Pete Rawley, his arm still in a cast, assumed the tour manager role, relieved that he didn't have to be left out of our adventure just because he couldn't play.

My dress was delivered with a flourish, right before we left, and it fit perfectly. I stood in the middle of the bandstand, bathed in stage lights, modeling my beautiful self for the band. I was instructed to close my eyes, and a fuzzy object, with a familiar weight and feel, was placed in my hands. That's how I ended up with my famous "leopard-skin pillbox Strat" with the foot-long fringe. Richie had come up with a form-fitting leopard slipcover, held together with tiny silver hooks, that fit over the body of my guitar, with openings for the strings and knobs—and I could actually play just fine with the darn thing on. I have to admit I ended up thinking it was pretty cute. It would certainly get attention at the Patsy show. There was even enough fabric left over from my adored bathrobe for a matching jacket.

Richie fussed over my outfit, and my guitar's outfit, until the very last second. I finally had to tell him we were going to miss our plane if he didn't hand them both over and let me get in the truck and go to the airport. I literally had to pull my fringed gloves out of his hand.

Chapter

8

HOAGY TOLD ME TO CLOSE MY EYES AND LED ME across the threshold of our mystery destination. Why did I think I would open them to find my parents together and happy, or Bobby Lee Crenshaw holding a room service rose, or the embodiment of some other deep longing I never even knew I had? Instead I saw Hoagy's grin, surrounded by a bunch of weird merchandise, every last item imprinted with George Jones's face. Not surprising, since we were in the George Jones gift shop, across the street from the Barbara Mandrel gift shop, in what was apparently the Celebrity Gift Shop District of Nashville. In fact, I'd even heard that the Cindi-Lu Bender gift shop, soon to be remodeled, was going to feature a real-life replica of the star's boudoir, in which fans could get themselves photographed in Cindi-Lu's bed. But back in George Jones Land, Hoagy was practically wetting his pants with delight. He knew I was a huge fan, and I didn't have the heart to tell him I'd been here before, quite recently, with Amy and Kathleen.

We'd been having what we called a "girl's day," blasting around town shopping for stage clothes and peculiar souvenir items to drag around with us to a couple of cities and then inevitably leave in some hotel room later on. Seeing all the George Jones ashtrays and refrigerator magnets and ballpoint pens made me miss those days viciously. It was so safe, hanging out with my girlfriends, singing what I was told to sing, and getting my weekly paycheck. Now that I was back in Nashville, I doubted I was cut out for this new country-sweetheart/bandleader role, expected to compete with the big kids. Lately the stress had even been upsetting my stomach with alarming, almost constant indigestion. But I thanked Hoagy sweetly and stuffed a basket with a pile of dumb merchandise.

We met up with the rest of the band at the Bluebird Cafe. Pete was proud to have scored us a reservation at the famous Nashville institution. Hoagy, Lee, Lloyd, and Pete appeared to know everyone in the noisy, crowded bar—and all of their pals seemed to know my parents. I was told time after time that I had a smile "just like your mama's" and that my father was "acting like a damn fool, you'd best believe it." Apparently Allie had fueled many a sideman's fantasy in her road days, and everyone still adored her. They sent her love, kisses, fishing invitations, marriage proposals, and demo tapes—Nashville's ubiquitous version of the business card.

One in particular, a dark-eyed cutie named Jimmy Clearwater, seemed deeply interested in Allie's welfare. Jimmy was a very successful songwriter perpetually trying to break through as a performer and always just missing. His latest song, "The King of Breaking Up," was a huge hit—for George Jones. He'd been nominated in the Songwriter of the Year category and would be appearing in the show just after me. In fact, he'd recruited Hoagy and Lloyd to supplement his band of Nashville regulars.

Jimmy pulled me away from the raucous gathering, into a corner near the pay phones, a concerned look on his handsome face. I couldn't help noticing his beautiful Nudies shirt and the long purple velvet scarf wrapped dramatically around his throat.

"How is your mom, really?" he whispered.

"It's complicated," I whispered back. "She's having a rough time, but basically I have to think she's going to be fine. There are good days and bad days." Then: "Hey, why are we whispering?"

"I have to save my voice for the show," he answered conspiratorially, "so I really shouldn't talk anymore. But I'd like to connect with you later, 'cause I'm really concerned about your mom. I've always had very special feelings for her, you know."

You could've fooled me; as far as I knew, she'd never mentioned him. But I agreed to look for Jimmy at the after-show party, so we could continue our conversation.

The Patsy show was staged in the old Ryman Auditorium, home of the Grand Ole Opry before they moved over to Opryland. It's a gorgeous old theater, smaller in person than it looks on TV. I drifted around in the buzz of pre-show excitement, imagining what I'd hear if the walls could talk about the musicians who had played in this room. I was awestruck that I was about to join their ranks, and doubly grateful for my band of old pros when I saw the lead singer of the new Nashville "hat" band Wildfire near tears because he couldn't get enough guitar in his monitor at sound check. For us, it was a given that we would sound basically like shit—there's no way to sound great on live TV, especially in a show with so many performers, if you're not the star. The trick is to look comfortable and have fun and not worry about it, but I figured it wouldn't hurt to turn a little charm on the sound guys. They always appreciate it, and you never know. So while the guys tuned up and posed and postured for their pals, I wandered off in search of the right roadies to suck up to.

I found Hoover, the sound tech, easily enough. He was deep in conversation with the stage manager, identified on his laminate as Mouse. These two, legendary in Nashville circles, often worked as a team. I'd met them a couple of times before, and I knew we'd be in good hands.

"So who does that asshole think he is, anyway?" Mouse sputtered.

"Cool your jets, dude. It's Cal, remember? Just say yes and do whatever you want. Don't let him get to you, man."

"I know, I know, the guy just pisses me off. He's got some nerve asking for a—

"Hey, Sarah Jean! What's happening, babe? It's good to see you. Cute song, by the way."

"Yeah," Hoover chimed in. "Mouse thinks it's about him."

"Which, of course, it is." I smiled. "Mouse inspires all my songs. How are you guys, anyway?"

"Peaking as usual. So, Country Western Bitch Goddess, what can we do for you?" Hoover said.

"A little extra reverb, crank my vocal in the monitor, and I'll love you till the end of time."

"I'm not cheap, but I'm easy. Hey, Mouse, would you tell Gary to ride the vocal level on the monitor in segment six?"

"You got it, babe," said Mouse. "Then I want to ride Cal Hooper over a cliff. Anything else?"

"Ooh, just one thing, but it's no big deal, only if this is real easy. I forgot to bring any percussion stuff, and there's this one little part of the song—"

"How about a beer bottle and a drumstick?" Mouse suggested.

"That'll work fine, thanks."

"No problem. Think I'll go tune up your instrument right now." The ever-resourceful Mouse grabbed a beer out of the cooler under the mixing board, took a long swallow, and wandered away.

Hoover's cell phone rang, and he made a face as he answered: "Yeah, Cal. Right. Okay. Yup. Sure. No problem. . . ."

I blew him a kiss and found my way backstage.

I had fun watching Greg, who was having an absolute blast fighting off women, and Hoagy, ever on the lookout for old pals who owed him money. Lloyd was deep in conversation with a dapper older gentleman in a Western shirt and bolo tie. Hoagy identified the man as Don Helms, Hank Williams's steel guitar player, there to accept a Lifetime Achievement Award. Jimmy Clearwater, still wearing his purple velvet scarf in spite of the hot stage lights, stood in the wings applying throat spray with a cut-crystal atomizer. I stifled a giggle, wondering if Hank Williams, Ernest Tubb, and the other ghosts who roamed the halls of the Ryman had ever been that precious with their throats. I mean, when you got right down to it, we were all just honky-tonk singers trying to liven up a Friday night for hardworking folks. Sometimes the trappings of country music celebrity looked pretty ridiculous to me. But there was something charming about Jimmy in spite of his weirdness. I shot him a smile across the stage.

He smiled back, beckoning me to follow him.

"Listen," he whispered urgently. "I have reason to believe there's a conspiracy afoot. If you win tonight, watch out for the crutch. That's all I can say. Forget who told you this, but don't forget to say hi to your mom for me, right?"

"Hey, Sarah Jean!" Pete called out. "We're up to sound check! Get your butt out here."

"I'm on my way." When I turned to say good-bye to Jimmy, he was gone.

"What are you doing back there with Jimmy Clearwater?" Hoagy asked. "Is he trying to sell you on one of his bizarre conspiracy theories? Don't listen to that wanker. Come on, we're next."

We ran through our song without mishap, and in spite of the delightful people-watching opportunities, I decided to wait out the pre-show festivities in the dressing room. Knowing that Cal and Cindi-Lu were on approach was making me nervous. A young associate producer led me backstage, telling me the story of her life in under a minute. Jamee was a petite, fast-talking, big-haired blonde in a tight sweater and high-heeled boots. She packed a clipboard and a walkie-talkie, and she knew how to use 'em.

"My dad was a musician—I grew up singing. Came to Nashville to become a star. Thing is, I didn't realize I'd have to take a number. Ended up answering phones for a concert pro-moter to pay the rent—at least I get to meet a lot of people this way. By the way, I love your song—were you really a backup singer for Cindi-Lu Bender? Isn't her voice amazing? But I wish she'd pick better songs sometimes—why doesn't she sing your songs? Listen, here's my pager number if you need anything. Oh, I was wondering, your drummer, is he single?" She waved a cheery good-bye and closed the dressing-room door behind her. I sat for a long time with my head between my knees, fighting off nausea.

The theater quieted as performers finished their sound checks and went out to eat. Greg poked his head in for a minute to make sure I was okay before he disappeared with Jamee. I begged off dinner with the rest of the band and their buddies and wandered around the beautiful old theater for a while, then into the inevitable gift shop. It was filled with an amazing array of Patsy Cline memorabilia, but I selected cardboard Ryman Auditorium fans, the kind you see women using in Southern churches, for Allie and Perle. Considering how much time they spent discussing hot flashes, I figured they'd come in handy. I wondered what Patsy herself would have thought of all this, and her namesake awards show.

"What do you suppose Miss Patsy would think of all this?"

I jumped, startled to hear a voice echo my thoughts. Behind the counter stood a severe-looking older woman with perfect posture, gray hair pulled back in a bun. She wore a silver nametag that said *Mildred Martin, Winchester, VA*. She looked far too elegant and stuffy to be working behind the souvenir counter at a tourist attraction. "Well," I answered, "I guess part of her would be flattered. And probably another part of her would think it was all pretty ridiculous, that people were somehow missing the point."

"No, young lady. This is the point, the whole point. Without money, fame, and commercialization, this music wouldn't survive, and don't you forget it. Are you here for the show?"

"Yes, I'm nominated for the Newcomer of the Year Patsy."

"Newcomer of the Year, hmmf. They come, they go, and none of those girls have any talent or staying power. They end up getting chewed up by the Nashville machine and spit out again. You the gospel singer or the drug addict?"

"Neither. I'm Sarah Jean Pixlie, the man-basher."

"Well, at least you have something to say. Let me give you a word of advice, girlie. Don't expect these Nashville sharks to keep their promises, and don't expect this award, win or lose, to make one bit of difference. No, mark my words: It won't make any difference at all. You want to buy those fans? How about a Grandpa Jones stickpin, half price. We're supposed to unload these before they do inventory. See? I'm wearing one myself."

The woman was a piece of work, but I added a stickpin to my pile of souvenirs and remarked that Grandpa Jones looked lovely on her green silk blouse.

"Calvin Klein, on sale at Castner's, downtown. They come in all colors. But if you're nominated for Newcomer of the Year, it'll be a while before you can afford Calvin Klein, even on sale. Cheating youngsters out of their money is Nashville's best trick."

Maybe she had good reason to be bitter and maybe not, but I didn't appreciate her attitude. She was doing her best to ruin my big day, and I felt compelled to fight back.

"Did you know that Patsy Cline was his mother?"

"Whose mother?"

"Calvin's. I hear he changed the way he spells his name so no one would know, and he could make it in the fashion world on his own merit—and, you know, have credibility with the Jewish guys on Seventh Avenue." God, I couldn't believe I was lying to this nasty old lady. What kind of horrible person would do that?

"Are you telling me, honestly, that Patsy Cline was Calvin Klein's *mother?* For real?"

"That's what I hear. I have no reason not to believe it."

"Well, I'll be . . . and no one in Nashville knows this?"

"I was kind of under the impression everyone knew."

Her eyes softened, just a little.

"Well, mercy, I went to school with Patsy, worked with her awhile at Gaunt's Drugs. But you know, people drift apart sometimes, and what with her career and all, we lost touch. But why not? I guess it makes sense. Miss Patsy had quite a sense of style, you know. I never saw anyone quite as clever with a scarf."

Backstage, I found Greg's cell phone lying on a chair and decided to check in with Allie. She roared with laughter over the lady in the gift shop, and went on to dish the dirt about Ira, the Pillbox Players' director. His latest indiscretion, with the woman contractor in charge of rebuilding the playhouse, had been discovered when the entire high-school jazz ensemble caught the two making whoopee in the band room. Hearing Allie laugh out loud for the first time in weeks, I suddenly loved Patsy, Calvin, and even foolish old Ira. I was about to tell her about meeting Jimmy Clearwater when Aunt Perle grabbed the phone, interrupting us to check on whether I'd remembered to wash my hair with beer and eggs for extra shine, and to deliver an urgent message from Richie about my bustier—as though I couldn't figure out how to put on my own underwear. The backstage area started filling with people and my band came slamming in from dinner, so I said good-bye and got off the phone. It was time to get dressed. It was also apparently time to witness an occurrence that most women never get to see: the transformation of nice, intelligent men into full-tilt road morons.

"Greg, honey, there you are, just in time. Hey, can you zip me up?" I asked.

"Greg, honey, can I zip yours down?" cried Hoagy in falsetto.

"Ooh, Greg," added Pete. "Can I zip it in?"

"I'll bet that's not the first zipper he's messed around with today," Lloyd chuckled.

"I'd like to be zipping that one over there," mused Lee.

"Aw, man, you're just jealous. By the time your groupies get in here with their walkers, we'll be back in California."

I remarked that Greg did look radiant.

"Oh yeah, he's radiating, all right."

"Steamin' baby."

"Fuckin'-A."

"As long as he has some strength left to play."

"Did you use sticks or brushes, man?"

"You oughta know, Pete, you oughta know."

"Come on, pal. Give us old farts a thrill. What's she like? Did you get any Polaroids?"

"Well, did you?"

"Hey, man, a gentleman never tells." But Greg was beet red, which told us everything we needed to know. "Pull your tummy in, will you?" he scolded me. "There you are, all zipped. Can you breathe in that thing?"

"I guess. Does it look okay?"

They all assured me I was gorgeous. Richie's leather, lace, and velvet combo was beautiful, the leopard gloves and guitar providing the final magic touch. I had to admit the guy was brilliant. For the first time that day, I felt as though I belonged in the Patsy Awards lineup.

We were to perform "Heartaches for a Guy" near the top of the show, then take seats in the audience. Later on, when the Newcomer award was announced, I would either run from my seat to the stage to accept the little Patsy Cline figurine, or sit there trying to look pleased for the winner on camera, a far more likely scenario. The other Newcomer nominees were Kellie Griffin, a heavily produced Nashville teenager with her first single, "Rodeo Heartthrob"; Bunny Soules, a young pedal steel guitarist from Oklahoma, whose song and album were called "Buyin', Beggin', and Steelin'"; Marvella Claxton, a gospel singer with "Jesus Is My Lawyer Now," a crossover hit on the country charts; and humor writer Elroy Blunt III, whose novelty recording of Bob Wills's "Roly Poly" had charmed most of America completely by accident, kind of like my song. I was secretly rooting for Elroy, myself.

Marvella was up first, I guess since she sang about Jesus. She walked out from the wings, a dark-skinned beauty, a tiny thing on that huge stage, and bowed her head in silent prayer as the organist played a standard church hymn introduction. Then a huge, breathtaking voice came floating up out of that little body as she began to sing.

> When I find myself in a sorry state
> Tempted by the devil to negotiate
> The Lord says there's no need to litigate
> I keep my eye on the prize and my hand on the plough
> 'Cause Jesus, oh Jesus, is my lawyer now
>
> I don't need a sub rosa investigator
> And I don't want no subrogation either
> I don't need no expert witness or no Latin conjugation
> I got my Wonderful Counselor, and I'm His congregation
>
> He's my lawyer (He's my lawyer),
>   He's my savior (He's my savior)

Counselor of my behavior
Oh Jesus (Jesus!), Oh Jesus (Jesus!)
Jesus is my lawyer now

Deliver me from worldly inquisition
And when Saint Peter comes to take my deposition
I will testify, and shout about the truth —
All objections overruled, and Jesus is the proof

When that final gavel falls on Judgment Day
And they ask how do I plead I will surely say
I have retained His services, and He showed me the way
Not guilty, saints, not guilty, since Jesus took my case
I am here to testify to His amazing, saving grace

He's my lawyer (He's my lawyer),
  He's my savior (He's my savior)
Counselor of my behavior
Oh Jesus (Jesus!), Oh Jesus (Jesus!)
Jesus is my lawyer now

Well, of course, by the end of the song she had us all on our feet and people were yelling "Hallelujah!" and "Amen, sister!" all over the place. Jesus had become everyone's lawyer during the call-and-response part, including mine. I would have given Marvella Claxton the prize right then and there and headed for the after-show party, but of course I wasn't in charge. There were a couple of welcome speeches, a tech award or two, and then it was our turn to play.

We ran out onstage. I grabbed my guitar, remembering not

to get tangled in leopard fringe, and counted off the song. Greg was right there, everyone was right there, and as always when I hit the zone, the rest of the world got smaller. It was the guys and me and we winked and smiled at one another, and I remembered that Perle had said to make love to the camera and I tried, even though I wasn't exactly sure what she meant. My rhinestones sparkled in the stage lights, my eyes sparkled in the TV monitor, and we could even hear ourselves pretty well, thanks to Mouse and Hoover. It felt like about four seconds and the song was over and we ran offstage pumped and breathless.

We might have been done, but the Patsy Awards weren't, not by a long shot. The show went on. And on, and on. Not only did the nominees perform, but the winners felt obligated to thank everyone who had ever entered their lives. Some thanked their mothers; most thanked their managers; everyone thanked God. One or two even remembered to thank their wives and kids. And then they were ready to announce the Newcomer of the Year.

The way it's supposed to work is the Newcomer of the Year award is presented by last year's winner, who, historically, over the course of a year, has become an established country star. However, the previous winner, Trixie "Cowgirl" Ryder, had just gone into drug rehab and couldn't make it. And the Patsy organizers thought it would be big fun to have the award presented by an honest-to-goodness country legend, America's favorite fucking heartthrob, the one and only Cindi-Lu Bender.

She walked out in her bouffant hairdo and high-heeled boots and heaving Wonderbra'd cleavage, and the entire place was on its feet with a five-minute stomping and screaming ovation. She smiled. Then she did her famous little dimpled wink, and spoke:

"It's an honor and a pleasure to be here tonight, y'all!" Screaming and stomping from the audience. "I know you all join me in sending up loving prayers for our sister in song, Trixie Ryder, to aid her in her journey back to our Nashville family." Like she actually gave a shit. More screaming and stomping. "And speaking of family, a former member of *my* beloved touring family is up for this award tonight, so let me quickly run through the nominees, since I personally can't wait to find out if she's won."

She repeated all of our names as a clip of each song was played, then tore into the envelope.

"And the winner is . . . Sarah Jean Pixlie, 'Heartaches for a Guy'! Honest, folks, I didn't rig this one! Come on up, honey. Here she is—the newest Newcomer of the Year!"

I ran up to the stage, realizing that I'd been so sure I wouldn't win that I hadn't bothered to prepare a speech. Cindi-Lu smiled from ear to ear, but her eyes were dead cold. I gamely smiled back and reached for my trophy. Was it my imagination that she held on to the little Patsy figurine a second or two longer than necessary before handing it over, or that she whispered unrepeatable words as she lovingly kissed my cheek? I turned to the microphone.

"I didn't prepare a speech, because I never thought I'd win. I mean, didn't you all think Marvella was incredible, really?"

"Amen, sister, praise the Lord," from the audience.

"And after all, I'm sure none of the men here voted for me." Hoots and laughter from the women. "But I'd like to thank my family, my wonderful band, and most especially, Miss Cindi-Lu Bender, for her love and support. And sorry, Elroy, I was actually rooting for you, but hey—that's a lot of heartaches for a guy, I guess." And, feeling like the world's most disgusting hypocrite, suddenly queasy again, I smiled and waved and walked offstage.

The band was in the wings, with shouts and hugs and kisses, and then, standing off to the side, there they were: Kathleen, Amy—and Bobby Lee Crenshaw. Kathleen and Amy were crying a little and I was, too, and we hugged and giggled and shushed each other like the old days, and made plans to meet later because they were about to go on with Cindi-Lu. Then they drifted away and there was Bobby Lee. He smiled and touched my hair, and I was about to melt into his arms or some corny old thing, when my queasy stomach finally won. I looked down to catch my breath, and before I could stop myself or turn away even, I threw up—all over my beautiful dress and his brand-new Tony Lamas.

The general band consensus was that although it was a damn shame I had to toss my cookies all over Bobby Lee's boots, it was damn lucky that I hadn't done it onstage, on live TV, down Cindi-Lu Bender's cleavage. Only a few people saw, and none of them took pictures. Porter Wagoner, who was about to go out and introduce "Magnolia Heart," handed me his hanky, and I cleaned off as much as I could. Dolly Parton winked and slipped me a Tic-Tac. Bobby Lee gave me this completely unreadable look, stepped out of his boots, and walked onstage barefoot; what else could he do? Which is what earned him a footnote in the Wallace brothers' *Complete Encyclopedia of Country Music Award Shows* and the undying respect of my bandmates.

"Now, that's a pro," sighed Hoagy to Pete as they watched him take his place on stage and pick up his Martin. He started finger-picking the acoustic introduction to "Magnolia Heart." Every note, every squeak of his fingers on the fret board was as familiar as my breath. Watching from the wings, I sang along quietly as the girls came in.

In a cabin in the country, in a county out of time
Lived a family so happy, though they didn't have a dime
They loved each other fiercely and vowed they'd never part
Most of all they loved the girl, lovely little Magnolia Hart

The magnolia is a flower, beautiful and white
A blooming piece of heaven on earth that burns so bright
It's a delicate creation that doesn't last too long
Though it comes from a tree that is solid and strong

Magnolia Hart, lovely by the lake—Magnolia's heart was
there to take
Standing in the sunlight, a sight to make you ache
Picked up by the wind, to fall to ground and break

How many times had I heard that song as overproduced manipulative schlock? How many jokes did we make on the bus, imitating Cindi-Lu's vibrato and laughing about "Magnolia's parts" and "Magnolia farts"? Yet hearing her voice soar magnificently above the band, then drop to a throaty whisper as though she were telling us all her deepest secrets for the very first time, I was astonished to find that the lyrics moved me to tears. This was really weird, since they don't make a whole lot of sense to begin with. I guess I was crying for myself, the loneliness of standing in the wings watching my friends onstage, and the surprising disappointments in this moment that most musicians would give anything to have. But a big old part of me would have given anything, right that minute, to trade my new life for my old one.

* * *

MY SADNESS LINGERED AS THE SHOW ENDED AND WE WERE taken to the after-party. The party room was large and crowded, with festive decorations and a lavish buffet. We posed for pictures, and the guys ran for the open bar while I stood alone looking at people I would ordinarily have been ecstatic to meet. Miserable, wishing only that I could go brush my teeth, tired of fake smiles and small talk, I just wanted to crawl into a hole.

Cindi-Lu, fifth-time Country Legend winner, stood next to Cal Hooper, surrounded by admirers. She was radiant, patiently indulging her fans with handshakes and smiles as she posed for photos with her Patsy statuette. I couldn't get close, even if I'd wanted to. I tried catching Jimmy Clearwater's eye, hoping to finish our conversation about Allie, but he was busy with the publicist from his record label and seemed to have forgotten about me. I did have a nice chat with Marvella Claxton, who accidentally spilled her tumbler full of Jack Daniel's down the front of my dress as she fumbled for a pen so we could exchange phone numbers. She was sweet, and seemed genuinely pleased that I'd won, not to mention grateful that I'd praised her in my acceptance speech. Elroy Blunt III drifted over with a bottle to refill her glass, and a few minutes later as I made my solitary getaway, I noticed her sitting cozily on his lap in the corner. And they called me the winner? I may have been Newcomer of the Year, but I sure felt like a patsy.

Back in my room, I ran a hot bath, tore off my clothes, and rubbed the angry red welts that control-top designer panty hose had imprinted on my belly. I just gave in and let myself feel like total shit, which was actually kind of a relief. I must have fallen asleep in the tub because when the phone rang, my hands were wrinkled as prunes.

"Hey, girl, where are you? We're waiting down in the lobby bar."

"Kathleen! Yikes, I fell asleep. Sorry, I'll be right there."

THEY WERE BOTH TALKING AT ONCE, FILLING ME IN AS WE found a small corner table. "So then she said you were the one who decided to leave," Kathleen explained. "We never believed it, of course. But you know what was weird? Bobby Lee Crenshaw threatened to quit the band after you got fired. He was furious. Cal had to kind of strong-arm him—you know, remind him he was under contract until the Patsy show. Tonight was his last gig with us. He's a nice guy. I'm gonna miss him."

"Yeah," Amy chimed in, "he was booked out of here at midnight, I think. It's just as well for him. He got a Japan tour with Randy Newman, and I think he was getting fed up with Cindi-Lu, anyway."

"So, ladies, how's the new redhead?" I was aware that my voice sounded carefully cheerful.

Amy rolled her huge dark eyes.

"You know what she does?" Kathleen made a face. "She counts up how many parts each of us sings per set, and complains if it doesn't come out even. Can you believe it? Like if Cindi-Lu throws me the solo line that Rosemary Butler did on the 'Magnolia Heart' single? It drives her crazy, 'cause that means I get five more seconds of spotlight than she does."

"Doesn't she realize she's lucky to have this gig?" Amy added. "And the parts work so much better if we all get along. But she keeps her distance and worries about stupid stuff and hogs the dressing-room mirrors and she never wants to go do fun stuff with us. Remember when we used to go look at Barbie doll outfits to get fashion ideas for stage, or go wig shopping? She never wants to do that stuff—she's not much fun, period, and she doesn't sing any better than we do. The worst part is, I hear she's actually fucking Cal."

"Eeeeuuuuwwww!" Kath and I had the exact same reaction.

"She must have misunderstood his request for a blow job," Kathleen laughed, "unless she thinks this is a career move or something. I still remember how totally shocked I was the first time he showed up at my door in the middle of the night."

"Tell me about it! It's the only thing I don't miss about touring with you guys," I said.

"I feel left out. Nobody ever hits on me!" Amy whined, then shrugged. "All I know is that Hoover saw the redhead coming out of Cal's room at about five one morning, looking furtive— and that's Hoover's word, not mine. He thought it was pretty funny, but of course I didn't ask him what *he* was doing wandering around the hotel at five A.M."

Was that an ever-so-slight blush creeping across the demurely married cheeks of my friend Kathleen? Oh, my. I felt it'd be wise not to go there. So we laughed and gossiped and ate hotel bar pretzels until they kicked us out.

"Ooh!" Kathleen shrieked at one point. "I almost forgot to tell you guys. I heard the most amazing thing about Calvin Klein. . . ."

THE NEXT MORNING, WE HAD A BAND MEETING IN WHICH everyone agreed it was important to honor our commitment to play at the Nashville Palace, even though I wanted desperately to go home. I was still feeling lousy and didn't think I'd be able to get through a four-set gig, even for just a couple of nights. It turned out that Cindi-Lu's band had a week's vacation, and Amy and Kathleen were staying in Nashville to catch up on laundry and rest. They put it this way: If I promised to see a doctor when I got home, they'd sing with us for free, allowing me to take as many breaks as I needed. It was the perfect solution.

The Nashville Palace was similar to the Dewdrop in size and atmosphere. The crowd, a mixture of tourists and local musicians, appeared to enjoy our sets of country standards laced with my originals, but the showstoppers each night were "Heartaches for a Guy" and "Take It from Me." Jamee came every night, sweetly mooning over Greg, who seemed to be losing interest. He was impeccably polite to her, which in my experience is not a good sign for the future of a relationship, and I can't pretend I wasn't secretly relieved. It was clear that Greg and I were just friends, true, but that didn't mean I was ready to share him with a serious love interest, especially a cute one with Nashville connections. Funny thing: As it became clear that Jamee was no real threat, I began to feel increasingly sympathetic toward her. Struck by the hopelessness of her situation, I scribbled some lyrics on a bar napkin and finished the song back in my room. It was a straight-ahead Southern-style rocker that took the band about five minutes to learn. With cool backup parts for the girls, we were able to add "Put Me on the Guest List (To Your Heart)" to our second set the following night. Jamee walked in as if on cue, just as the band played the introduction.

I heard you were playing the Palace on Saturday night
I got all dressed up and you know I was feeling all right
Went downtown to meet you but I didn't know
It would cost so much to catch your show

When the bouncer said, "Baby, better come up with
    some dough"
I looked in my pocket but I didn't even have a buck
    (Uh-huh — Oh no)
I smiled real pretty but he said I was out of luck
    (Uh huh — Oh no)
Now you know, sweet baby, it gets kinda old,
Sitting on the sidewalk out here in the cold
So put me on the guest list, I want to rock and roll

Put me on the guest list to your heart
Put me on the guest list if you're smart
I can't afford a ticket, my oh my
Your cover charge is much too high
So put me on the guest list to your heart

"Wow, that guest-list song's killer," Jamee gushed during the next break. "I'm going to be in a talent show at my high-school reunion next month. Do you mind if I do it?"

Relieved that she wasn't insulted, I wrote out the lyrics and a chord chart for her. Jamee insisted on seeing us off at the airport the next morning, and I had the feeling as we boarded the plane that she was the only person in Nashville who was genuinely sorry that we were leaving.

Chapter

9

"**S**O, WHEN DID YOU SAY YOU HAD YOUR LAST PERIOD?" It was a little hard to answer Dr. Terri, because she had a tongue depressor down my throat.

"Oh, a couple of months ago. I've been on the road for a year, though, and that doesn't exactly make for regular periods."

"Uh-huh. Is there any chance you could be pregnant?"

"Nope, absolutely not. I don't have a very exciting life these days."

"You're sure?"

"Well, there was this one night—but it was right after my last period. That's supposed to be safe, isn't it?"

"You said it yourself," Dr. Terri reminded me. "Road life doesn't make for regular periods or ovulation. I'm going to do a blood test, of course, but I'll bet the only thing wrong with you is a normal, healthy pregnancy. How do you feel about that?"

I really didn't know.

I took the long way home from Dr. Terri's office, indulging in a leisurely drive around most of Clear Lake. I stopped for a while to sit by the water and stare at looming Mount Konocti, steeped in mystery and Pomo legend. I tried to remember its various creation stories, learned by every schoolchild in the county, usually mixed into one rambling narrative about when giants roamed the earth and the Indian princess Lupiyoma wasn't allowed to marry because her father disapproved. There was a fight in which both the father and the lover were killed. Lupiyoma threw herself into the lake; her tears became the pieces of volcanic obsidian that children gathered in the countryside, or, in some creepier versions, eyeless fish in hidden underground lakes. Lupi's father became our famous mountain, eternally standing guard. Her lover—hmmm, I couldn't exactly remember what happened to him.

At home I waited for Dr. Terri's call before saying anything to my family. Of course, the blood test was positive—I knew it would be. Suddenly everything from weight gain to nausea to peanut butter cravings made all kinds of sense. The only thing that didn't make sense was that pregnancy was the one possibility that hadn't occurred to me.

It was Monday and the club was dark, so I was able to make my announcement to the family off-mic, thank goodness. No one seemed upset when I shared the big news.

"Honey, I thought you were starting to get a little glow," was my mom's reaction.

"Now someone's going to have to drive to the city for some really good folic acid," was Aunt Perle's.

"Awesome! I'm gonna be an uncle!" crowed Greg.

No one asked about the father. No one suggested an abortion, which was an obvious alternative due to the fact that I was a single, unemployed woman and/or country music's Newcomer of the Year with a tiny window of opportunity to cash in. They all fussed over me; Allie put my feet up on embroidered pillows while Perle made peach tea.

Later, I walked to the lake with Greg. I told him the whole story, about Bobby Lee Crenshaw and the Wild Turkey and the wild night—and the fact that Bobby Lee was currently on tour in Japan, and due to that and other circumstances, we had not really spoken since I left his bed the morning I got fired. We talked about single parents and one-night stands and abortions and my new flash of stardom and how hard I should or shouldn't try to get in touch with Bobby Lee. Greg was amazed and horrified when I admitted we hadn't used any kind of birth control. It had been hard enough to knock on the guy's door in the middle of the night holding his shoes, forget about packing a condom. Where would I have put it? It would have been totally embarrassing. I knew he didn't screw around a lot, so I wasn't worried about catching anything—he'd just been dumped by a longtime girlfriend who got tired of not having him around on Saturday nights. So I'd decided not to worry about the fact that, right after he promised to be very careful, he exploded inside me. At the time, it seemed like the right thing to do. Both times. Actually, all four. It was all coming back in precise detail.

"You have to let him know," Greg insisted. "I would want to know."

"Of course, it's only fair to tell him. But guess what? I barely know the guy. I have no idea how to get in touch with him. He's in Japan with Randy Newman right now."

"Oh, right, suddenly you don't know how to use a phone? Look, Cindi-Lu's played in Japan. Get out an old itinerary and call the hotels. There's probably only one or two in each city where the bands stay. Come on, I'll help you."

We found Randy Newman's tour schedule on the Internet. And sure enough, there was a Robert Crenshaw registered at the second hotel I called in Tokyo. Greg tiptoed out of the room as I waited, heart pounding in my ears, for the operator to put me through to his room. The phone rang and rang. Finally someone picked up.

"Hello?" A woman's soft voice answered. Oh, no.

"Is Mr. Crenshaw there?" I was trying desperately to keep my voice from shaking.

"No, I'm sorry, but he's out right now. This is his wife. I'll be happy to take a message."

I pretended I was from Cindi-Lu's business office, calling about a tax form. Sorry, but I wasn't about to say, "Why, how nice. I'm the mother of his unborn child. Let's get together some time." So shoot me.

I THOUGHT ABOUT HAVING AN ABORTION. I WOULD BE ABLE to go on with my budding music career after a few days of taking it easy, according to Dr. Terri. Having always been adamantly pro-choice, I was surprised by my own feelings—an abortion seemed too sad. Given the state of my love life, I didn't know if I'd ever have another chance to have a baby. And, of course, I wasn't exactly alone in the world. My baby would be born into a loving, if bonkers, extended family. In a year or so, when the BMI checks for "Heartaches" started rolling in, I'd have a nice little income, and how many kids get their start in life with a house band in a honky-tonk? Having a baby would be fun. It would take Allie's mind off what was now looking like her impending divorce. It would take my mind off my own stupid self. It was, like everything else that had happened recently, a total accident. But it wasn't necessarily bad. And so, with exactly the same amount of thought I'd given to jumping into bed with Bobby Lee or writing a hit country single, I decided to become a mother.

Aunt Perle had a few suggestions for me, of course. Actually, more like a few million. I was to avoid sugar, alcohol, and air travel. I was to eat tons of leafy greens along with more tons of everything else except milk. If I showed any signs of a vaginal yeast infection, I was to treat it not with medicine but with the topical application of homemade yogurt—strawberry is best—and who was I to argue? I was suddenly her pet project, and she was in her element. Perle didn't have a very high opinion of doctors; she thought they were all under the evil influence of food industry lobbyists or worse. But I made a secret pact with Dr. Terri: prenatal care in exchange for a concert to benefit her favorite local charity, the Lake County Family Literacy Project. It seemed like a good deal all around.

Richie, vindicated by the fact that he hadn't screwed up my measurements after all, started designing a maternity stage wardrobe. Greg spent a half hour a day talking to my naked belly. And Allie, in the first act of pure domesticity I'd ever witnessed from her, tried to knit a baby blanket.

UNICORN ENTERTAINMENT DIDN'T QUITE SEE THINGS my way. Now that they'd finally gotten used to the idea of a real, live hit-producing country-western recording artist, they felt it was their duty to work me to death. They wanted an album, a tour, and a shitload of promotional appearances, all of which I'd have been happy to do under different circumstances. The VPs had some "image problems" with my pregnancy, since it would indicate that I didn't hate men all that much after all. They had actual meetings about this. But the bottom line was, I didn't feel very well and couldn't have handled being on the road. They had to be satisfied with my promise to complete a solo CD, somewhere close to home and with no firm deadline, using my own band. So, queasy and tired, I spent most of October helping out at the Dewdrop, happily eating tons of food, and taking long walks to the lake, more often than not in order to sneak down to the Soft Serve for a hot-fudge parfait. Or sometimes two.

When bouts of morning sickness sent me to my room, I amused myself by going through the box of old papers and letters I'd saved, the one Allie had almost given away to the library. I found some pretty cool stuff in there—a diary I'd faithfully kept at age ten, in which I'd chronicled weekly meetings of the "Boy Haters Club," and my report card from kindergarten, which might have been describing me last week:

Sarah Jean is a friendly child who is perhaps overly concerned with getting people to like her. She enjoys making up clever rhymes and especially enjoys music corner.

And there was the first song I ever wrote, at age four:

I'm a Jet Plane
I feel like all the transportation things
With my car right here I could be all kinds of things
'Cause this car here is magic when I hop into it,
    you know what I am?
I'm a jet plane, Australia Airlines, it's all right if I'm in the
    Southern Plane
I'm a jet plane, I'm a jet plane

Even then I had an understanding of verse and chorus, defined in my mother's handwriting at my request, in the margins.

I found some wonderful photos of my parents as a young couple, Allie sweet and pretty with flowers in her hair; Dad in stage clothes, always the handsomest one on the bandstand. There was a ridiculous press clipping about my first band, the Surgeons of Sound—we performed in puke-green scrub suits and surgical masks, not great for vocal clarity, a point that was noted repeatedly by the snotty reviewer.

There were pictures of me in other bands, too, bright-eyed and smiling; stuffed into a low-cut glamour dress, leather pants, or cowgirl drag; surrounded by serious young men trying to look like Elvis Costello, Johnny Cash, and/or Merle Haggard; looking startled by the camera's flashbulb; holding on to my Stratocaster for dear life, more because I needed something to do with my hands than because I was any kind of a great player; and backlit, sincere as the day is long, belting out the blues.

I dug through the box, sorting things into piles, taking my time and letting myself recall the reasons I'd saved these particular scraps of paper in the first place. It was fun, soothing, completely absorbing. And then I found something incredible.

At the very bottom of the box was a bundle of papers much older than the other things, older than my things. It was tied together with frayed white satin ribbon. There were some letters and a couple of yellowed newspaper clippings, coated with a fine purple dust. A wrinkled black-and-white photo fell out of the little parcel. My mother's impossibly young face beamed up from the glossy, faded surface. Next to her was a handsome dark-haired stranger, bare-chested in jeans and boots, his arm draped casually around her shoulders. She held a bouquet of ragged flowers in her hand. She looked radiantly happy.

At the time I rationalized my invasion of Allie's privacy, deciding that because the letters were in "my" box they were fair game; later I decided it was hormonally impaired judgment due to pregnancy. Really, I have no good excuse to offer for digging through her secret stuff, I just did it. As I read her letters, I recalled Jimmy Clearwater in Nashville and his "special feelings" for Allie, and the way all the sidemen I met lit up when I mentioned her name. Now here was another one! Perhaps my mother had more secrets than I'd ever imagined.

July 1966, Denver

Of course I remember you, silly goose. Just hate writing. Didn't have your address for a while, but I'll always remember those special times with a very special lady. Don't know if I could ever do it, but I admire your courage going into the Peace Corps— bet you broke every heart in Borneo when you split.

Love from your old friend,

Artie B.

P.S. Try to make it to Newport, OK? They're finally putting me on the bill—not the main stage, just a workshop, but it'd mean a lot if you could be there. —A

I was startled, since by July of 1966 Allie was married to Dad and soon to be pregnant with me. This letter, and the yellowed clippings referring to the new release of an album by folksinger Artie Blond, led me to ask around about him.

"Artie Blond?" Hoagy laughed out loud. "I haven't heard that name in years. What made you think of him?" He put down the Les Paul he was stringing. "He made a folk music record back in the sixties that was pretty good. There was one song on it about the 1871 Chicago fire; actually, it was one long, goofy version of "Hot Time in the Old Town Tonight" with a talking blues riff and a plot twist that involved Mrs. O'Leary's cow smoking reefer. Big cult hit, but that was pretty much it for him. I knew him a little back then. He was a great picker, but there was this other side— he'd worked as a carney and a rodeo clown, dealt a little pot and acid when that was happening. He was a sad cat in a way, always seemed to be running away from something, but funny, and he loved women. If he'd had better clothes, they'd-a called him a playboy. In fact, yeah, we used to sometimes party together in Cambridge back when I played with John Koerner and Eric Andersen. I wouldn't be surprised to hear he died in a barroom fight or stabbed by a jealous husband or a drug deal gone bad, you know? Yo, Pete, remember Artie Blond?"

Pete had wandered in toward the end of Hoagy's speech, to drop off some PA equipment.

"You mean the Artie Blond who took my fiancée skinny-dipping over at Baker Beach in '66, talked her into driving to Denver with him instead of showing up at our wedding, then ditched her for a stripper in Bakersfield? The one I almost sued for alienation of affections?"

"In his case, that lawsuit would have been class-action," Hoagy chuckled.

"Nah, never heard of the guy," Pete grumbled. "But he still owes me money from one time when we went to the dog track."

Later, driving her to the health-food store, I asked Aunt Perle.

"Artie Blond," she mused. "Yes, doll, he was on the radio for a while, some long, funny song about a cow in a fire. God knows

I ought to remember it; Allie played his record enough. She was a big fan. Handsome, on the album cover, one of those deals where the eyes follow you around the room, loaded with sex appeal. But he looked like he could be trouble." Aunt Perle didn't seem to know that Allie had ever met Artie Blond.

I tried one more person.

"Artie who?" asked Greg.

At the library, *Who's Who in Folk Music* listed Artie Blond only as a performer in one or two of the festival programs from the sixties; there was no discography or contact information available. A Web search turned up nothing except others trying to find him. The guy appeared to have dropped off the face of the earth.

I didn't ask Allie, because she'd been intensely moody and it was impossible to guess what would or wouldn't upset her. The routine was, she sulked and Perle walked around muttering about how much better Allie would feel if she ate less sugar and took regular coffee enemas. Anyway, I had to concentrate on my upcoming recording sessions. Artie Blond had to be somewhere, but for now, he'd have to take care of himself.

Chapter
10

THE GENIUSES AT UNICORN ENTERTAINMENT EMERGED from several weeks of meetings with a plan. They were right about one thing, and that was that the only thing disappearing faster than my waistline was my chance at country music stardom. I had to find a way, they said, to keep my fans interested in me. If I wasn't willing to go out on tour, we'd have to think of something else, like a video in heavy rotations on CTV and TNN.

"We can book the soundstage next Tuesday," said the young director on the phone. "Our designers are working round the clock to make it look like an authentic cowboy bar. We even found a mechanical bull in Agoura— Wait a minute, I'm about to go through a tunnel here—call me back if I lose you." I didn't have the heart to disillusion him about the mechanical bull. This piece of rodeo practice equipment was the novelty item once placed in the corner of Mickey Gilley's club in Houston that had somehow become the symbol of the *Urban Cowboy* craze of the early eighties. But the idea of going to Los Angeles to perform in a bad replica of my actual living room seemed ridiculous. If I could lure him to the Dewdrop, I felt sure that we could convince him to shoot the video there. But I had to make him think it was his idea.

"Wow, a real Hollywood soundstage?" I gasped. "I just can't wait. Can we have lunch in the commissary and meet some stars? I promise I won't embarrass you, but if you could introduce me to Regis and Kathie Lee, or the cast of *General Hospital,* I'd love that!"

"Well, you know, it's unlikely we'd have time—"

"Oh, this is all so exciting." I added a bit of Southern twang for effect. Heaven knows I'd heard Cindi-Lu, all-time Southern belle champion of the Western world, do this enough times to imitate her in my sleep. "Could we ride in a stretch limo, too? Can you get me tickets to Jay Leno? Hey, can you get me *on* Jay Leno?"

"Our publicist is working on that. I have to take another call. My girl will get back to you with all the details, okay?"

"Okay, but don't y'all forget about Regis and Kathie Lee now, promise?"

Hoagy and Greg, working on the PA wiring, looked at me as if I'd gone batshit until I explained my plan. Sure enough, within a half hour I got a call from Unicorn's brand-new VP of Artist Development. It seemed the young director was very concerned about my being unclear on the concept of producing a video, and was flying up that very day to talk to me.

We spent the rest of the afternoon gathering the troops, making sure the bar would be full for Mr. Hollywood's arrival. Richie brought his mother, aunt, and sister, Allie called the cast and crew of the Pillbox Players, and the guys called all their buddies and ex-wives. By the time Mr. Hollywood hit the Dewdrop Inn, the sun was going down, the band was warming up, and there was a large and lively crowd pointedly ignoring him. Pete sauntered over to the door.

"That'll be a five-dollar cover charge, pal."

"Oh, I'm sure I'm on the guest list. Harlan Harris from Videophile Productions."

"Guest list, huh? Hey, Allie, you seen a guest list around here anywheres? This dude says he's on it. Funny, he don't *look* too cheap to pay five bucks."

"For heaven's sake, Pete, let the poor man in. He's obviously come a long way. Welcome, Mr. Harris. I'm Allie Pixlie, Sarah Jean's mother. This is our old friend Pete Rawley."

As Harlan entered the bar, I heard one of the regulars remark that in his getup, he was all set for Halloween.

"You'd better be sweet to this one, Wonderboobs," Richie whispered to me. "That's the first Hugo Boss shirt this town has ever seen. Except for mine, of course." He then proceeded to identify the manufacturer of every visible item of clothing on Harlan Harris's very fit body. In addition to the black Hugo Boss shirt buttoned at the neck, he wore tinted wire-framed Oliver Peoples glasses, Gucci loafers with no socks, a Ralph Lauren suede jacket, and soft, bleached Calvin Klein jeans.

"Hey, Richie, did you know about Calvin Klein being Patsy's—"

"Don't you dare even start, Sarah Jean," Richie hissed. He flounced away before I was able to ask how he could recognize a pair of Calvin Klein jeans from that distance.

Allie jumped up onto the bandstand and kicked off the first set with "Stay All Night, Stay a Little Longer." She introduced each band member as she cued his solo, then called me up to the stage. Inspired by the scene at the door, I counted off "Put Me on the Guest List (To Your Heart)." It was the first time we'd done it since Nashville, and we got a good crowd out on the floor. We followed with "Heartaches for a Guy" and then slowed things down to waltz tempo for a ladies' choice on "Take It from Me." By then Harlan Harris, local brew in hand, was looking more relaxed.

I turned the stage back over to Allie and went to rescue Harlan from Richie's relentless fashion chatter. We walked back to the office and closed the door.

"So, when do I get to come to L.A.?"

"Sarah Jean, I hope you won't be too disappointed when I tell you this, but—"

"But what? You mean we're not doing the video?"

"No, no, babe. It's just that, well, this place is so deliciously authentic, you dig? Call me crazy, but I had a wild idea we might shoot the video here."

"You mean no Regis and Kathie Lee? No lunch? No limo?" I tried hard to sound heartbroken.

"Sweetheart, I know it's a disappointment. But comparing what it would cost to try and recreate, um, this—we could do three videos here for the price of one in Los Angeles. Can you understand that?"

"Well, I guess it does make sense," I sighed. "I can always meet Regis and Kathie Lee another time."

"Great. Now, if only we can get that mechanical bull up here."

A WEEK LATER, HARLAN, A VIDEO CREW, GRETCHEN PEA—THE most sought-after and expensive set designer in the industry— and the mechanical bull took up residence in the cabins at the

Skylark Shores Resort on the edge of Clear Lake. They spent money and tipped well, so the locals welcomed them with open arms. But Harlan's impeccable fashion statements and fussy mannerisms became easy targets for us. I'm not especially proud of the fact that we made him the butt of endless jokes; even invented a new dance called the Harlan, mimicking his walk. Even so, I kept up my smarmy, exaggerated Southern belle routine, as we found his earnest responses hilarious.

Somewhere during the planning stages it had been revealed that there was no actual studio mix as yet for "Take It from Me." Harlan wanted to try capturing a live performance of the song on video while actors played the roles of the characters in another part of the club. It was an ambitious idea that required multitrack audio and impeccably timed synchronization of activities. Allie recruited the Pillbox Players, once again, to act in my video. Most volunteered their services in return for a hefty donation from Unicorn Entertainment to the Pillbox Players' building fund. They were planning to stage *Carousel*, and Monster Truck damage repair was proving costly due to the rapid turnover of female contractors.

Harlan cast our band as the guys in "Heartaches," with footage from the Patsy show, where I'd been relatively slim, to be edited in. Hoagy was the lead, and the others were convincing enough as his poker and bowling buddies. The casting for "Take It from Me" was trickier. Even though the song was for and about Allie, she simply looked too young to play the role of a woman who'd been left by her husband of thirty years. Perle, just a few years older, had a more grown-up appearance with that indefinable New York edge. It took some doing to talk her into playing the part, but once she agreed, she took her role seriously, driving everyone crazy with intense discussions about motivation and the Method.

The wayward husband was more of a problem; the guys in the band were simply not capable of the arrogant posturing required for the role. Then the infamous womanizing Ira stopped by to drop off some flyers, shirt unbuttoned to reveal several gold chains nestled in dark, curly chest hair. As always, he stood a little too close and looked a little too intently into my eyes. Harlan hired him on the spot, despite Aunt Perle's protests that she wasn't sure if she and Ira would have the requisite onscreen chemistry.

HARLAN AND I WERE IN AGREEMENT ABOUT CASTING, BUT HE remained convinced that the mechanical bull was necessary. Gretchen Pea, a six-foot blonde who wore silk Chinese robes and about eighty pounds of exotic jewelry, finally persuaded Harlan to drop the clichéd idea after a long conversation with Greg that involved an excessive amount of hair tossing and smile flashing on both their parts. To say that Greg was charming the socks off the Hollywood contingent would be a remarkable understatement. He became our spokesman and our secret weapon. No one could understand what he was still doing in Lake County playing in a country-western roadhouse with a bunch of old guys.

"Some people," he explained when I expressed similar concerns, "just don't understand about loyalty. That must be it, 'cause it sure ain't the sex."

The day of the shoot, Richie showed up with two assistants and approximately forty gallons of makeup. The cast gathered, sipping coffee and reading their papers while the lighting crew spent hours making the Dewdrop look like it was midnight. I'd learned by then not to ask what seemed to be an obvious question: Why not just wait till midnight?

The phrase of the day was "Hurry up and wait." Flurries of activity were followed by long periods of nothing apparently happening while a scene was set up, lights and levels and camera angles adjusted. Greg was fascinated by the technology; I enjoyed watching the people.

Harlan was in his element, eyes sparkling as he put us through our paces. Whatever else you might say about the guy, it was clear he really loved his job. He was a good director— encouraging, supportive, and funny. Gretchen Pea, cool and elegant, contributed constant minuscule adjustments that somehow made an enormous difference. Richie's energy level was scary as he flew around the room wielding powder puff and mascara wand. The Drifters, all lifetime experts at playing themselves, did great. The only rough spot occurred when Perle found Ira's hand on her thigh under the kitchen table and decked him with the frying pan she was using as a prop. Richie's industrial-strength makeup covered the bruise.

It really was midnight by the time we wrapped, and I walked Harlan out to his rental. As Gretchen Pea settled herself in the car, I impulsively gave him a hug.

"Thanks," I said. "You might not believe this, but I'm glad they put you in charge of my video."

"Hey, babe, it was fun. But next time you try out the dumb-country-girl routine, there's something you ought to know."

"What are you talking about?"

"Regis and Kathie Lee tape their show in New York, not Los Angeles. Any real fan would have known that."

"I didn't fool you for a minute, did I?"

"Not for a second. There's a lot of heart and intelligence in your songs; no one smart enough to write them could be that stupid. But the guys at Unicorn said to do whatever you wanted, so I went along with it. People care about you more than you think, babe. Look, it was a blast and we have a dynamite product here. Oh, by the way, I just called the club owner in Agoura. He says he wants you to keep the mechanical bull as a gift. His wife is a big fan."

"But—"

"With my compliments." Harlan smiled. "Neener, neener, neener. No backs."

He adjusted his Oliver Peoples, gunned the engine, and drove into the night, the glamorous Gretchen riding shotgun. I found myself surprisingly sorry to see them go, especially since the mechanical bull stayed. We plugged the thing in once so Greg could try it, and after that it became the bull of a thousand uses. Aunt Perle sorted vitamins on its back. Richie draped sequined fabric on its horns. Allie named it Frisky and talked to it every now and then. But mostly, as time went on, it became the receptacle of choice for everyone's laundry.

THEY RUSHED THE VIDEO OF "HEARTACHES FOR A GUY" into rotation on TNN and CTV, and we made plans to record "Take It from Me" for real, in order to time my solo CD with the video's release. I needed to include more songs, and chose "Put Me on the Guest List (To Your Heart)," "My Baby Used to Hold Me (Now He's Putting Me on Hold)," which I'd finally finished, and some older stuff I'd been working on for a while: "Hell on Heels" and "Baby, Hold On." Depending on time, I thought I might add my high-tech parody of the Muddy Waters blues classic, inspired by Greg's obsession with his laptop computer, "Got My Modem Working." We'd round things out with a couple of cover tunes. I was thinking of "Tall Tall Trees" and "Pick Me Up on Your Way Down," two songs I loved to sing, which always went over well at the Dewdrop.

I started planning the sessions, wishing that Kathleen and Amy were around to sing harmony. We'd had a special chemistry with our vocal blend. The fact that we were good friends might have helped, but I suspect it can also go the other way. Playing or singing well with someone can connect you in amazing ways, cutting through a lot of the things you'd normally have to do to make friends. Singing harmony has always felt particularly intimate to me.

The band caravanned to San Francisco in my pickup and a couple of cars, and set up headquarters at the Hotel Phoenix, Bay Area home to the low-budget touring rocker. Although they were paying for the sessions, Unicorn didn't have much production guidance to offer; everything from choosing the songs to arranging the sessions was up to me, as long as I stayed within the budget. I booked Poolside Studios in the Marina District. I'd worked there on my demo and remembered that Dave, the chief engineer, had been the guy who walked "Heartaches for a Guy" across the hall, getting it into that movie sound track in the first place. He had a good ear for instrumental tracking—my weak point, since I'm always focusing on the vocals. Dave worked fast, and knew how to step in without stepping on toes. We had only one week to record all the instrumental and vocal tracks for my CD.

The greatest luck of all rolled through town on our first night, in the petite form of gospel singer Marvella Claxton. She happened to be performing at a Youth for Jesus convention and was staying at our hotel. Elroy Blunt III was there, too, having somehow talked an editor at a men's magazine into assigning him to cover the event. The two seemed as cozy as ever. Marvella and I stayed up late working on a new song, and I impulsively decided to include it on the CD when she agreed to sing it with me. I recruited her for backup vocals, too, while we were at it.

Dave helped me get basic rhythm tracks to all the songs on the first day, and overdubs over the next two. On the fourth day, the guys all went record shopping while I did my lead vocals. The fifth day I worked with Marvella and session goddess Keta Bill on background parts. They weren't Amy and Kathleen, but they weren't exactly chopped liver, either. We had a blast, especially on "Hell on Heels," loosely inspired by Perle and Allie's girlhood stories, which features a feisty call-and-response vocal arrangement. They were total pros, and the blend was lovely.

I saved the duet with Marvella for last.

We'd decided to try recording the old-fashioned way, with both of us singing live into the same microphone. We slipped on our headphones, Dave rolled tape, and we sang. Marvella, better acquainted with both God and Jack Daniel's than I could ever hope to be, sang her little heart out, and I did my best to keep up as we rolled into the last verse and chorus.

When my time is ended here, lift a glass for me
Fill it full and raise it high for everyone to see
Thank God for Jack Daniel's, he's why I'm here today
Thank Jack for helping me see God, and send me on my way

Jack's got my front, God's got my back
Together we can fight off whatever may attack

Praise the Lord and Mr. Daniel's, we're doing fine so far
I've got my eye on heaven and my butt is in this bar—Amen

We nailed it in a couple of takes, and even in my heavier, rounder state I felt lifted off the ground. Marvella beamed, listening to her own incredible voice on playback.

"You are amazing," I gushed. "Where did you learn to sing like that?"

"In church, where everyone learns to sing in Hope Springs, North Carolina," she answered. "I'm nothing special in my choir back home, really. Some of those sisters can *sing*. You should hear our pastor. I just got lucky is all."

Marvella told me about growing up in a small town in the South, where church was the center of family and community life. She'd been singing ever since she could remember, probably before she could walk. She joined the choir before she was out of knee socks. Her grades were good enough to win her a college scholarship, and she met someone in school who hired her to sing on songwriter demos. Producers who heard the demos hated the songs but loved her voice. Soon she was offered a deal with a small gospel label. The rest was a matter of luck and timing. She was as surprised as I was to have a hit record.

"I'm envious. I've always wished I had a big gorgeous voice like yours."

"Well, your voice might not be as big as mine, but it sure is pretty," she said. "And you can do some things I can't. I wish I had your ear for harmony; the way you can pick up parts instantly is pretty special. Where did you learn to sing?"

I actually remembered the day I learned to harmonize. I was eleven years old on a lazy Saturday afternoon, sitting at the kitchen table with my favorite book of Greek mythology, running my tongue over the new braces on my teeth. My parents, home between road trips, were going through piles of mail.

"Hey, gals, look what Waddy sent us," Dad said as he pulled an LP out of its cardboard mailing sleeve. A guitarist pal in L.A. had apparently played on the recording sessions. "Zevon—I've been hearing about this guy. He's supposed to be pretty good." The man on the album cover looked like one of my mischievous musician uncles, only perhaps more cynically urban. He wore round glasses and a pageboy haircut, elegant against the deep red color of the photo's backdrop. Dad carefully lowered the turntable needle on the title cut, and from the first notes of the intro, the three of us were on our feet, dancing around the kitchen and laughing. Then these magnificent background vocals kicked in, and I grabbed a spatula and pretended it was a microphone, singing along.

"Oooooh-waaaaah-oooooh! Oooooh! Excitable boy!" I sang over and over, along with the lovely women's voices on the record.

"Johnny, listen," my mom shouted over the music, "Sarah Jean's singing a third. She's actually harmonizing."

Dad started the song again from the beginning. Allie sang with the girls on the record, demonstrating the different vocal parts and how they worked together, then coming up with some new ones that complemented the existing parts. She and Dad each took a different note. I stayed on the third and we played the song again, each keeping the thread of our individual lines. "Oooooh-waaaaah-oooooh!" over and over, laughing at the excitable boy who couldn't stay out of trouble. The homicidal content of the lyrics wasn't disturbing in the least, since it echoed many of the plot lines in *Clarkson's Anthology of Greek Myths for Young Readers.* Allie picked up the album to look at the credits.

"Wow, great choice of singers. You have to respect a man who knows how to arrange background vocals." Something about her tone of voice got it across that in my parents' band, this had been an Issue. "This is a good record," she sighed, and proceeded to have a secret crush on Warren Zevon for the rest of her life.

The kids I knew latched on to "Werewolves of London"— Leslie Jane Schoonmaker even wrote a play about them—and my folks loved "Lawyers, Guns and Money." But "Excitable Boy" became my favorite song in the whole world that year. I always sang along with the record, over and over again. After a while I decided to branch out and try harmonizing with other songs I liked. But when I think about harmony, either the musical or the family kind, I drift back to that Saturday, my orthodonture sparkling in sunlight from the kitchen window, singing into a spatula with my mom and dad.

"You miss your dad a whole lot, don't you?" Marvella asked kindly.

"I do. I can't believe I'm going to have a baby and he won't be around. It feels so wrong." The hormonal tears that were never far from the surface threatened to burst through.

"Oh, Baby." Marvella took my hand. "I don't know if you usually do this, but let's take a minute to pray about it. Then let's go get a drink."

THE GUYS RETURNED, LOADED DOWN WITH BAGS FROM Amoeba Records, bragging about the used vinyl rarities they'd found in their favorite Berkeley store. Dave, Marvella, and I, having been cooped up in the studio all day, were more than ready for a walk around the corner to the Balboa Café. The guys wanted to hear the vocals we'd done and said they'd meet us in a few minutes. The trendy Marina District joint gets busy singles pickup action at night, but at four in the afternoon it was nearly deserted. The hunky young bartender was—of course, who isn't?—a singer-songwriter, and as he chatted with Dave about his latest CD project, I checked out the beautiful old room and the one other customer sitting at the bar.

He had one of those remarkable faces. Long gray hair framed tanned, rugged cheekbones; he had deep laugh lines around his mouth, and bright blue eyes. His nose looked as though it had been broken in several places. He reminded me of the guys in our band—he was about the same age—but someone else, too, I couldn't quite place. He nursed a whiskey straight up and seemed lost in his own world until his ear caught part of Dave's conversation with the bartender.

"'Scuse me, man, I don't mean to butt in, but it sounds like you know some shit about digital recording. This is all new to me; I haven't been inside a studio in twenty years. Could I ask you a few questions?"

Dave nodded, mentioned that he ran the recording facility around the corner, and began chatting with the stranger. I took the opportunity—always welcome, in my condition—to run to the ladies' room, dragging Marvella along with me. We returned in time to see Dave hand over a business card. The man scribbled something on a cocktail napkin while he finished his drink, gave the napkin to Dave, and left the bar.

"What a weird cat," Dave said as he turned back to us. "Says he made a few records about twenty years ago, then got sick of the business and quit. Have you ever heard of him?"

He showed Marvella the cocktail napkin and she shook her head no. She passed it to me. On the napkin, scrawled in handwriting I'd seen before, with no phone number or any other information given, was the stranger's name: Artie Blond.

I DECIDED TO KEEP NEWS OF THE ARTIE BLOND SIGHTING TO myself until I could actually talk to him, and since I didn't have a way to get in touch with the guy, there was no point getting everyone all excited. I asked Dave to give me a call if Artie got in touch.

I rounded up all the Dewdrop Drifters except for Hoagy, who was staying on to help with mixing and mastering, and headed home a week before Thanksgiving.

OR AS LONG AS SHE'S OWNED THE DEWDROP, ALLIE
has maintained a peculiar Thanksgiving tradition. The
club is closed to the public for the entire long weekend
and the band gets time off. She hosts a huge feast for a hundred or
so of her closest friends on Thanksgiving Day, followed by a talent show in which the word *talent* has a broader definition than
usual. Then we have the place to ourselves until Saturday evening,
when that old-traditional Dewdrop Harvest Dance is held. It's
called a private party so kids can come and stay all night, but
everyone's invited, and the whole town generally turns out for an
evening of great music performed by a roots music band from
Austin, L.A., or San Francisco—anywhere but Lake County.

This year, in a gentle act of rebellion against Dad's well-
known musical preferences, Allie announced that she had booked
a Zydeco band, mumbling something about how everyone eats
too much all weekend and Zydeco seemed like the most aerobic
kind of music for dancing—really, she was just contributing to
community health and fitness. Sunday and Monday are recovery
days, then back to business as usual, gearing up for the holiday
season's special events.

We returned from San Francisco to find Allie in high gear organizing her annual bash, the one time of year that she actually cooks. There were recipe books and weird ingredients everywhere, and she was experimenting with a new culinary invention.

"Salsa roll-ups?" asked everyone who made the mistake of wandering through the kitchen.

"Try one, they're good. Look, it's just salsa baked inside rolled-out cornmeal batter. I put a little too much baking soda and sugar in these, but you'll see. This time next year there'll be an Auntie Allie's Salsa Roll-Up Stand next to every Mrs. Field's in the mall," Allie informed us as Perle, Greg, and I inched toward the door. But there was no escape without trying a salsa roll-up.

"Ugh, these are truly disgusting," Greg whispered as he discreetly disposed of his in a napkin.

"If only Mama had taught us how to cook," wailed Perle, "instead of telling us we could pick that up from books, and that it was more important to learn how to flirt." She turned to Greg and me. "Our mother bought us red lace underwear for our thirteenth birthdays, can you imagine? She said we should always remember that 'the boys like to see a little panty every once in a while.' But cook? Forget it, she wasn't so good at it herself, and didn't teach us a thing. This—" she wrinkled her nose in disgust, holding a salsa roll-up at arm's length—"is the sad result. At least she could have used whole-grain flour."

But I was pregnant, and the weird combination of spicy, sweet, savory, and buttery flavors with a bitter undertone of baking soda tasted wonderful. I had eaten six of the strange little things before I could tear myself away. Allie commandeered the club's industrial-sized oven and kept 'em coming. It seemed to cheer her up some. Even Aunt Perle, secretly horrified at the lack of actual nutrition in a salsa roll-up, knew better than to get between a pregnant woman and her cravings. She boosted my vitamin formula and hoped for the best. She needn't have worried.

ON THANKSGIVING DAY, WE STOOD AT THE FRONT DOOR of the club greeting guests. Although most of the regulars normally enter through the back door off the parking lot, Allie dictates that for this occasion everyone use the front entrance "like ladies and gentlemen." It seemed that my recent TV exposure had given this year's feast some extra drawing power. Our comfortable, casual dinner had suddenly become a hot ticket, and we were expecting a full house. Allie and Perle had been cooking for days, bickering about ingredients to their hearts' delight. The large dance floor was filled with candlelit tables, decorated in a style Richie described as "Martha Stewart on Acid." Every random large piece of fabric in the place had been pressed into service as a tablecloth. Every loose nonflammable object we could find, from shoehorns to obsolete computer program disks, had become a candleholder.

Greg seemed especially nervous. Not only were his parents coming up from Bakersfield, but Jamee from Nashville had called to announce that she was going to be in the neighborhood visiting family and would love to stop by, a huge surprise, since we're not exactly in anyone's neighborhood. He'd basically forgotten about Jamee the minute our plane from Nashville hit home turf. She was a nice person, he explained, but their relationship had been just a road thing, and being familiar with road things myself, I understood. Greg seemed to have very little contact with his parents, the busy Central Valley business owners—it was a surprise to everyone that they'd accepted the invitation. We worked out a secret "rescue me" signal and vowed to stay within eye contact of each other at all times.

Lloyd was also a little jumpy. Although they'd still not met, he and SWF 34 had been talking on the phone almost daily, and we could tell he liked her a lot. She'd responded to his holiday invitation with a card explaining that she was supposed to entertain out-of-town guests but would try to make an appearance later in the evening. Lloyd was settling in for a long night with his eyes glued to the door, and I was jealous. Hormonally sentimental, I found the sad fact that there was no one I was expecting, or even wanting to see that intensely, incredibly depressing.

Hoagy returned with a copy of the finished CD master, and we played it in the background as the club filled up with old friends and familiar faces. I served champagne and hors d'oeuvres, my job ever since I could remember. I found that most of our neighbors were more interested in my autograph than my canapés. I had just signed a paper napkin for Mr. Bagatelle, the produce man, when I heard an ear-shattering screech.

"Floppytoes! Sweet little Picklebelly! You look absolutely, completely divine!" The paint-scraper voice belonged to a voluptuous blonde in a floor-length mink coat, who had Greg in a vise grip. Standing next to her was a tall man with a bodybuilder's physique, wearing purple polyester opened to reveal so much gold jewelry that I was afraid he might have rolled Ira in the parking lot.

"Hi, Mom," Greg answered weakly, just as Jamee took a breathless running dive into his arms, having pulled up in a taxi a moment earlier. The poor guy was a goner.

Little Max, my pal since kindergarten, when he was only a few inches shorter than he is now, arrived looking gloomy and tense. He followed me around the room trying to get my attention, and I made an effort to focus on him, but was constantly interrupted by people I hadn't seen in ages. I turned around after signing a Patsy show listing in *TV Guide* for my dentist and nearly tripped over Little Max.

"Here, party girl, I have a present for you." He placed a tiny plastic vial in my hand. "It's the best crystal meth around. I know the guy who makes it, and there's plenty more where this came from, too."

"Actually, Max, I was never really that much of a party girl. But that doesn't matter. Here, take it back, it'll just be wasted on me." I had to make an effort to be gracious, still annoyed at the way he'd tried to hit me up for money at the Honda dealership.

"Oh, all of a sudden you're too good for my present? Well, fine." Sulking like a toddler, he withdrew to a corner table where, in between his frequent trips to the bathroom, he started ostentatiously flirting with a young woman I'd never seen before.

I helped serve, then sat down with a plate full of salsa rollups, watching everyone eat. It had not been an easy day for Allie. The first holiday season of her life without Dad had begun. She was brave and charming, trying to have a good time, but anyone who knew her could see she was fighting tears. Greg was drinking too much, flanked by Jamee and his mother, neither of whom seemed to have noticed the other's existence. Hoagy crossed the room and plopped down next to me.

"Why so glum, Beautiful?"

"I don't know, Hoagy. People are acting weird, staring at me and asking for autographs. I know I've been on TV and everything, but I'm still the same Sarah Jean. Even Little Max was following me around, offering me speed. I don't do drugs with Max anymore. It's not that I'm a prude or anything—we did our share on the road—but even if I weren't pregnant, Max always gets shitty stuff. Now all of a sudden it's like it means more to him. He's really insulted that I said no."

"It feels like you haven't changed but everyone around you has somehow, doesn't it?" Hoagy said. "People give the time they spend with you more importance than it deserves—no offense—because of what your fame and your music mean to them. It's a big responsibility for you. You have to be careful not to believe your own press and turn into an asshole."

"Maybe I already have."

"Nah, you're fine so far. But you're lucky—you have people around who will care enough to let you know when they start seeing the telltale signs. It's not fair, but you're going to have to put out a little extra effort to make other people feel comfortable around you."

"I'll say it's not fair," I grumbled. "Not that it's at the same level, but I'm starting to understand why Cindi-Lu Bender spends so much time alone in her hotel room."

Dinner ended and the band assembled onstage for Allie's All-Star Thanksgiving Day Talent Show. The deal was that no one was supposed to show off his or her usual talent. The Drifters were exempt because they were needed to back everyone up, but I was expected to come up with something ingenious that didn't involved singing or songwriting. I was planning to lead the whole group in the Chicken Dance and had to sneak off and watch from the hallway as I slipped into my feathers and tutu.

Allie gloried in her role as emcee. She put on her seasonal glitter top hat and walked up to the microphone.

"Welcome, everyone, to the All-Star Thanksgiving Day Talent Show, featuring our house band, the Dewdrop Drifters.

Let's have a special round of applause for long-suffering musical director and bandleader Hoagy Guitarmichael. These guys are here for *you* tonight, so if you haven't signed up yet, talk to Pete over there with the list. Come on, Pete, stand up so everyone can see where you are."

Pete half-rose from his chair with his bashful "I'm a little drunk but I can do this" smile, waving a crumpled-up sheet of paper in the air.

"All right, then, I'd like to welcome our first guests. Dave and Michelle both work at Bruno's Market and they've collaborated on an original song. Without further ado, let's hear a big round of applause for their "Supermarket Fantasy.""

They both looked about nineteen years old. Blushing adorably, Michelle handed chord charts to the band while Dave counted off a perky little two-step.

M: *I let you squeeze my melons down at the produce stand*
D: *I loved the way you held that ripe zucchini in your hand*
M: *You helped me grind my coffee*
D: *You sweetened up my tea*
BOTH: *We've never met but you're my supermarket fantasy*

I got the weekly special when you rolled your shopping cart
Out of farm fresh vegetables and right into my heart
I don't even know your name but I like what I see
We've never met but you're my supermarket fantasy

D: *Cakes and pies, big brown eyes, are pretty as can be*
M: *You're so hot, what you got meets all my baking needs*
D: *If I walk up and say hello, please answer with a smile*

BOTH: *And maybe someday, darling, we'll go walking down the aisle*

I got the weekly special when you rolled your shopping cart
Out of farm fresh vegetables and right into my heart
I don't even know your name but I like what I see
We've never met but you're my supermarket fantasy

The crowd, totally charmed, gave them a standing ovation as they bowed and returned to their seats. Allie sprinted back up to the microphone. She consulted her clipboard.

"Please put your hands together for the second performer of the evening. She's a first-time guest and must be a proud, proud mama. Her son is Greg Carson, drummer of the Dewdrop Drifters. Let's have a warm welcome for Monica Carson. We hope to see a lot more of her around here."

Mrs. Carson wiggled out of her fur coat to reveal a skintight spangled evening gown. She appeared to be Allie's age or a little older, and had a smashing figure. She knew it, too, as she sashayed up to the bandstand and handed out sheet music. The band played tentatively at first but hit their groove by the end of the first verse. Mrs. Carson's voice was soft and breathy in the microphone.

I was sitting on my barstool when you lit my cigarette
You thought it might be worth a try to see how far you'd get
Your eyes were on my Wonderbra, your hand was on my thigh
Cool your jets, you hunk o' love, you're not my kind of guy

As she sang, she sauntered around the stage. Everyone seemed enchanted by her performance except Greg, who was suddenly pale. Ever the professional, he kept on playing, keeping perfect time with his brushes.

She kissed the air as she ended the first verse. One shoulder strap slid down her arm as she removed her long gloves in a fetching manner and draped them, one by one, on Hoagy's guitar strap.

> *You're plying me with liquor, you're licking me with plyers*
> *You've bought me seven rum and Cokes, that's Diet Coke*
> * with Meyers*
> *But I'd prefer a Mai Tai with a little pink umbrella*
> *Stop drooling in my cleavage, dude, you're not my kind*
> * of fella*

Struggling to stretch the glittery tutu over my recently expanded belly, I got tangled up in the straps of my neck and head feathers, and was only half paying attention as her cinch belt hit Lloyd's amp with a thunk. So it wasn't until she actually started removing her dress that I realized Greg's mom was doing a strip act. She undulated out of her gown and wrapped it around Lee's neck while leaving a large lipstick smudge on his left ear. Moving to the edge of the stage, she beckoned Pete, whose Adam's apple started bobbing up and down as he approached. She hiked her satin slip around her waist and slowly, ever so slowly, rolled her panties down to the floor, daintily picking them up and placing them in Pete's pocket while planting a big fat kiss on his cheek as she pushed him away from her. Then, turning her scrumptious behind toward the audience, she slowly pulled the slip over her head and threw it over her shoulder. There was a mesmerizing tussle with bra hooks and the purple lace Maidenform Underwire was flung offstage into a lap that unfortunately belonged to

Richie (who immediately checked out the label and gave his usual look of disgusted resignation when confronted with a "fashion don't" of this magnitude). Still singing, she turned around to face the crowd and I saw the Drifters' awed reaction as they got the rear view. I gave up trying to adjust my tangled feathers and watched from the doorway, mesmerized.

You want me to go home with you, but that just ain't my scene
'Course, I could be persuaded if your currency is green
We'll wake up in the morning, your flag will be unfurled
Well, guess what, babe, I lied to you, I am that kind of girl

She ended the song with a classic bump-and-grind maneuver. Then, in the tiniest of pasties and G-string, she stepped daintily down from the bandstand and finished her song perched on the lap of Reverend Walter Little, the new pastor from the Light of Zion church in Clearlake, to appreciative whoops and hollers.

Allie returned to the bandstand.

"Uh, when I said we wanted to see more of Mrs. Carson, I didn't think she'd take it quite so literally, but hey, nice job, Monica. Next up is someone we all know well. Lorenzo 'Greengrocer' Bagatelle and Rufus the singing dog. Drum roll, please!"

But Greg was gone. Sheet white and shaking and a little too drunk, he'd slipped off his drum stool and wandered outside. I found him sitting on the gravel next to the mailbox, out at the end of the driveway.

"Hey, buddy, you okay?" I asked as I sat down next to him.

"Fuck, no. Would you be okay if your mom just took off all her clothes and wiggled her tits in the minister's face? Shit, she promised she'd behave herself. What am I going to do about her?"

"Where did she learn how to do that? I mean, she's really good."

"She's been doing it forever. That's her business. She and my dad own a famous strip club in Bakersfield, Monica's Boom Boom Room."

"Look," I reassured him, "everyone's fine about it. But you might have mentioned the nature of their 'thriving family business.' That's where you learned to play drums and developed your marvelous concentration, isn't it? And that hair-tossing you do—it's a stripper thing!"

"I do not toss my hair like a stri—"

"Oh, you absolutely do too. I know it must be embarrassing, but we love you." There I was, trying to have a heart-to-heart talk with my dear friend, wearing tangled-up chicken feathers and a tutu. It was not exactly my best, most levelheaded look. "No one cares if your mom needs to show off, and besides, she's great at it. If she's going to do it, she might as well be good, right? And your dad was there. He didn't seem to mind."

"He thinks it's delightful. Shit, he's her manager. But she promised."

We heard a door slam, and a sweet female voice.

"Greg, honey, are you all right?"

"Is that your mom?" I whispered.

"No, it sounds like it might be Jamee, though," he whispered back. "Oh man, what am I going to do with her? When it rains, don't it just fuckin' pour?"

Chapter
12

THE NEXT DAY, GREG USED HIS PARENTS' VISIT AS AN excuse to avoid Jamee, and Jamee as an excuse to avoid his parents, while he hid out in my room. Allie and Perle did some aggressive damage control with Reverend Walter Little, who quite honestly didn't seem terribly upset. Monica promised to keep her clothes on, and pretty much did. She was having a great time and decided to stay for a few extra days after her husband, who had said all of three words the whole time, returned to Bakersfield. She said she wanted some extra time with her "snuggle-wumpkin." In fact, Monica and Allie seemed to have forged a surprisingly tight bond overnight. Being middle-aged women in the nightclub business, however different the clubs, gave them a lot to talk about. They went for long sisterly walks to the lake and exchanged enough eye-rolling looks across the table to make their children quite uncomfortable, and Perle a little jealous.

SWF 34 and Lloyd missed each other again. A flat tire had kept her in Ukiah on Thanksgiving, but she was going to try to make it up later in the weekend. Lloyd sat by the phone for hours then decided he needed to run a quick errand in town. Restless, I jumped into the car with him. Like most pedal steel players I know, Lloyd is not a real talkative guy, but there's no one better at companionable silence. We went to the bank, the post office, the tackle shop, and the used bookstore. It felt good to be away from Dewdrop Inn Soap Opera Central for a short while, with an old friend who didn't require a lot of sparkling repartee. I found myself lingering at the bookstore, not wanting to go back quite yet, until Lloyd insisted. He was afraid he'd miss his phone call, which of course is exactly what happened.

A heavy four-four drumbeat hung in the air as we entered the bar. Monica's voice boomed, "No, no, ladies, move it like you mean it!"

Monica, in a flesh-colored body suit, held the CD player's remote control device in one hand, a black lace bra and G-string in the other. She stood in the center of the bandstand, bathed in a blue spotlight, with Allie and Perle on either side. Allie was wearing red-checkered boxer shorts, a tank undershirt, white ankle socks with high-heeled pumps, and my fringed leopard gloves. Perle wore her usual drawstring getup and pink Reeboks. Since Allie had commandeered my gloves, Perle was stuck with quilted orange oven mitts.

"Posture, ladies, posture," Monica screeched. "How many times do I hafta tell you, boobs up, nipples out. What parta that do you not understand?"

"When do we learn how to twirl the tassels?" Allie whined. "That's really all I wanted to know."

"Listen, ya gotta crawl before ya can walk, right? You can't be a tassel twirler if you don't know how to carry yourself, doll. Besides, I didn't want to disillusion you or nothing, but tassels kinda went obsolete quite some time ago, around when Velcro revolutionized the industry, not that there's any connection. I can still show you how to do it. I always carry some pasties around with me for sentimentality. But nowadays the classy places just want the bra off by the end of the second song. The dives, they expect the girls totally butt-naked doin' lap dances and whatever. Nobody cares about old-fashioned values anymore." Monica hit the pause button, the better to be heard. "In my place, the girls know how to dance. They put on a theatrical striptease show—you know, with costumes and props and everything. If we lose a little business to Eddie's Town Pump down the highway, well, I gotta live with myself, so screw them. Plus I'm not going to put my girls at risk. It's all about attitude, anyhow. Well, attitude and tits, of course. You don't have to have big ones, either, if you know how to use 'em. Like I said, posture is everything. See? Just do what I do."

Monica turned the music back on and demonstrated an adorable butt-wiggling half-turn toward the door, which Allie and Perle tried to imitate with absolutely pathetic results.

"Sorry, doll, but if you worked in my club, the customers would be hollering at you to 'Put it back on! Put it back on!'"

"I give up," sighed Perle.

"No, Sugar, you'll get it. Just hang in there a little longer. Here, let's crank it up and start again. Shoulders back, heads up, tits out. Don't forget to smile; eye contact gets you the big tips. Wiggle that hip—no, from the waist. Okay now, turn slowly—that's a little better. Remember, it's all about promising something they're never gonna get and you both know it. You're in total control of the situation."

And they tried the turn again. This time it was almost—well, if you squinted, it was almost a little bit sexy.

Lloyd and I hooted our applause from the doorway.

"Hi, kids," Monica shouted over the music. "Hey, Lloyd, that gal from Ukiah called. Said she'd be home until three."

It was 3:05. Lloyd rushed to the kitchen phone. He returned a moment later, looking dejected.

"I missed her again, damn it. Did she leave any other message?"

"No, Sugar. Sorry."

"I have to meet this woman. If anyone asks, I'll be in Ukiah," Lloyd called over his shoulder, as he slammed out the back door.

"Hey!" Allie yelled from the stage. "Monica's teaching us her sexy stripper moves—come join the fun."

I figured, What the hell? I took off my T-shirt and with Monica's help, attached tassels to my industrial-strength maternity bra, then pulled my drawstring pants down low around my hips, exposing my gently rounded belly. Allie wasn't giving up the gloves, so I found another set of oven mitts and completed the ensemble with a chicken feather boa around my shoulders. I jumped onstage to join the workshop: You never know when a skill like that will come in handy.

An hour or so later we were still at it. We'd gone about as far as we could with butt wiggling and were up to flirtatious glove removal. Despite the awkwardness of oven mitts, I thought we were beginning to get the hang of removing them with a kind of saucy joie de vivre.

When we were interrupted by a timid knock at the front door, I ran to open it, not thinking about how I would look to the stranger standing outside. She had long, straight honey-blonde hair and a pretty, heart-shaped face. A shiny stretch limousine was parked in the driveway.

"Hi, is Lloyd Sanders around?" asked the woman.

"No, but he should be back later," I told her. "Do you want to leave a note or something? Who—Oh my God, you must be SWF 34. He just took off for Ukiah to see you! We have no way to reach him, but you're welcome to wait here. In fact, we were just learning some swell professional stripper techniques from our friend Monica. Come in and join us if you want."

SWF 34 looked through the open door and took in the scene: a blue-lit stage on which three women were writhing around, one of them looking very sexy and, from this distance, very undressed in her flesh-colored leotard. Half naked, wearing oven mitts and chicken feathers, we appeared to be acting out a gourmet chef's sex fantasy. She looked startled and a bit confused.

"Lloyd told me he worked in a music club," she said, "not a strip joint. No thanks, I have to get back to my weekend guests."

"Would you like to leave a note or anything?"

"No, I don't think so. Thanks anyway." Her voice sounded tight and small.

Before I could explain, she was gone.

GREG AND I WERE SETTING UP FOR THE HARVEST DANCE, AND Allie and Perle were cleaning up the kitchen when Pete dumped the soggy pile of Saturday mail on the table. It was the usual assortment of bills, ads, and magazines, a postcard from Amy and Kathleen in Orlando, and a torn wet envelope that had been forwarded to Aunt Perle from her New York address. The San Francisco postmark bore an unsettling date; it had been mailed more than two months before.

A lavender scent filled the air as Perle tore open the envelope. Inside was a handwritten note on thick, old-fashioned stationery. Silently, she showed the first page to her sister.

"Oh, my." Allie handed the letter back to Perle. "This is big. Would you all excuse us for a few minutes? Someone seems to have died."

A tiny card fell out of the envelope onto the table, adding to the mystery:

Miss Samantha Jasmine Eustace
Recreational Retreats for Women
Discretion Guaranteed

"Who's that?" asked Greg.

I had never heard of her, and neither had Pete. Monica, carefully explaining the structural differences between Hanes and Fruit of the Loom thong underwear to Jamee as the two strolled into the room, picked up the card.

"Hmmm," she said thoughtfully. "The name rings a bell. I just can't place it." No one had time to ponder that particular mystery, because Perle and Allie returned with the news that yes, someone had died, and Perle was to receive an inheritance.

Dear Ms. Cohen,
You don't know me, but I certainly feel as though I've known you for a long time. I hope you will excuse this intrusion.

The letter was from a woman named Samantha Eustace, who had instructed that it be delivered after her death. It had gone to Perle's home address in New York and sat on a table in the lobby for a long time until finally it had been forwarded by a thoughtful neighbor. Miss Eustace wrote that she had been a subscriber to my aunt's *Living Well—Naturally* newsletter and felt that the information she received over the years had prolonged and enhanced the quality of her life after she discovered she had a terminal illness. A successful small-business owner with no heirs, she wanted to leave a chunk of her assets to Aunt Perle. The arrangements were somewhat complicated, however, and would have to be explained by the executor of her estate. There was a San Francisco phone number given—Perle had already left a message and was waiting for a call back. In the meantime, there was nothing to do.

MOTORDUDE ZYDECO ROLLED IN SATURDAY EVENING FROM San Francisco. I'd done a few shows with them over the years, and it always felt more like running away with the circus than going to work. Our old friend Billy, almost seven feet tall, was the accordion player and bandleader. The guy just loved to play, being even more of a gig-slut than I was, and his enthusiasm was completely infectious. I jumped onto the bandstand to sit in on the first song, while he counted off a Cajun two-step, and by the end of the first verse, the floor was packed with lively dancers.

> *Come on, honey, there's lots to do,*
> *cookin' up some gumbo and cornbread, too*
> *Gonna dance, gonna sing, and have a lot of fun,*
> *'cause Billy's bringing his accordion*
> *Sing all day, dance all night,*
> *when Billy plays everything's all right*
> *There's no such thing as too much fun*
> *when Billy brings his accordion*

Little Pierre said Ellie May
  would never give him the time of day
Now they have a daughter and a son,
  'cause Billy brought his accordion
Sing all day, dance all night,
  when Billy plays everything's all right
There's no such thing as too much fun
  when Billy brings his accordion

The leaders of the world could not agree,
  poised on the brink of World War Three
But the fighting stopped and peace was won,
  when Billy brought his accordion
Sing all day, dance all night,
  when Billy plays everything's all right
There's no such thing as too much fun
  when Billy brings his accordion

I left the stage and the band rolled into "Big Oakland" followed by *"Mon Coeur Fait Mal."* The dance floor was jumping; people lined up three deep around the bar. Allie was bartending alongside Fawnee and David, her weekend crew. She pushed auburn curls off her face as she smiled and joked with the customers, constantly keeping her eye out for problems. She'd been on that famous old heartbreak diet and looked delicate and intensely capable. Her slim hands poured whiskey and her boot kicked an empty carton out of the way, while her eyes signaled to Pete to check out a potential problem in the corner, all the while laughing at a regular's silly old joke. The bar business is tough, and she worked hard and cheerfully and well. In my heightened state of pregnant weepiness, I found it incredibly touching. A few minutes later, she stepped around the bar and over to me.

"It's a good night. You're doing great," I whispered. "Everyone loves the band."

"Thanks, sweetie," she answered. "I'm learning how to trust my instincts a little, running this place without Johnny. Tonight I had this feeling—it's a little hard to explain—just the idea of being where I'm supposed to be. Keeping this place going for people and watching what goes on every night is a privilege. Look, there's Linda from the bookstore and Phil from the body shop. They've been eyeing each other for weeks and he finally got up the nerve to ask her to dance. And over there—Jenny and Fred broke up last month and he just waltzed in with his new girlfriend, so she's trying to make him jealous by flirting with Pete, who's going for it because his ex-wife just showed up with the karate teacher. And see those old dolls at the end of the bar, in the pastel pantsuits? Eunice and Teddie, they come every Saturday night after they get their wash-and-set at Tangles Salon. Those two have been coming in here once a week since way before we ever bought the place. They can drink anyone in this room under the table, and boy, do they have some stories to tell about the old days. It's a soap opera really, and I get to set the stage. Tonight someone will cry, you can bet on it. And someone will drink too much and get in a fight and feel very stupid in the morning. Someone else will walk in after almost having stayed home, expecting nothing but a beer and an early evening, and meet someone new and both their lives will change forever. It's incredible what can happen. Most of the time I don't notice or care, I just want the business to work out. Most nights I'm too busy even to think, back and forth between the bar and the band

and the door and worrying about running out of Red Hook and whatever. But tonight feels like magic. I want there to be magic. I wish—I hope that tonight all the people in this room get something they want."

Across the crowded dance floor, I spotted Greg laughing, waltzing with Audrey from the flower shop. Jamee, on the other side of the room, seemed to be busily making new friends. Lloyd, eyes glued to the front door, looked miserable. Perle, in a state of giddy excitement over her news, was plying him with gorse flowers to be held under his tongue, her supposedly surefire cure for depression.

As the Ball of Love turned slowly, sprinkling silver light on their shining faces, I made my own wishes. I wished for my dad to come home, for my CD to be a success, and for me to find someone to love—I didn't dare wish even in private for Bobby Lee specifically. And, patting my belly, I wished for everything to just come out all right.

Chapter
13

SUNDAY IT RAINED AND WE CLEANED UP. THEN ALLIE got out the holiday decorations so we could prepare the club for its busiest season. As usual, she had booked a number of private parties, in addition to expecting good crowds on weekends.

By late afternoon, the place looked clean and cheerful—all set for Christmas, Hanukkah, Kwanzaa, Ramadan, and the winter solstice. Allie was an equal-opportunity holiday decorator. Perle was with her in the basement looking for the chili-pepper hanging lights, Hoagy and Pete stood on ladders putting Santa hats on the buffalo heads, and Lloyd sat in the kitchen, trying to write a letter to SWF 34. Greg and I were wrestling with a seven-foot plastic cactus when we heard the crunch of wheels in the gravel driveway. A car door slammed and there were footsteps and a hard knock at the front door.

"It's open. Come on in!" yelled Hoagy from his perch.

A tall, gray-haired man, soaked from the rain, stood in the doorway.

"I got a message," he informed us. "I represent the estate of Samantha Eustace."

"You must be here to see my aunt Perle," I said. "Here, let me take your wet—"

"Hey, man, it's been a while! What brings you all the way up here?" Hoagy, grinning, jumped off the ladder and raised his hand for a high five just as Monica stumbled downstairs in her satin robe, in search of coffee, and spotted the man.

"Oh my Gawd!" she shrieked. "Wonderbuns!"

Allie entered the room, draped in strings of novelty lights. Her eyes went soft and the color drained from her cheeks. She moved slowly toward the stranger at the door.

"Artie? Artie Blond? It's me, Alice Cohen."

It seemed Artie Blond got around.

THE ROOM ERUPTED, AS YOU CAN IMAGINE. ARTIE HAD COME to see Perle about her inheritance, but everyone in the room had something to say to him first. In his position, I think I would have hightailed it out of there. Finally, Hoagy stood on a chair, stuck two fingers in his mouth, and silenced us with an ear-splitting whistle.

"Everyone shut up," he commanded. "Allie, get us all something to drink, would you? Greg, call the pizza place that delivers. Artie, you're staying for supper. Pizza's on me." He shot Perle a defiant look, about the pizza. "We're all going to sit down and have a nice visit, and everyone doesn't have to talk at once."

Allie plunked a bottle of Heradura Gold on the family table, along with lime slices and shot glasses, and all the leftover holiday desserts.

"Allie, what are you giving people to eat, poison?" Perle looked disgusted.

"I don't want to hear it now, Perle, I'm serious." Something about Allie's tone made Perle shut up for once.

Chairs scraped against the wood floor as we all gathered around the table to sort things out. Artie sat across from Perle, with Monica and Allie on either side of him. The rest of us—Hoagy, Lloyd, Pete, Greg, and I—found places where we could. I grabbed a bottle of water while Hoagy poured tequila for everyone else.

"Did you know about this?" Perle asked her sister, waving her arm in the vague direction of Artie.

"Apparently there's a lot I didn't know," Allie answered.

"Hey pal," Hoagy said to Artie, "take it from one who does know. Save yourself a shitload of hassle and tell all. These two won't let you get away with a fucking thing. You might as well just tell us your life story."

"Okay, here goes. I've known Alice here almost thirty-five years. And Hoagy, what a surprise, man. Monica, I'm still trying to get my head around all of you being in this room together." Artie swallowed a shot of Heradura and began.

"I grew up in a suburb in Massachusetts. As a kid I was always a nut for old country-blues guitar, and the second I graduated from high school, I hitched a ride to Boston and never looked back. I crashed on a friend's sofa, bought a used guitar, and practiced like crazy. It was my goal to memorize the picking styles of all the greats: Leadbelly, Blind Willie Johnson, and especially Fast Freddy Blouster."

"Who?" we all asked at once.

"Fast Freddy Blouster was an obscure Chicago blues man. I had this scratchy old '78 of him singing 'Hot Time in the Old Town Tonight' with amazing finger-picking in an open tuning, and I wouldn't rest until I could play that sucker note for note."

Hoagy was rapt. We women squirmed, impatient for him to get to the parts about meeting Allie and Monica.

"I guess I was a little obsessed with Fast Freddy. I used to hang out at this greasy spoon called Rascals Diner on Charles Street, just 'cause Freddy's niece, Josie Blouster, worked in the kitchen. She liked me and let me run a tab when I was low on cash—you could fill up on the best food bargain in town there, Josie's famous beef stew, because it came with three huge slices of bread for a buck twenty-five. This was before the whole Boston thing really kicked in, you know?"

He told us a little about Boston's folk music scene in its infancy—playing for tips at Club 47, the Loft, and the Golden Vanity. Artie became an accomplished guitarist, known for his humorous interpretations of obscure blues songs. His show-stopper was "Hot Time Chi-Town Talkin' Blues," in which he elaborated on Fast Freddie's version with several of his own verses suggesting that Mrs. O'Leary's cow caused the famous fire by smoking reefer in the barn. He worked the crowd like crazy on that song, drawing it out to last over ten minutes, and no matter how good he got at serious interpretations of country blues, it was the "cow song" that everyone wanted to hear. Artie's career as a folk music legend had begun.

"It was around that time I ran into a cute little girl from New York at the 1959 Newport Folk Festival." He grinned. "She was looking for a pay phone and I gave her a ride downtown. Let's see now, what was her name, Alice something-or-other? Smart as a whip, but I still managed to convince her that a twenty-year-old folksinging drifter was worth the time of day. I think I seemed glamorous compared to the boys back in high school."

"That's for sure," Allie agreed. "I was sixteen years old, and it was my first time away from home alone."

"You were how old?"

"Sixteen—actually almost seventeen. It was a few weeks before my birthday."

"You told me you were eighteen!"

"Well, I was trying to appear sophisticated. People always lied about their age. You didn't actually believe me, did you?"

"Oh, sweet Jesus, sixteen." Artie smacked himself on the forehead. "Anyway, this adorable girl spent the weekend with me, promised she'd write, and she did, but she forgot to put her return address on the letter. There was no way I could get in touch with her."

"Allie, that's so rude!" Perle was indignant, still processing the fact that Allie had let an eligible guy get away. "What were you thinking?"

"I guess I got scared," Allie answered thoughtfully. "I left the return address off that letter on purpose, Artie. I figured if you knew how to reach me and didn't write, I'd simply die of a broken heart. But if you spent the rest of your life searching the earth trying to find me and couldn't, well then, it wasn't really anyone's fault."

"I would have loved to see you again, you know," he said softly.

"It's so hard to explain," Allie answered. "You were a dream, my first glamorous bad boy. You jump-started the most exciting part of my life and I wanted to be with you, but not in my real high-school girl's life. Actually, even more than I wanted to be with you, I wanted to *be* you, so it was confusing and a lot easier to handle as a fantasy. It wasn't fair, but Artie, you were never exactly what I'd call prom-date material."

"So you two never saw each other again?" Perle wasn't letting it go.

"That's the funny thing, we did. We kept accidentally running into each other every once in a while. It was always wonderful. It happened a lot in the sixties, to everyone," Allie explained. "We would have called it cosmic. I'd be pulling into a parking space at a folk festival and Artie would be pulling out of the next one. Or I'd run down the street for coffee and he'd be buying rolling papers at the corner store."

Artie reached over and took her hand. She poured another shot of tequila into his glass and sat quietly for a minute, her dreamy eyes staring into his.

"Want to know the truth, Artie? I was surprised you even remembered me. You once remarked about the fact that I'd 'forgotten' to put a return address on that letter, and I played dumb. I was delighted by how happy you looked to see me. It always made my day."

"Mine too, Allie."

"So then what happened?" asked Hoagy. Even he was on the edge of his chair.

"Nothing. We went our separate ways. But now and then I'd see his name in the paper, playing at a folk club. I'd drag my friends with me because I'd get nervous. Remember, Hoagy, you came along a couple of times? We'd finally gotten around to exchanging addresses, but by then Artie was kind of a celebrity. He had that song everyone loved, and a big following, including a lot of very cute girls, so I was a little intimidated. Anyway, I went off to school and we didn't keep in touch. But the folk scene was starting to explode by then and it was actually a pretty small world, so I'd hear about him occasionally and every once in a while I'd get a postcard. Then I went into the Peace Corps and came back and met Johnny and . . ." Allie's voice trailed off.

Artie went on to tell us how he became a regular on the New England folk circuit, supplementing his income with a little side business of the herbal variety. In the mid-sixties his cow song caught the attention of some A&R guys at Folklore Records, not to mention Vanguard, Oracle, and Capitol. He signed with Folklore. By this time, Charles Street had become a real scene, and Rascals the number-one dining choice of the discerning starving musician. Hoagy recalled one particular afternoon in 1965. Geoff Muldaur, sitting at the corner table with Jaime Brockett, had been working his way through a bowl of the famous beef stew but hadn't finished his bread, when Artie burst through the door, eyes glowing with excitement. He had just signed his first record contract but didn't have $1.25 for lunch, so Geoff let him have his leftovers.

The cow song became a cult hit; the ridiculous story line about a stoned cow captured the imagination of hippie deejays everywhere. Artie got tons of airplay on the new free-form FM radio stations from Boston to San Francisco.

"And you two never saw each other until now?" I asked.

"No, not exactly—" Artie started to say.

Allie shot Artie a glance that I knew to be her "I'm warning you to shut up now or else" look, but since she wasn't his mother, he missed it.

"Don't you remember, the fall of '66? We played that gig together in Florida with Buffett, where I subbed on fiddle with your band 'cause Johnny was stuck in Kentucky. I'll never forget what happened that night."

"Oh, right," she said, glaring at him murderously. "But Artie, nothing happened that night."

"What? You mean you don't re—" He finally got it. "*Riiiight*. I was thinking of another time, with another girl, because yes, you were married by then. Of course, my mistake."

Even Perle wasn't going to touch that one.

"That explains Alice and Artie, but what about Mom and Miss Eustace?" Greg was quick to change the subject. "Neither of them seems to have been part of the sixties folk scene."

Artie poured everyone another shot before continuing with his story.

"My second album bombed and the label dropped me. Man, that was a lousy time, 'cause right after that I got busted for possession with intent to sell and spent the Summer of Love, not to mention the fall, winter, and spring, in the slammer. When I got out I decided to hitchhike west. So there I was in a truck stop on I-76, nursing a cup of black coffee and waiting for the rain to stop, or at least that was my excuse. What I was really doing was listening to the Louvin Brothers on WWVA and trying to pick up the waitress." He winked at Monica. "It'd been a long time since I'd seen anything as pretty as her rear end when she bent over to pick up a napkin off the floor. She wasn't bad from the front, either, and she'd undone a few extra buttons so the edge of her black lace bra showed. She wore this little ruffled cap and a plastic name tag that said 'Molly Pancake, Wheeling,' and I fell in love."

Artie said he'd shot her his best sideways grin and asked when she got off work. An hour later she'd stashed her frilly cap and apron behind the counter and they were headed for California in her brother's old Ford station wagon.

"Now, this particular waitress had two remarkable quali-
ties," he continued. "Molly Pancake was her real name, and she
absolutely hated wearing clothes. You can imagine my surprise
when she wriggled out of her uniform and undies and tossed
them into the backseat. Shit, I almost drove right off the road. But
hey, I'm an open-minded guy. So I drove the next two thousand
miles listening to loud country-western music with a gorgeous
naked woman riding shotgun. It coulda been worse."

"You drove to San Francisco like that?" Perle was undoubt-
edly weighing the health benefits of wholesome nudity versus the
potential for catching a chill.

"Nah, we didn't get that far. The Ford bit the dust in
Bakersfield and we got a cheap room for a couple of days so's we
could figure out what to do next. Molly liked to go out and sun-
bathe by the pool—topless, of course—and one day the owner of
a strip joint noticed her, uh, résumés and offered her a job. She
had no previous experience, but she was a natural. Pretty soon she
was headlining, had a private cubicle backstage with a star over
the mirror, the works. It was time for me to move on, so I kissed
her good-bye and hit the road."

"What happened to Molly?" Pete wanted to know, once
again validating all those dumb drummer jokes.

"You have to ask? Her new boss changed her name to
Monica Boom Boom. I believe you've made her acquaintance.
Monica wowed 'em in Bakersfield, where she soon married a club
regular named Sonny Carson. When the owner died he left her
the club, and they've been running the place together ever since.
They even had a son, who became the house drummer. Talented
kid, too."

IT WAS ALMOST MIDNIGHT, AND WE'D BEEN SITTING THERE for hours, everyone except boring pregnant me getting drunker and drunker. Monica wanted coffee and we were out of milk, so I offered to make a run to Safeway. It felt great to get out alone for a few minutes. I pulled the truck into the nearly deserted parking lot and turned off the engine. As I stepped down from the cab, I felt the tiniest flutter inside my belly—so soft and subtle but so unmistakably there—and then again. I looked down and patted my stomach.

"Hi, sweetheart," I whispered.

"Hi, Mom," my belly replied with a breath of movement, gone almost before it began.

I held completely still for a moment or two, but there was no more belly action. The rain had stopped. Wanting a little more time in the cool air, I stood quietly in front of the supermarket, and the newspaper vending machines lined up in front of the window caught my eye. The *Midnight Examiner,* a tabloid, boasted the headline: *World-Famous Fashion Designer Revealed as Country Legend's Love Child.*

I returned with the paper and some milk to find Perle sitting on the table, eyes closed, in full lotus position. Lloyd was asleep on Pete's shoulder, and Hoagy, Monica, Greg, and Allie were rapt, listening to the rest of Artie's story.

He finally made it to San Francisco, where his uncle invited him to the Playboy Club for dinner. He immediately hit it off with one of the bouncers, who helped arrange an audition with the house band. He spent the next couple of months playing acoustic rhythm guitar in a jazz combo and became great friends with a Bunny called Jasmine, a leggy brunette with a background in theater. When she invited Artie to share her apartment, he jumped at the chance.

"It was cool to be able to say my roommate was a Playboy Bunny. Plus she saved the extra rent money to invest in a business of her own. She wouldn't ever sleep with me, and God knows I tried, but we were best pals till I left town with some guys to start a bluegrass band. Anyway, my friend Jasmine finally quit the Playboy Club and opened a little bed-and-breakfast joint in the Sunset District. Many years later, she invited me back to California to help her run the place—she was too busy to handle it alone. Then out of nowhere she got sick, some kind of weird, rare neuro-shit. There wasn't anything the doctors could do, but before she died, Jasmine asked me to administer her estate. And that's why I'm here."

Artie tried to get Perle's attention by waving a thick manila envelope in front of her face.

"Perle, wake up," Allie hissed. "Artie has papers he needs to go over with you."

Perle slowly opened her eyes.

"I'm awake, Allie. And it's about time someone told me what any of this has to do with me, or with Miss Eustace, for that matter."

"Jasmine's real name was Samantha Eustace," Artie explained. "And you might say she was kind of like your groupie. She read everything you wrote, listened to your tapes, followed your advice to the letter. She started having dizzy spells and memory lapses—turned out she had this incurable virus that attacks the nervous system. She died believing that you helped her maintain a quality of life she wouldn't have had otherwise. See, her condition wasn't diagnosed till it was way too late to do anything, but the treatments would've been worse than the disease, and she probably wouldn't have lived much longer, anyway. Following your advice, she was active almost until the very end. The doctors couldn't believe it—said it was a miracle."

"They never can," Perle muttered under her breath. "It's always a miracle."

"Anyway, Ms. Cohen, I'm here to tell you that except for some charitable donations to women's groups and such, you and me are Miss Samantha Jasmine Eustace's sole heirs. She was smart with her money, you know. In addition to her business, she had some nice investments and a couple of rental properties. You have to agree to a couple of conditions and sign some papers, and the inheritance is yours."

It was late and we were so tired. But we ended up sitting around the table most of the long night, partly because Artie's stories were too good to miss, but partly, I realized, because sleeping arrangements were up in the air. I had the feeling that if they'd been alone, Artie would have ended up in Allie's bed hours ago. But in front of her pregnant daughter, her bossy big sister, her band-brothers, and another of Artie's old girlfriends, she was understandably reserved. What with Jamee and a bunch of Zydeco musicians staying upstairs, we had so much company that for the first time since I could remember, we were out of extra bedrooms. Monica complicated matters by moving closer and closer to Artie, as bits and pieces of her outfit found their way to the floor. It was easier to stay up all night and keep on talking. So I asked Artie to tell us more about Jasmine.

"Jasmine continued to work at the Playboy Club for some time, despite her budding social consciousness and awareness of sexual politics. She simply couldn't make that kind of dough anywhere else. She saved her money, and after a while had enough for a down payment on a cottage in the Sunset District with a garden and a rental unit. It was time to put her plan into action.

"She decorated the rental apartment with a big brass bed, blackout window shades, and lots of frills. The medicine cabinet was filled with nail polish and makeup samples, the refrigerator with health food, the bookshelves with anything and everything. She put the word out to her married mom friends—the room was available for relaxing weekend getaways, at a reasonable price, to women who needed a break."

Allie remarked that this seemed like a great idea.

"See, the way it worked," Artie explained, "was a gal could sign up for a couple of days of R&R. Jasmine would plan activities for her if she wanted, but most of 'em were happy just to lie around reading or napping or walking on the beach. Some of 'em even liked to putter in the garden. She was one of the first people I ever knew to buy a VCR, and she kept a bunch of corny romantic chick flicks around, and face creams and other girlie stuff. The gals loved it, word got around, and she was booked for months in advance most of the time. Only problem was that the husbands didn't always understand. So that was where her acting experience came in. She got out her makeup case from the old theater days and turned herself into Aunt Samantha. Based on the theory that a chick could get sprung easier if she was caring for an elderly relative than if she was gonna be walkin' on the beach and doin' her nails, you know? She even provided holiday cards from 'Aunt Sam' and picture postcards from Miami Beach for her regular customers. You can imagine—she did great. But that was nothing, compared to later on."

Artie couldn't exactly remember when, but sometime during the seventies, Samantha's business changed. A regular customer confided that she and her husband were experimenting with the then-fashionable concept of open marriage, and it was driving her nuts. It wasn't jealousy so much as a privacy issue, she claimed. Her husband's endless chatter about the hot sex he was having with his girlfriend was boring. There was a guy she was interested in, but she'd be damned if she was going to give her husband the detailed reports he expected about her sexual adventures with a new lover.

Well then, said Samantha, *why don't you bring him here? I can keep a secret.*

And that was the understatement of the century.

"For the next fifteen years, Samantha and her little rental cottage were the best-kept secret in the history of female infidelity," Artie went on. "'Aunt Sam' became the cover for thousands of weekend trysts, usually a secret even to the male participants, who thought they were really the guests of an elderly and understanding auntie. Samantha left breakfast trays and cut flowers at the bedroom door and stayed out of the way. She had found her calling. She made a fortune. Eventually she bought the lots on either side of the house and added a couple of extra cottages, nestled in foliage, for holiday weekend overflow."

Allie wondered aloud about the potential for breaking up families.

"Actually," said Artie, "I think she always believed she was helping families stay together. This little safety valve she provided helped the ladies go back and deal with their lives easier, or at least that's what she said. She was just trying to even out the playing field, was how she put it."

"But it's so weird," said Allie. "The burden of all those secrets, the acting, the lies—how could she keep all their stories straight?"

"She was a really smart and talented lady," Artie said softly. "She got off on it. Besides, no one ever said she wasn't also off her nut. Now, would you like to see the terms of the will?"

Perle snapped to attention. "I was wondering when you'd get to that. How much money am I going to get?"

"That would be nice to know, wouldn't it? I almost forgot to mention it. There are certain conditions, some choices to be made. We can go over all of the papers tomorrow, when we're sober," Artie offered. "But assuming you are willing to meet the requirements, your share is just shy of six million dollars."

That was when Perle fainted. So we covered her with a blanket and offered Artie her room.

I was screaming tired as I dragged myself off to bed. But I thought I saw him squeeze Allie's hand and kiss her softly on the top of her head.

"It's good to see you again, Artie," she whispered.

"Hi." He smiled. "Want a ride?"

Chapter
14

ARTIE LEFT LATE THE NEXT MORNING WITH A LOT TO think about. He told Hoagy that he'd never expected this simple errand to ram him headfirst into so many ghosts, never mind memories of a summer weekend in 1959 and a certain bright-eyed redhead. Why did seeing her again make him feel so old and sad? Hoagy couldn't come up with an answer to that, but was able to help him master a tricky chord progression, which he figured was almost as good.

Aunt Perle had a lot to think about, too, because the conditions of Miss Eustace's will required that she take up full-time residence in the Sunset District house and transform the picturesque cottages into a center for alternative healing. It was a lifelong dream, but would mean changing her entire life—giving up New York as well as Lake County and her new position as the self-appointed boss of my pregnancy. She'd never been especially driven by money, and wasn't sure what to do. Artie told her she could take her time; he wasn't in any hurry for an answer. Left unsaid was the fact that Perle's indecision would give him plenty of excuses to come visit.

Allie looked wistful as she walked Artie to his car and said good-bye. For the rest of the day she was so distracted that she didn't even notice when Perle threw all the holiday leftovers down the garbage disposal. Monica hitched a ride to the airport with the Zydeco musicians a few hours later, leaving us in a poof of perfume and boa feathers, with big lipstick smudges on our cheeks and the astonishing news that I had potential as a stripper and was welcome to come work for her once I got my figure back.

That left Jamee. She pulled Greg aside for a serious talk in which she informed him that their brief affair in Nashville had been nothing more than a "road thing." She was so sorry, but she'd discovered she had strong feelings for someone else: drummer-turned-bouncer Pete Rawley. He was as surprised to hear the news as we were, but he didn't really mind.

THE THING ABOUT FAME AND FORTUNE IS THERE'S NO guarantee they'll kick in at the same time. I was getting famous all right, but the income from royalties would not roll in for a while, and that was assuming Unicorn Entertainment didn't subscribe to the various rock-and-roll methods of creative accounting that can prevent artists from ever seeing a penny. But everyone in town suddenly expected me to have loads of cash, and whenever I went out, I found myself spending more than a comfortable amount so that no one could accuse me of being cheap or greedy. I was mystified by the whole financial process and secretly afraid that when my ship finally did come in, I'd be at the airport.

Perle was still trying to make up her mind about the inheritance, and Allie was trying to work out a reasonable agreement with Dad that would allow her to retain sole ownership of the

Dewdrop Inn, so although our family's future looked bright, we spent the holiday season maxing out our credit cards and waiting for the mail.

"If bills were snow, we'd have a blizzard for Christmas," Allie sighed, going over the accounts with Hoagy in the office one afternoon, while I tried to make sense out of my bank statement.

"I don't know about you two, but I'm having a credit card Christmas this year," I said.

"Ooh, baby, hold me back. I feel a song coming on!" yelled Hoagy. *"Davey wants a bicycle, Linda wants some skis—I'm the guy who's got to buy the presents and the tree!"*

"Then we have to trim it, but I've spent up to my limit," Allie added.

"Whoever said 'Joy to the World' was free?" sang Hoagy. "Come on, Sarah Jean, you're the songwriter. Where's our hook?"

"It's gonna be a Credit Card Christmas again," I sang, *"Just so I can satisfy my family and my friends. / 'Tis the season to ignore what we really can afford."*

"And it's a Credit Card Christmas again!" we all shouted in unison.

Last year I made a New Year's resolution,
    to pinch each dime and get us out of debt
I thought it was an excellent solution,
    but a year's gone by and it hasn't happened yet
We paid our bills on time and started saving,
    but life can undermine the best-laid plan
To satisfy my family's every craving,
    it's not enough just doing the best I can

It's gonna be a Credit Card Christmas again
We've got to go out shopping for our family and our friends
'Tis the season to ignore what we really can afford
And it's a Credit Card Christmas again

Shining eyes and eager little faces
*   will gather round the family Christmas tree*
Expecting every toy that's made of plastic
*   and advertised on Saturday TV*
The experts say America's in trouble,
*   we've got to watch our spending carefully*
But the experts don't go shopping for my children,
*   and Santa doesn't do his thing for free*

It's gonna be a Credit Card Christmas again
We've got to go out shopping for our family and our friends
'Tis the season to ignore what we really can afford
And it's a Credit Card Christmas again

Because she stands beside me through the ups and downs
*   of life*
I need a special something for my sweet, supportive wife
I'm so desperate to please her that I'm maxing out my Visa
Should I get her diamonds or a Ginsu knife?

It's gonna be a Credit Card Christmas again
Just so I can satisfy my family and my friends
'Tis the season to ignore what we really can afford
And it's a Credit Card Christmas again

When we sang it for the rest of the band, Lee responded by quoting Johnny Mercer: "I coulda eaten alphabet soup and shit better lyrics."

But guess what? "Credit Card Christmas" became the Dewdrop Inn's most requested song that season, finally beating "Grandma Got Run Over by a Reindeer"'s ten-year winning streak. It was something to be proud of.

ALTHOUGH IT WAS LATE IN THE YEAR, UNICORN RUSHED production of my solo CD to hit stores for the last three weeks of the holiday gift-buying season. Somehow they got it out in time for the video release of "Take It from Me," and even more miraculously, people were buying it.

The cover photo was a live shot of me in my beautiful dress, strumming the leopard-skin pillbox Strat onstage at the Patsy show—mouth slightly open near the microphone, eyes large and looking to the side at Hoagy, who was grinning slightly out of focus on my left. The back cover was a great shot, too, taken by Greg at the end of our video shoot. I sat cross-legged, small and alone, in the middle of the large dance floor, strumming my guitar, the Ball of Love overhead, the empty bandstand behind me. The track list was printed in white over an expanse of empty dark wood dance floor. It was quite effective.

One thing I'd never anticipated was fan mail. Every week or so, Unicorn sent a large envelope stuffed with letters from all over the country from people who'd heard "Heartaches for a Guy" on the radio. About 10 percent were from men who thought I should basically be shot for encouraging their wives to laugh at them. But most were supportive notes from women who enjoyed my song and wished me luck, health, and happiness. News of my pregnancy had leaked into *Country Music Today*'s gossip column, and I started receiving homemade baby gifts and baked goods. But my all-time favorite was this note, received just two days after my CD hit the stores:

> *Darling Girl,*
>
> *We got such a laugh over your songs. The nurses here at Pine Ridge Residence have learned they must play your record over and over during recreation hour. But we have one question, and that is what kind of wax do you use to get your floors to shine so? It's too late for us, but we would like to tell our daughters to buy that kind of floor wax.*
>
> *Your Fans,*
>
> *Eleanor, Bertie, and Victoria (our combined ages equal 268 years and we're gunnin' for 300!), the Pine Ridge Cuties*

Perle, who'd been getting her own fan mail for years, volunteered for the job of reading, sorting, and answering these letters.

MY BENEFIT CONCERT FOR THE LAKE COUNTY FAMILY Literacy Program was to be held in mid-December, and the newest Unicorn Entertainment VP suggested we call it a CD release party. The label brass wanted to do something splashier than "just another night in your shit-kicker bar," as they delicately put it, and booked the dinner theater at the nearby El Rancho Resort and Casino for my big night.

El Rancho is quite a place. Sprawled over a hundred or so acres, the resort boasts every lakeside amusement you could imagine, plus indoor and outdoor concert venues, golf courses full-size and miniature, lodging, shops, and restaurants. It's a place where you can see Merle Haggard or James Brown in the showroom and "Weird Al" Yankovic in the amphitheater, and it doesn't matter how much you drink because a shuttle bus will take you back to your room when the show is over.

Seeing as it's a dinner theater, the showroom tries to be elegant, and by Lake County standards I guess it succeeds. But there's a crazed sloppy-drunk undertone that comes with the territory when no one has to worry about who's driving home. On the other hand, it's a room where major acts play, and I had never done a show of this magnitude as a headliner. I was unusually nervous, worried that I would somehow find a way to screw things up— the only question in my mind was how. Jumping onstage to sing a song or two at home was one thing, but putting a headline act together for El Rancho was another. Since I didn't know where to begin, I'd avoided making any decisions until the very last minute. It was now time to get my ever-expanding ass in gear.

The Family Literacy program had printed up flyers:

Presenting Lake County's Own
"Man-Bashin' Sarah Jean" and Special Guest
December 12
The Showroom at El Rancho Resort and Casino
Doors at 7 P.M. $25 to benefit the Family Literacy Program
of the Lake County Library

The ticket price seemed exorbitant in view of the fact that folks could hear me at the Dewdrop anytime for the price of a beer, but that's the way it is with a benefit.

After listening to dozens of demo tapes, we finally found the "special guest" when Greg called in a favor and arranged for friends of his, a group called Red Meat, to come up from San Francisco to open the show. Little Max was furious that we didn't choose his plodding and derivative blues band. To calm him down I blamed my record label, because I could.

I was at that stage of my pregnancy where my belly had just begun to pop out, so instead of looking like a luscious mama-to-be, I looked like my regular self with twenty extra ungainly pounds. Richie came up with a slenderizing bias-cut calf-length dress with a matching fringe vest and boots that worked with my leopard Strat, and saved the entire day to help with hair and makeup. I even made an appointment for a manicure at Tangles Salon.

Figuring out a set list was easy by comparison. I had to do songs from my CD, of course, building up to "Heartaches for a Guy." We could add a few Dewdrop Inn favorites with lead vocals from other band members, and with Allie in the lineup, background vocals were covered. Everything was looking good: The Family Literacy people said that advance tickets were selling well; the band was rehearsed and excited. But I couldn't shake a sense of misgiving as the day approached.

OUR SOUND CHECK WENT A LITTLE TOO SMOOTHLY, according to Allie. She had this residual "bad dress rehearsal equals good show" theory left over from her theatrical training. I wasn't going to worry about a good sound check, though. The stage techs at El Rancho knew what they were doing and did it in record time, so Allie and I spent a long afternoon relaxing in the resort's spa. We were to meet the rest of the band backstage an hour before show time.

The showroom is in the resort's main building, accessible from the spa by a long underground corridor, and I was able to find my way without going through any of the public rooms. As I approached the backstage area, a perky blonde from our local TV news team and her cameraman stood waiting near the dressing-room door. She ran her tongue over her lips, smiled at the camera, and spoke into a hand-held microphone.

"I'm Patti Larson here at El Rancho Resort with tonight's headliner, Lake County's hottest resident, Sarah Jean Pixlie. Your song's caused quite an uproar here tonight. Are you still having the relationship problems that inspired your hit, 'Heartaches for a Guy'"?

"Well, Patti," I stammered, "I wasn't aware of any uproar. And that question sounds a bit like 'Are you still beating your wife?' you know? There's just no good answer."

"How courageous of you to share your history as a battered wife with our viewers. I know they join me in wi—"

"No! I would if I was but I'm not. Battered. I have no relationship. That is, I don't think you understand—"

"Thank you, Sarah Jean Pixlie. That was Lake County's new man-bashin' country music sweetheart courageously coming out of the closet about her abusive relationships. Now let's move to the action outside."

"What action outside?" I wanted to know.

"You haven't seen them? It's making local history—SNAG and SMUG together for the first time. Where have you been? This is big news."

"What are SNAG and SMUG?" I asked thin air. Patti Larson was already running toward the front of the building, heels clicking on the polished tile floor.

I turned to see Hoagy and Greg, coming from the other direction.

"There she is!" cried Greg. "Come on, we've got to get you backstage. The mob out there is going to bust right through the door."

I pleaded for someone to please tell me what was going on.

"In a minute, let's get you safe first," Hoagy insisted.

The band was packed into a small dressing room meant for half our number. It was magnificently equipped with the usual cracked mirror, torn sofa, lackluster cheese platter, and a couple of six-packs of Budweiser. Hoagy filled me in on SNAG and SMUG, two local men's activist groups. SNAG, for Sensitive New Age Guys, had a reputation for sponsoring men's sensitivity-training groups and weekend vision quests. Their position papers earnestly explained their mission to raise consciousness about negative male images in the media. SMUG, for Smart Men Use Guns, was a rough-and-tumble group advocating a vigilante militia, and didn't know what a position paper was. Their leader, a dentally impaired bruiser who called himself Major Booty, was himself a ripe candidate for the Family Literacy Program. For the first time ever, these groups were united in their hatred of one single entity: Man-Bashin' Sarah Jean.

Greg and Hoagy reported that the two groups had set up camp in the large parking lot in front of the resort's main lodge, keeping the sell-out crowd of literacy-loving ticket holders at bay. On one side of the parking lot, several dozen SNAGs, dressed in flowing natural-fiber shirts and Birkenstocks, pounded on conga drums and handed out colorful flyers explaining their philosophy. On the other side, an equal number of SMUGs held court in flannel shirts, jeans, and work boots, conducting belching contests and drinking beer.

In the middle of the parking lot was a portable boom box connected to two large speakers. Earlier in the day this setup had been used as a public address system with the addition of a plastic microphone, the finest Radio Shack had to offer. But one of the SNAGs had given a long-winded, heartfelt speech about the sexual politics of organic gardening, and a SMUG threatened to cram the mic up his ass if he didn't shut the fuck up. In the tussle that ensued, the microphone was broken. Now the boom box was being used by the SMUGs as God intended, to play Marshall Tucker's greatest hits.

Except that the SNAGs wanted to hear Yanni.

ALTHOUGH THE PROTESTERS BLOCKED EL RANCHO'S front entrance, most of the ticket holders quickly realized they could just walk around to the other side of the building and come in through the back door. So by the time Red Meat took the stage, five hundred women, who felt they had risked their lives to get in, were expecting a great show.

The literacy program's star pupil was to introduce my set. Constance Villena had recently learned to read bedtime stories to her four young children with the help of a volunteer tutor and donated books. She was one proud lady as she began her prepared speech, piped into the dressing room through a tiny speaker, about the many ways in which literacy had changed her life, including helping her find a better job. In fact, we were all starting to tear up a little, when we heard a shot ring out in the vicinity of the parking lot, followed by a gut-wrenching scream.

Of course I assumed the worst. Someone had been killed because of my stupid song, and we would be next. I like to think it was the animal force of pregnancy hormones that made me stand up and announce, "That's it. I'm not going on. Please tell the nice literacy people that I'm very sorry but we'll have to give everyone's money back."

They all just sat there on the sofa.

"Hey"—my voice sounded shrill in my own ears—"I said let's go. We're not doing this gig. It's my show and I say we're leaving." And I started gathering my belongings.

They continued to sit there. Lee opened a bottle of beer and took a long swallow. Allie picked up her guitar and plugged it into her electronic tuner. Hoagy combed his hair.

"Shit, what's wrong with you people?" I shrieked. "This is my show and my CD and I say we're leaving!" And I walked toward the door.

"You're not going anywhere, young lady." Allie looked over at Pete, who stood up and blocked my path to the door, while Hoagy gently held on to my shoulders. "I did not raise my daughter to act like a snot-nosed diva when there's a show to do," she said calmly. "We've all worked very hard to get you here tonight, and there is no way you are not going to play this gig, little princess, so dry your tears and get the fuck out there." And she stood up, walked over to me, and kicked a hole in the dressing room wall.

"Hoagy, help me," I collapsed, sobbing, in his arms.

"Remember back when you asked me to be sure and let you know if you started acting like an asshole? Well, this is it," Hoagy said. "Your mother is right. You have five minutes to pull yourself together. Go wash your face."

"Greg?" I pleaded.

"I know you're scared," Greg said gently. "And you don't

owe us anything. But think about that lady who was just talking out there. If she can learn to read at her age you can play a few songs with a bunch of morons yelling in the parking lot. Look, I'll go out there and find out what really happened. If nobody died we'll play, okay?"

It sounded reasonable to Allie.

Greg came back to report that as far as he could tell, Major Booty had gotten so sick of hearing the SNAGs whine about their Yanni CD that he'd shot the boom box.

"See," he said, "it just goes to show how much music means to people. And these people came to hear your music, so I think you should get your butt out there and play."

"I'm sorry, I just can't do it," I sobbed. "Let's go home."

Hoagy stood up. I assumed he was coming with me to the truck, so I gave him a grateful look, but instead he turned toward the band.

"Everyone onstage," he announced. "We'll start with 'Hell on Heels.' Just hang on the intro till Sarah Jean comes out, and then we'll kick it into the verse with a drumroll."

They calmly took their places onstage, and Hoagy counted off the introduction to "Hell on Heels." They played it again and again and again as the crowd's roar turned to puzzled murmurs.

I stood paralyzed in the wings. I'd forgotten all the lyrics. I just wanted to go home. I started to cry.

Allie glared at me from the stage and signaled to Pete with her eyes. He walked over and took my hand.

"Looks like you need a little help. Come on." And he picked me up like a sack of potatoes with his good arm and deposited me in the middle of the stage.

The crowd went wild.

I still couldn't remember the lyrics!

It must have been only a minute until Allie took pity on me at last and walked up to the microphone, but it felt like an hour and a half.

"Hey, tell us about your baby sister," she teased.

The lyrics came back to my brain in a flood of relief and I was able to sing.

My baby sister wears her skirts up high
Got a five-dollar haircut and a million-dollar smile
She hates peace and quiet and she can't sit still
Tearing down the turnpike to the next big thrill
The girl's about as subtle as a jumbo jet, she's political—
  but she's not correct
Never tells a lie, man, you know she's for real
She's gonna drive you crazy, she's hell on heels

I was mediocre at best, but I'm not sure anyone in the audience noticed. They were appreciative and generous with their applause. I did the set, terrified, holding back tears the whole time, a frightened mammal protecting her young. I'd never felt anything like that before.

Back home, I thought I'd made it through free and clear—no one outside had really been hurt, no one inside had complained about my performance—until, buried under my pink comforter, I turned on the eleven o'clock news. There was a long shot of the El Rancho Resort's parking lot, then a close-up of a nervous-looking redhead with a forced smile . . . oh, my! It was me!

"What one word best describes your past relationships?" I heard Patti Larson's voice ask off-camera. My own face, fearful and confused, answered on-screen: "Battered."

"This show is a benefit for the Lake County Family Literacy Program," said Patti Larson's voice. "What is your connection to this worthy group?"

"I have no relationship," said my face on the TV screen.

THE REST OF THE HOLIDAY SEASON PROMISED A WHIRLWIND of anxious planning, eating (me), drinking (everyone else), and mood swings, both pregnant (mine) and menopausal (Allie's). Jamee, back in Nashville, started a hot e-mail correspondence with Pete. Lloyd and SWF 34 made up after their first fight but continued to miss meeting each other, and "Take It from Me" hit the country charts at number twenty. It amazed me, as I patted my growing belly, how little that changed anything. Perle kept vacillating about whether to accept the inheritance. The rest of us went about the sloppy business of getting on with our lives. After all, what other choice did we have?

Chapter

15

MY DAYS WERE BUSY, WORKING AT THE DEWDROP
and preparing for the baby. But at night I was often
overtaken by an itchy restlessness. I'd drive around in
the hills for hours blasting Merle Haggard tapes, holding my
head out the window like a big old dog to feel the night breezes.
My companion on those drives was Bosco, which was the name
I'd given my fetus. We had some good long talks. I explained the
absent-daddy situation as best I could, and Bosco didn't seem to
mind too much.

I told myself I didn't mind too much either, but sometimes
I'd start really missing my dad, and it broke my heart for Bosco's
sake that his father was also missing in action. On the nights when
I thought about that my tears could have rivaled those of Princess
Lupiyoma, the legendary and frustrated loser whose tears are
a spring that fills Clear Lake. But mostly things were fine, really.

Then my father called a week before Christmas.

"How's my little team player?" he asked.

"Okay, Dad, but I'd be better if you were still on the team."

"Aw, I know. And don't think I don't miss you every single
day. It's just—I had to do this. I'm really in love with Rainbow."

"Rainbow? Her name is *Rainbow*?"

"What's wrong with that? Her parents were hippies."

"How old is she?"

"She's about your age. But Rainbow is a very old soul."

"Who are you and what have you done with my father?" I had never heard him talk that way before.

"Maybe it's hard for you to understand, but I love Rainbow. Try to have an open mind about her. I hope that once things settle down, you'll be able to be friends, but whether or not that happens, she's going to be my wife and I'd appreciate it if you'd treat her with a little respect. Anyway, she really wants to say hello to you. I'm going to put her on the phone now—don't make me sorry I did."

"Oh, barf," I answered, with all the sophisticated acceptance I could muster.

Her voice was breathy—she sounded about fourteen years old. She said she was very much in love with my father and that she hoped we could end up being friends, especially because she was a big fan of my music. She knew deep down in her soul that as hard as the breakup had been for my mom, it would prove to be a growth experience for all concerned.

"Yeah, I think Allie would love to grow you a black eye right about now," I said. "What makes you so sure that in a few years my dad won't get tired of you, too, and find another pretty young girlfriend?"

"That will never happen because Johnsey and I are true soul mates, not like your parents. I mean, I'm sure your mother is a wonderful person in many ways, but apparently they had, like, zero going on in the bedroom."

That wasn't what I'd heard, but what was the point in bursting her bubble? And *Johnsey*? Puh-lease!

"Oh, there's no need to worry about Allie. She's kind of seeing someone and she seems pretty happy these days," I offered in as peppy a voice as I could manage. I heard her whisper something, and Dad got back on the line.

"See, what did I tell you?" he asked eagerly. "Rainbow's a beautiful woman, inside and out. And she loves your music, too—you can't beat that. Now, what's this about Allie having a boyfriend? Is it anyone I know? Don't tell me Hoagy finally made his big move. He's had a crush on Allie since high school."

"Actually, no," I answered. "It's an old friend of hers who just showed up one day. I don't know if you know him. Did you ever meet a musician named Artie Blond?"

I heard shattering glass, and the phone went dead.

"Well, Merry Christmas," I said to nobody, on the other end of the line.

I HATED TO ADMIT IT, BUT DAD AND RAINBOW DID NOT have the distinction of being my only troubled relationship during that time. As Hoagy had predicted, now that I was somewhat famous, people seemed to assign more importance to their encounters with me. I had to make an extra effort to be gracious—it wasn't so hard with acquaintances, since my mama raised me to have very good manners, but it could be difficult with old friends, whose agendas were complex. My struggling-musician pals wanted to be happy for me, but I could see frustration and envy in their eyes. Little Max kept inviting me to his band's Friday-night gigs at the bowling alley. If I showed up, he'd find some way to make nasty jokes about me from the bandstand. If I didn't show, he'd call and whine about not feeling supported. I finally gave up—stopped going, and stopped returning his calls—turning his fears that I was "too busy" for him into self-fulfilling prophesy. There was just no getting through to the guy.

ON CHRISTMAS EVE, CINDI-LU BENDER AND CAL HOOPER announced their engagement on nationally syndicated Christian Family Values radio. It was all over the papers, and there were splashy photo spreads of the happy couple in *Entertainment Weekly* and *People.* Marvella Claxton, who called every now and then to check in, reported a less-than-idyllic scenario, however. She'd been performing on the same show the day they appeared, and she overheard Cal hitting on a young segment producer in the green room, while Cindi-Lu was in makeup. (Most performers don't require makeup for radio, but this was Cindi-Lu.) This wasn't so unusual for show business people, of course. Five minutes later, when he went on the air with Cindi-Lu to talk about the importance of monogamy in Christian marriage, Marvella said it made her want to puke.

Then Richie, usually the source of the juiciest gossip, checked in with a tidbit I found hard to believe. Someone at the hair salon had told someone at the bait shop, who told Richie's sister, who told Richie that "that guy who's marrying the country star from Sarah Jean's old band" had been spotted checking into the El Rancho Resort with an attractive redheaded woman. A couple of people around town wondered if it was me! It wasn't, of course, but the whole idea of Cal coming up to Lake County for a secret tryst was laughable—an idea so farfetched that I wrote it off as a case of mistaken identity.

IN A GRAND GESTURE DESIGNED TO IMPRESS ALLIE, ARTIE Blond came up with a fabulous Christmas present for her. He'd secretly called in some favors and arranged for an incredible lineup of musicians, many of whom had starred at the folk festivals they'd attended when they were young, to play at the Dewdrop on New Year's Eve. As we prepared for the big night, the chemistry between Artie and Allie was electric. They blushed and giggled; we could almost see sparks flying as their hands touched. I'm sure they both thought they were acting perfectly normal, but anyone could tell that those two had been hit by the Crush Bomb. I asked Greg to follow me upstairs when I was dismissed to rest up for the evening. He sat on the edge of my bed, fiddling with the TV remote control.

"Greg, I just had the weirdest thought."

"What's that?"

"What if Artie Blond is really my father?"

"What? That's crazy."

"No, it isn't. Remember that first night he showed up here, when we were all listening to the Alice and Artie Story?"

"More like the Alice and Artie and Monica and Jasmine Story . . ."

"He said something about being together while Dad was stranded somewhere else, and she gave him one of her looks and he backed off, remember? And that timing goes along with some old letters I found. Well, that could have been around when I was conceived. And don't you think I look a little bit like him, too, around the eyebrows?"

"No, I don't think you look like him, but that's beside the point. What I can't imagine is Allie screwing around. She was a newlywed, and crazy about your dad," he reasoned.

"I know," I said, "but she's always had a thing for Artie. You can tell just by looking at the two of them. And it was the sixties. Everyone screwed around back then; you were supposed to. I don't think it meant the same thing as it does now, and they didn't have any of the really horrible diseases yet. I was born during the Summer of Love, you know."

"So, you going to ask your mom about it?"

"No way. I was thinking maybe you—"

"Are you crazy? Hey, I have an idea. Why don't you go on *Ricki Lake* with everyone and have them do a paternity test on the air?"

"Who's Ricki Lake?" I wanted to know.

"Wow, you really have been on another planet. Hand me the *TV Guide*, will you? It's always on somewhere." Greg flipped on the TV and channel-surfed till we found a rerun of *Ricki Lake*. There on the stage was Calvin Klein, explaining to the live studio audience that his mother was really a sweet little old lady from Queens, and not Patsy Cline. He even brought his real mother out from backstage and introduced her to everyone. There to refute his claim was Mildred Martin from Nashville, with the story about her dear friend Patsy's secret love child. When questioned about the fact that there was only a ten-year difference in their recorded birth dates, the interviewee had sniffed that Patsy Cline would not have been above lying about her age, and anyway, there were certainly occasional sad instances of ten-year-olds giving birth. At the end of the show, the studio audience voted on which story was true. Mildred Martin won. As educational as it might have been, an appearance on *Ricki Lake* didn't seem like a viable option for my family.

Jack Elliott, the Burns Sisters, Jaime Brockett, Roger McGuinn, Richie Havens, and Judy Collins all graced our stage that night, along with Marvella and Elroy. Harlan Harris had heard about our plans and asked if he could film the evening for a VH1 *Harvard Square to Honky-Tonk: Where Are They Now? Folk Legends of the Sixties* special, and showed up with his entourage and crew. He coaxed Artie into performing the famous cow song for the cameras; many of us were hearing the cult folk hit for the first time, since Artie hadn't played it since the seventies. He started the song by finger-picking the traditional melody in Fast Freddy's trademark open tuning.

Late last night, when we were all in bed
Mrs. O'Leary left her lantern in the shed
Well, the cow kicked it over, and she winked her eye and said
There'll be a hot time in the old town tonight

For dramatic effect, he coaxed the audience to shout out, "Fire! Fire! Fire! Fire!" at the end of the first verse, then the finger-picking shifted into a more traditional talking blues progression, and Artie took it from there.

Well, you know Chicago is known for the blues
Known for its pizza and its windiness, too
How 'bout that fi-ire a long time ago
Cow kicks a lantern and what do you know

The whole town bu-urned, the whole town bu-urned
The whole town bu-urned, right down to the ground

Hay in the barn, flame in the lantern
Mrs. O's Holstein made one wrong turn
That cow wasn't mean, he was sweet as can be
Mrs. O gave his hay a li'l special recipe

Some green in his feedbin, from her own private stash
Mrs. O shared her best weed with the livestock out back
And they were so mellow, they were never unkind
And didn't get anxious when she came around

Well, that big ol' bovine was gettin' it on in the stall
With a sweet sweet heifer who didn't mind it at all
Then his flank swiped the lantern as he mounted his gal
I bet they didn't take notice till they were medium rare

The whole town bu-urned, the whole town bu-urned
The whole town bu-urned, right down to the ground
Oh, let me burn
(Audience: Fire! Fire! Fire! Fire!)

When you hear those bells go ding-a-ling
All join round and sweetly we will sing
And when the verse is through, in the chorus all join in:
There'll be a hot time in the old town tonight!

The Burns Sisters, a contemporary folk trio from New York, contributed startlingly beautiful harmonies on "Dance upon the Earth" and "No More Silence" that made me teary for Amy and Kathleen. Hoagy provided death-defying guitar licks, and Lloyd, eyes glued to the door on the lookout for SWF 34, played pedal steel solos bursting with love and longing. Halfway through Judy Collins's set, he was rewarded at last. Breathless and pretty, SWF 34 burst through the door and walked up to the bandstand. Lloyd, ever the consummate professional, looked at her, smiled slightly, almost flubbed a note, but recovered quickly and continued to play his solo on "Someday Soon." After all the months of writing, talking on the phone, fighting, making up, and missing connections, they finally met face-to-face, and it appeared to be love at first sight. For the rest of the evening, they held hands every minute he wasn't playing. During his sets, Aunt Perle cornered the poor woman and extracted her entire life story.

It looked like SWF 34 would fit right in. She had a name—Rita—and she played the accordion. She was also about to become an author. *I Drove 'Em to It: Stories from the Front Seat,* a humorous account of her experiences driving a limousine, had just been acquired by a major New York publisher. She loved pedal steel and seemed quite taken with Lloyd.

"How many responses did you get to your ad?" Perle grilled her as Allie, Lloyd, and I joined them at the family table during a break.

"A lot, at least thirty or forty. I used to be an English teacher, so I really notice bad grammar and spelling. I made my first cut on the basis of that—I discarded all the letters with spelling mistakes. I figured that was as good a requirement as any, for me." She beamed at Lloyd. "His letter was perfect! No misspelled words, and an impeccable balance between self-confidence and vulnerability. I was intrigued."

Both Allie and Perle puffed up with pride as Lloyd's face turned crimson. I felt the sharp toe of his cowboy boot hitting my shin.

On the stroke of midnight, Judy and Marvella, alternating verses, led everyone in a breathtaking a cappella chorus of "Amazing Grace." After closing time, we sat up for hours, laughing, talking, and singing until we all finally went upstairs to bed. A short while later, too wound up and restless to sleep, I came back downstairs to take my usual insomniac's drive into the hills, and heard soft laughter. It appeared that Lloyd and SWF 34 had found yet another use for the mechanical bull.

Part Two
⤜ 1994 ⤛

Chapter
16

"**Y**OUNG LADY, IT'S TIME WE DISCUSSED YOUR CHILD-birth options," Aunt Perle said. She was holding a sheaf of notes and looked like she meant business.

I groaned and lifted myself off the sofa in Allie's bedroom, where I'd been hiding out.

"What do you mean? I've been seeing Dr. Terri. I just assumed I'd go to childbirth classes at the hospital and she would deliver the baby."

"There's a problem with that. Dr. Terri is very medical in her thinking."

"Well, she *is* a doctor," I reminded Perle.

"You see? That's exactly what I mean. Now that you're starting your third trimester, there's no time to lose. I think you should consider an alternative."

"And what would that be?"

"The Bhalahdi community. You remember Desi, the English guy who fixes our dishwasher? He's one of them. That's where I do my nutrition workshops; I know the spiritual leader from Brooklyn. A couple of his wives are pregnant right now, and they are holding natural-childbirth classes with their own midwife.

Usually they don't allow outsiders in, but since Harvey and I go way back, he said he'd make an exception for you."

"Who's Harvey?" I asked.

"The teacher, the community's spiritual leader. I know around here he goes by Avatar Di O Bhalah, but to me he'll always be Harvey Kirshbaum from Flatbush Avenue. All I ask is that you come up there with me one day and give it a try. You can always go back to Dr. Terri if you don't like them."

A little research around town delivered the information that Avatar Di O Bhalah had been a child tap-dancing star—he once appeared in purple sequins on the *Ed Sullivan Show*—then a promising dental student, before finding God and starting his own religion during the seventies, up in the hills above Kelseyville. The commune supported itself with a virtual monopoly on home-appliance repair in Lake County. Theologically, they borrowed liberally from various Eastern philosophies, with a bit of Yiddish folk wisdom thrown in.

Perle insisted on driving me over to take a look on a chilly February day.

There were no signs marking the entrance to the Bhalahdi community. On a small wooden plaque next to the driveway leading into the compound were carved three words that appeared to be used as a kind of all-purpose greeting, similar to "shalom" or "aloha." These words were LIFE GOES ON. This was how community members greeted one another when they passed by on strolls through the beautiful Japanese-style gardens, or entered the main house for meditation circle or the assignment of daily chores. Members of the community appeared to be universally slender, clear-eyed, and serene. They wore rubber flip-flop sandals and seemed to like to dress in purple, the brighter the better.

It was a tranquil, quiet place, so it surprised me to see Perle slam the car door and run through the gate, yelling, "Yo, Haaaarvey, we're heeeere! Come on outa there, you spiritual old fart!"

A smiling, bald-headed man with wire-rimmed glasses appeared at the top of a flight of stairs on the side of one of the buildings. He was decked out in the obligatory saffron robes of a religious cult leader, but otherwise he looked like a dentist from Brooklyn.

"Perlie, Perlie, how's by you? I see you finally brought your beautiful niece along," Harvey gushed in an unmistakable New York accent. "Hi, sweetheart, I must tell you we love your music up here. Just yesterday we played 'Heartaches for a Guy' at the end of Prayer Circle. That one gives me a chuckle every time I hear it. Maybe sometime you could bring the band up here and play for us? Not next week, because we have to practice for our soccer tournament with Swami Sammy's Temple of Insecurity, but anytime after that. Meanwhile, you'll want to meet Molly the midwife—she's an absolute gem, that Molly. I don't know what we'd do without her. Come, come with me now, darling. Our morning meditation is about to begin."

"Morning meditation?" I whispered to Perle. "It's past noon."

"Harvey always likes to sleep in," she explained. "Come on."

We slipped out of our shoes and entered the main building, then walked down a hallway to a large domed room. I sat quietly in the back, next to two other pregnant women on folding chairs. Perle assumed full lotus position at my feet.

I'd guess there were about seventy or eighty of them, chanting quietly. Then deep purple curtains were opened to reveal a raised platform covered with flowers, fruit, crystals, and framed photographs of Harvey. Most of the photos portrayed him in his Swami getup, but a couple appeared to be posed shots with celebrities seated around tables at Trader Vic's. I thought I spotted one in which Harvey had his arm draped casually around Muhammad Ali's shoulders. Harvey himself entered through a side door, and everyone rose to greet him. He raised his arms in benediction and chanted to the assemblage:

"Ooooooh, Bha Lah Di. Oh, Bhalahdi!"

"Ooooooh, Bha Lah Di. Oh, Bhalahdi," they responded. Then, "Ooooooh, Bha Lah Da. Oh, Bhalahda."

And Harvey repeated, "Ooooooh, Bha Lah Da. Oh, Bhalahda!"

He brought his hands together in prayer, bowing from the waist.

"Life Goes On!"

"Life Goes On!" repeated his followers, who then joined in a high-pitched chant. "Laaaaaaa Laaaaaaaa Laaaaaaa Laaaaaa."

"Life Goes On!" he cried, and then they did the whole thing over again, about thirty or forty times.

As the chanting ended, Aunt Perle scooted over and whispered, "Here comes the moment where Harvey blesses everyone with a thought for the day. Pay attention, it's the best part."

Harvey cleared his throat. "My lesson for the day is this. Always remember, the clothes do not go through the water, the water goes through the clothes."

"Ahhhh," said the gathering. "Oh yes, so very true."

"What's that supposed to mean?" I whispered to Perle.

"Don't forget how they make their living. They own the best washing-machine repair service in the county. That's why Harvey is known as the 'Spin Cycle Swami.' For this group, those are words to live by."

Harvey bowed again.

"Life Goes On!" he shouted.

"Life Goes On!" was the crowd's joyful response.

"Turn to silence!" he yelled.

"What does that mean?" I whispered.

"It's one of their mantras," Perle explained. "Harvey found those words on a knob in back of a toilet, in the early days. More words to live by, if you think about it."

"Let's have lunch!" cried Harvey.

After meditation, we had a vegetarian feast with Molly the midwife, and a tour of the compound that included their birthing tent. Molly explained some of the peculiarities of their theology. The Bhalahdis believe in an afterlife that takes the form of the last song you heard when you were alive. So, for example, if you checked out in the middle of Buck Owens's "Truck Driving Man," you'd end up in a very different heaven than someone who was listening to Aerosmith. For this reason, their musical environment was under Harvey's strict control. I should consider it a great honor, Molly said, that he liked my song and had invited the band up to play. I was polite, but I couldn't wait to get Perle alone in the car.

"Come on, Aunt Perle, spill," I said as we were driving away. "That was pretty elaborate for a practical joke. What's the deal?"

"What do you mean? That place is no joke. They're serious, committed people and they are absolutely lovely. Why do you think it's a big joke?"

"Ob-La-Di, Ob-La-Da—that's a Beatles song. You can't seriously tell me that your pal based a whole religion on a Beatles song, can you?"

"So all of a sudden you've got something against The Beatles?"

"Anyway, he forgot the 'bra.' It goes, 'Ob-La-Di, Ob-La-Da, life goes on, *bra* . . .'"

"Nitpicking, always nitpicking," Perle grumbled. "No bras up there, sweetie. They don't need them 'cause they do yoga."

The thing is, I really liked it there. The birthing tent looked like a wonderful place to have a baby, much cozier than a hospital room. When we got home, I dug out my old copy of the *White Album*, to brush up on Scripture.

THEY WERE PRETTY EXCITED OVER AT UNICORN ENTERTAIN-ment. My CD sales were exceeding expectations despite the fact that I wasn't touring, and there was interest in a couple of my songs for sound-track usage.

"We've even caught the attention of a big international distributor who handles all the Nashville product," exclaimed the new Artist Relations VP in a phone call. "Those guys wouldn't give us the time of day a year ago. I'm thinking of going with them for the second release."

"Aren't you happy with the distributor we have? I thought they did a great job rushing my first CD out for Christmas. I think it makes sense to stay loyal to them," I argued.

"Yes, they did an awesome job. But they're not in the Nashville loop. These other folks understand the C&W market a whole lot better. They're making some tempting offers."

"You guys are the pros. It's your call," I said. "Anything else?"

"Yeah, one more thing. There's this fellow with a movie in production. He needs a safe-sex cheating song for a bar scene and we can't find one. Has to be classic sounding but not a ballad. Got anything up your sleeve?"

I told him I'd think about it and get back to him.

The next phone call I received, later that day, was from my dad's girlfriend, Rainbow. She was nearly hysterical.

"You're the only person I feel I can talk to about this," she sobbed. "Johnsey hasn't been the same since he heard about your mother and that Artie Blond guy. He's been depressed and uncommunicative, and last night he didn't even bother to come home. I think he's cheating on me."

Despite the fact that I didn't hold a great deal of sympathy in my heart for Rainbow, it was clear that she genuinely loved "Johnsey" and that she was in pain. I put my feet up and listened while she talked. Then I told her a little bit about Bobby Lee and how he'd turned out to have an unexpected wife in a Japanese hotel room, but I was already madly in love with our baby. Finally she became calmer.

"Thanks for talking me down," she said. "I owe you one. I should have listened to you in the first place. After all, if he cheats on one, he'll cheat on two."

"No problem, Rainbow. And thank *you*," I said as I slammed down the phone and ran to get my notebook and guitar. Two days later I had my "safe sex cheating song."

> *You say you've met the most enchanting lover of your life*
> *He'd be perfect if he didn't have two children and a wife*
> *They just don't understand him and he needs some sympathy*
> *But you better watch it, darling, just take a tip from me*
> *If he cheats on one, he'll cheat on two—*
> *You can bet your boots these words are true*

Though you do the best you can, when you love a married man
If he cheats on her, he'll cheat on you

When those stolen nights of passion slowly fade into the
* dawn*
You'd better be darn careful that he has protection on
For you may not be the only one with whom he likes to stray
And you don't know where his wife is
On the nights that he's away
If he cheats on one, he'll cheat on two —
You can bet your boots these words are true
Though you do the best you can, when you love a married man
If he cheats on her, he'll cheat on you

We threw a demo together in Lee's basement studio, trying to get as classic—which means as derivative—a "Ray Price shuffle" sound as possible. The movie producer was happy, and I was the hero of the hour at Unicorn Entertainment.

Never willing to waste a good song, I started performing "Cheats on One" regularly when I sat in with the Dewdrop Drifters. Though it was a silly song inspired by the words of a silly woman, everyone said I sang it with more heart, deeper feeling, and greater vocal range and style than ever before. It was true that I couldn't sing it without thinking of my own story—the fact that I'd unwittingly fallen for a married man, made love to him with no protection, and was now pregnant with his child. I silently dedicated those verses to one foolish night, a man I had loved for a few careless minutes, and the child I already loved forever. Layers of hope, regret, and passion came across in my performance—classic country music material.

LLOYD ASKED SWF 34 TO MARRY HIM EARLY THAT SPRING, around the time my feet disappeared. We'd all been cranky for various reasons. Perle was talking to lawyers about her options, should she decide to accept Samantha Eustace's inheritance, and felt it was taking up way too much of her time. Pete was frustrated because in spite of months in a cast followed by physical therapy, his arm was far from good as new—he was clearly not ready to play drums four hours a night. I was relieved that Greg would be around for a while—it was scary to think about what I'd do without him, if and when Pete resumed his role as the house drummer. Greg and I had continued with our easy and intimate friendship, which still involved a fair amount of naked, sexless pillow fighting. But Pete needed some kind of official position. Allie offered him a partnership in the Dewdrop, along with the position of VP/Head Bouncer. This made the issue of settling finances with Dad all the more urgent, causing my parents to argue about how to divide their property. Allie was also seeing a lot of Artie, who came up with one excuse after another for his frequent visits: He needed bee pollen available only at a local farm; there was a country music video he'd been wanting to see, and his San Francisco cable company didn't offer TNN; his dog had died, and he wanted its ashes scattered over Clear Lake; he had found a little owl for her collection (what collection?); he was doing some investigative legwork for a friend who was an undercover cop; he was moonlighting for ASCAP and wanted to make sure Allie was paying her jukebox fees. The closer Artie got to Allie, the more Hoagy sulked. Dad was right—he'd had a thing for her for years. How could we not have noticed?

So a wedding was just what we all needed, and plans were under way. We couldn't help but notice a certain synchronicity between Lloyd's wedding plans and Cindi-Lu Bender's, scheduled for the same Saturday in April. Every week the tabloids reported another juicy tidbit. SWF 34 planned to wear a ninety-five-dollar Hawaiian number she'd picked up on vacation, with some clever alterations provided by Richie as a wedding gift; Cindi-Lu's sixteen-thousand-dollar gown was to be made by a world-famous fashion designer. Cindi-Lu and Cal were going to be married by Billy Graham; Lloyd and SWF 34 were going to be married by Peter Rawley, who remembered he'd once been paid for a gig with a certificate of ordination from the Temple of Man. Cindi-Lu's bridal party was a who's who of country music royalty, including Reba McEntire, Lorrie Morgan, and Pam Tillis; SWF 34's consisted of her sister and her dog, Boo Boo. Cindi-Lu and Cal were to be married at the Beverly Hills Hotel, but Buck Owens and Merle Haggard were throwing Cal a bachelor party in Bakersfield the night before the wedding. Stretch limos adorned with huge steer horns would transport the groom's entourage to Beverly Hills the next day. In fact, Monica would be unable to make Lloyd's wedding because she needed all hands on deck for Cal Hooper's bachelor party at the Boom Boom Room. Lloyd's wedding would be held at the Dewdrop. The bachelor party would also be held at the Dewdrop, so limos were not required, although there would be one—the bride's—which she would drive on the honeymoon.

THERE WASN'T MUCH PRIVACY AT THE DEWDROP INN, BUT ONE afternoon everyone was out doing various things in preparation for the wedding, and I found myself blissfully, deliciously alone. I had decided to spend some quiet time working on a new song when I heard the door slam and Greg's excited voice downstairs.

"Hey, anybody home? Look what I got!"

"Up here in my room," I yelled.

"My mom sent me a present—a digital camera, so we can e-mail her some pictures of the wedding. Come on; let's try it out. We don't have to save any of the pictures. I'll take some of you pregnant."

It was fun posing. We ran through a couple of dozen shots while I tried on different outfits, including my shiny purple satin Bhalahdi birthing robe.

"Let's go for some art shots, okay?" Greg suggested. "Come on, take your clothes off. I'll go get that fabric Richie was fooling around with for the wedding decorations." As he draped red velvet around my huge naked belly, his hand accidentally brushed against my breast. I held it there against my swollen nipple, and I saw his body respond through those tight leather pants. He gently kissed the back of my neck.

"Why don't you take your clothes off, too," I whispered.

"Are you sure? Can it hurt the baby?"

"No, not according to the midwife. She says it's actually good for the baby," I answered.

"Well, then, here's to the baby."

I helped him unzip his pants as his hand, then his head, disappeared under my belly, so huge that it hid all the good stuff. But I could feel his silky hair on my thighs and then his tongue everywhere. Who needs to see everything, anyway? The best part was that I felt great about being enormous, the life force, the O-Bhalahdi. I was Mother Earth; I was the Goddess. I was so hot for him! My nipples were enormous and tender, craving his touch. I was completely aware of his fingers, his tongue, his breath in my ear. And he was magnificently hard for huge, pregnant me. It was hours later that we surfaced, slowly making our way back to the real world, with Hoagy screaming his head off that downbeat was in ten minutes, and where was the fucking drummer?

I didn't cry, even when I realized that we'd made love for the very first time, or that we were going to have to replace nineteen yards of really expensive red velvet.

Oh Greg, who knew?

Chapter

17

THE MORNING OF THE WEDDING FOUND ALLIE AND Perle perched on eight-foot ladders, dressing the buffalo heads in white tulle veils. Audrey the florist arrived with the bridal bouquet of white lilacs and other April wildflowers, and "Sweet Lorraine," the caterer whose specialty was magnificent cakes, was arranging her creation. A cousin of the bride's made a tiny accordion and a tiny pedal steel guitar for the wedding cake's bride and groom dolls to play. Another cousin had found a wind-up dog that resembled Boo Boo. Richie was there to do his last-minute fixes on the bride's dress, and touch up her hair and makeup. He seemed to be bursting to talk to me.

"Cupcake, I heard some gossip about a friend of yours, what's that kid's name, Max?"

"Little Max? Wow, I haven't heard from him in ages, which has actually been kind of a relief. What's he up to?"

"Well . . ." Richie leaned into his story, gratified that he would be telling me something I didn't already know. "You know Harlan Harris, the video producer, the one with the great taste in shirts? He called me about working on a shoot for him in a couple of weeks. And he said that Max moved to L.A. to join a band with a major label deal."

"You're kidding me!" I said. "Good for him. What band?"

"Harlan didn't say. He ran into him at the farmers' market on Fairfax; said he looked a little out of it. Max told him the band was about to sign a major label deal, though, and meanwhile he's working in a music distributor's warehouse in the Valley. He asked about you."

"That sounds like Little Max, all right. I hope the band, who-ever they are, can handle a big coked-up baby."

"Oh, Bunnyboobs, they're probably all big coked-up babies. Come on, help me with this lace netting. We have to do the cake table."

Hoagy, the best man, was taking the opportunity to run the show, and Artie Blond was the unfortunate recipient of his bossi-ness. It was far more interesting to watch those two trip over each other's egos, competing for Allie's attention, than to think about Little Max in L.A.

A huge pile of festively wrapped presents appeared on the long table next to the cake as the club filled with well-wishers. Lloyd, eyes glazed over and smiling from ear to ear, greeted guests in one of his beautiful vintage Western shirts. As the bride's friends and family walked into the Dewdrop for the first time, their jaws dropped. It appeared that none of these deprived folks had ever set foot in a honky-tonk before. The best reaction was from her brother, a molecular biologist from Livermore. "I want to live here," he pleaded. Jamee showed up from Nashville and immediately began hanging adoringly on Pete's arm.

On the groom's side, we had a huge Americana music and pedal steel contingent, including Buddy and Julie Miller, Jimmy

LaFave, Dallas Wayne, and Bobby Black. Several others sent lame excuses like aunts dying, and ended up on the TV coverage of Cindi-Lu's wedding later in the day. Despite the competing event, we had an amazingly talented room full of people. The Dewdrop Drifters, all except Lloyd, who was deemed incapable of anything that required brain cells, were going to serve as the backbone for an amazing jam, to begin after the ceremony and dinner. The bride was being fussed over upstairs in Perle's room, while Boo Boo, a shy dog by nature, hid under the bar.

Then it was time.

Boo Boo had been well trained. At his mistress's urging, he trotted down the makeshift AstroTurf aisle, rings tied securely to the pillow in his mouth. Right behind him walked the bride, playing her own wedding march on the accordion. She did fine until the modulation, when everything started to fall apart. She missed a note just as Boo Boo noticed that a lot of people were watching him. He froze and refused to budge, and she tripped over his rigid torso, sending him careening across the dance floor, legs splayed, trying vainly to right himself on the slippery wood as his toenails clicked and slid across the shiny floor. Lloyd rescued the bride seconds before both she and her accordion would have tumbled into the cake, and led her to the bandstand. Meanwhile, Boo Boo darted back under the bar, where he would stay until after the ceremony, when the smell of hot hors d'oeuvres would become irresistible. Pete, assisted by Harvey Kirshbaum, performed the shortest marriage ceremony in Lake County history.

He cleared his throat ceremoniously.

"Lloyd buddy, you sure you want to do this, now?"

"You bet, Pete."

"And you, honey, you down with it?"

"Yes."

"Okay, got the rings?" It took a minute to find Boo Boo and wrestle the rings out of his jaw. "Go for it, kids. By the power vested in me by the State of California and Avatar Di O Bhalah Da here, I now pronounce you husband and wife. Go on, kiss the bride and let's party!"

And party we did.

Hoagy and I waited until it was time for the toasts to present the happy couple with our special wedding gift, a brand-new song based on a certain person's personal ad.

HOAGY: *I turned off the TV show,*
    picked up the paper at my front door
Not much news, so I turned to the classifieds
Didn't want to buy a boat or a truck,
    bored to death and just my luck
Something in the personals caught my eye

ME: *Bright, pretty, slender, nice*
HOAGY: *Sounded good, so I read it twice*
ME: *I'd like to be your friend and maybe more*
Movies, music, theater too,
    I wanna be able to talk to you
And I'm only thirty-four

HOAGY: *I sat down at my computer,*
    hoping that this one was cuter
And smarter than the last girl I called mine
Some of the spelling caused me doubt

So I ran it through Spell Check and printed it out
And the ads were in my favor this time

ME: *I got a lot of letters from guys who sounded swell*
But I figured what the hell, at least this one can spell

BOTH: *I guess the rest is history*
HOAGY: *'Cause I love her and she loves me*
ME: *And as you know this is our wedding day*
BOTH: *So if you're feeling bored and sad,*
   just take out a personal ad
This is all you'll ever have to say

ME: *Bright, pretty, slender, nice*
HOAGY: *Sounded good, so I read it twice*
ME: *I'd like to be your friend and maybe more*
Movies, music, theater too,
   I wanna be able to talk to you
S-W-F, Thirty-four

The crowd went wild, and I made a mental note to include the song on my new CD. The bride threw her bouquet; it landed in Allie's arms. She hauled off and threw it back, and they both kicked off their shoes and played catch till the thing fell apart. When the inevitable jam began, every musician participated. Even the Reverend Walter Little joined in—once assured that no one would be naked, he agreed to play his harmonica, and he wasn't half bad.

Actually, for so many people onstage in a free-for-all, we sounded pretty good. But no stage would have been big enough to hold both Hoagy and Artie that night. Tension had continued building between those two. They were looking for any excuse to be pissed off at each other, and before long they found one.

The bride's sister had announced that her favorite country song in the world was "Silver Wings" by Merle Haggard, and I promised to sing it before the night was over. At one point we'd done a couple of up-tempo tunes in a row, and it seemed like a good time to slow the pace a bit, so I called out "'Silver Wings,' Charlie," meaning in the key of C, and counted off a medium tempo.

Now, "Silver Wings" is one of those songs everyone knows—or thinks they know. It's a deceptively simple, understated ballad about a lover leaving on an airplane, a song that has been played a million times by country musicians in every honky-tonk in America, right? On the original recording, Merle uses only three chords in the verse, C, D-minor, and G-seventh, and somehow with those three chords and the simplest of lyrics, he manages to evoke universal truth: every feeling of longing, every lost love in the history of the universe. But of course, if you were Merle Haggard, you could probably evoke the same emotions if you sang your grocery list or the phone book—the guy has a spectacular voice and an all-star band. Over the years, after playing the changes thousands of times, bar-band musicians began adding a B-flat chord to the last line, which makes it more interesting and musically hipper, I guess, if you're just trying to make it through a four-set night and you don't happen to be Merle Haggard. Whatever the reason, the standard bar version of the song has come to include the B-flat, unlike the original record, which does not.

Lloyd wasn't onstage at the moment, so both Artie and Hoagy started to play the classic introduction. Glaring at each other across the bandstand, both hit their volume knobs, beginning a game of musical chicken in which the first guy to back down by turning down would lose.

As they screeched into the last line of the verse, Hoagy, veteran of several thousand bar gigs, played the B-flat and Artie, Mr. Folkie Purist, who learned songs off scratched LPs, did not.

Hoagy walked across the stage, stumbling a little over some patch cords that weren't properly taped down, and said as clearly as he could over the noise of the guitars, "Flat-seven," indicating that Artie should play the seventh chord from the root, in this case the B-flat chord.

Artie understood exactly what Hoagy was trying to say, but he had no intention of playing a bastardized version, as he saw it, so he deliberately looked in the other direction and continued to play. But Hoagy was just as determined, and he stood there glaring until Artie was forced to look at him.

"It's two-minor, flat-*seven*, five, one," Hoagy said, rattling off bar musicians' code for the chord progression, when he was sure Artie was paying attention.

"There's no flat-seven in the song," Artie said quietly.

"That's how it goes," Hoagy insisted.

"Not on the record, it isn't."

It was getting embarrassing, because musicians aren't supposed to stand around arguing about how the song goes, on the well-known principle that the show must go on. As they drifted into the bridge, the two men glowered at each other, both playing Merle's beautiful tune at ear-splitting volume. Greg caught my eye and gestured toward the microphone, which meant he thought I should just keep singing and not let either of them take a solo. But here's the other thing about "Silver

Wings"—there aren't a whole lot of verses. In fact, there's only one, which I found myself singing over and over again, in between the one and only bridge. And every time I got to the middle of the second line, the part where the silver wings slowly fade out of sight, Hoagy would play the B-flat, Artie wouldn't, and they'd both snarl at each other and turn up. It was a nightmare.

Just when I thought I'd have to spend the rest of my life standing on the bandstand at Lloyd's wedding singing "Silver Wings" over and over again, Hoagy got right up in Artie's face.

"Who the fuck died and made you King of Musical Purity, anyway?" Hoagy looked proud of his witticism.

"You're telling me? I've been playing this song for years. It's totally fucked to make up your own version," Artie hissed.

"You think you've played more Merle than me, asshole? I've played this song night after night for—" Hoagy stopped for a minute to do the math in his head, how many nights he played a year, how many years . . ."

"Then you've been playing it wrong."

"Who the fuck do you think you are? I can play circles around you."

"Too bad the circles go in the wrong direction." Now it was Artie's turn to look pleased with his own wit.

"Wanna take it outside, asshole?"

"Shit, yeah, dickhead," was the thoughtful reply, at which both men took a minute to carefully set down their guitars, then stormed out the door into the parking lot.

"Uh, harmonica solo?" I asked the microphone, and Reverend Walter Little stepped up to the plate. No one heard him, though, because the entire wedding party had moved out to the parking lot to watch Hoagy and Artie go at it.

I told the empty room we were going to take a break, and followed the group outside.

The two men circled each other in the parking lot, easily dodging each other's attempts at throwing punches, until Pete pushed his way through the crowd to break it up.

"Hey, asshole," he reasoned, "is his black eye worth sacrificing your picking fingers? Same goes for you, dickhead."

I wasn't surprised to notice that both Artie and Hoagy looked a little relieved. It seemed the fear of hurting their own fingers far outweighed their intent on doing actual damage to each other.

LATER, AFTER THE PARTY HAD ENDED, STILL FUMING AND mumbling under her breath about "testosterone-poisoned childish moron assholes," Allie told them both to get out of her sight until they could learn to be nice, then plopped on my bed, joining Greg, Perle, and me to watch *Entertainment Tonight*'s exclusive footage of Cindi-Lu and Cal's wedding. The bride wore a hammered satin strapless gown, under a bolero with white mink-trimmed Peter Pan collar and cuffs. Mary Hart made a big deal over the fact that the sixteen-thousand-dollar frock had been designed by none other than Calvin Klein, who everyone knew was the secret love child of a beloved country music legend. Cindi-Lu looked beautiful but heavily sedated, and Cal looked like a guy who'd been up all night drinking. We spotted Jimmy Clearwater in his purple velvet scarf, as well as Amy and Kathleen, in the B-roll.

MONICA CALLED TO REPORT THAT CAL'S BACHELOR PARTY at the Boom Boom Room had been a total fiasco. It started out fine, with all her girls ready to perform their most elaborate theatrical routines. The bar was stocked with the best food and drink, the dancers were paid double-scale to stay all night. Tiffany did her ever-popular "Teacher Lets Her Hair Down" number. Peaches followed with "Whipped Cream Dominatrix." Louisa and Justine did their artistic and suggestively lesbian "Swan Lake Pas de Deux." Monica herself came out of semiretirement to star in the grand finale, a burlesque interpretation of the bride's country music career, called "Magnolia's Tits." The men loved it, and everyone was having a fine old time until Cal drank too much peppermint schnapps and decided he needed a blow job, administered onstage in front of everyone, by Monica herself.

"And you know, kid, that's not something we offer at the Boom Boom Room," Monica reminded Greg. "Never have, never will."

But Cal wouldn't take no for an answer, and started throwing chairs, bottles, and anything else that wasn't nailed to the floor. When that didn't work, he pulled down his pants and started waving his disinterested member at everyone. The evening ended with the place wrecked, three of the girls weeping in the bathroom, and Peaches getting hauled off to jail for participating a little too enthusiastically in the brawl and giving Moe Bandy a black eye when she accidentally socked him in the face with one of her silicone-implanted breasts.

"Needless to say," Monica concluded, "no tip. Give me conventioneers or smelly cattle ranchers any day. At least they understand limits."

But that wasn't all. The cops found a joint in Peaches's G-string and she was detained until bail could be posted on Monday. All the girls trouped down to the jailhouse where, in a gesture of sisterly solidarity, they stood under their colleague's window holding a beautiful hand-lettered sign reading FREE PEACHES. They received citations for the disturbance caused when a crowd gathered, assuming they were giving away fruit.

"Sounds like you all just redefined the term 'Peaches and Herb,'" Greg said.

"Some days are just like a big, scratchy label in your thong!" Monica sniffed.

"HAVE YOU BEEN PRACTICING YOUR SCALES?" HOAGY asked me. I was fighting the physical discomfort of my last trimester with an aggressive self-improvement campaign that included weekly guitar lessons.

"I try, but they are so boring. Why do I have to do scales? I just want to learn a couple of shortcuts, a tricky solo that looks harder than it is."

"But if you put in the effort now, you'll have the basics down so you can do much more stuff later," Hoagy explained. "I have an idea. What's your favorite rock-and-roll guitar riff in the whole world?"

"That's easy. Steve Cropper's intro to 'Soul Man' by Sam and Dave," I answered.

"Good girl. Now, just take that part and make it the exercise. Here, look." He took the guitar out of my hands and started to play the lead line. "See? Now you try."

I copied the placement of his fingers on the fret board and repeated the part he had played, slowly and out of tempo, but getting the notes right all the way through.

"Great. Just use that, up and down the neck, on every string. You'll be practicing intervals and getting the feel of the neck and you won't even know it. You'll think you're just playing your favorite song."

It was a good trick, and between childbirth classes at the Bhalahdi compound I was practicing the guitar riff from "Soul Man" whenever I wasn't in bed with Greg. He had moved into my room so we could have sex as often as possible. It seemed peculiar that even though I had gained fifty pounds and looked like a baby hippo, I felt sexier than ever before in my life, but it was true.

I'D ALWAYS HAD KIND OF A LOVE-HATE RELATIONSHIP with my body. A size twelve when I thought I should be an eight, like many American girls my age I thought having a voluptuous figure meant I was too fat. To make matters worse, most of the guys I met were scrawny musicians who often weighed less than I did. On the rare occasions when I actually ended up in bed with one of them, I was aware of constantly sucking stuff in, trying to appear somehow smaller. Not that they ever cared; men had always been interested in my body. It was my hang-up, but knowing it didn't help me get over it.

Pregnant, I had my own permission to be huge, beautiful, and horny. I spent the last month of my pregnancy naked in my room, having amazingly inventive sex with Greg.

"Look, your belly button's popped out. I wonder if that means the baby's done," he mused as he kissed my belly.

"I'm not sure it works like that, but wouldn't it be funny? Like a little kitchen timer. Hey, look, you can see something moving around in there. Hi, Bosco."

"What are you going to say about the father?"

"The truth, of course, eventually. But it'll be hard to explain. I hope that with all the grandmas and uncles and you around, it won't feel like anything's really missing. For a while I hope to get away with the line that there are all kinds of families, and we're just another kind."

I reached over to pull on my T-shirt.

"No, don't. I want to look at you some more. I can't get enough of that beautiful belly."

"How'd I get so lucky?" I asked, snuggling into Greg. "Really, you could have any gorgeous babe who walks into the club, any night of the week."

"It just so happens that I love you. Besides, I spent my entire youth in a room filled with gorgeous sexy naked babes. That's nice, but they all start reminding me of my mother after a while. I've always gone for a more exotic kind of beauty, I guess. There's something about you and your belly that drives me crazy."

I knew that Greg and I would love each other forever. But somehow I also sensed that a baby would bring an end to this little erotic vacation. My hormones and figure would go back to normal, and so would his ability to control his lust. We were in a little pocket of sex-heaven that would end soon, and I wanted to enjoy every second that was left.

"I'm so glad about that," I whispered, and we made love one more time.

Then my water broke.

I MUST HAVE MISSED THE PART IN MY CHILDBIRTH CLASSES where they tell you it's going to hurt. It *really* hurts, like nothing else hurts. I hung in there for a long time, breathing and screaming, sucking on ice cubes and having my back rubbed and my feet washed by supportive and loving Bhalahdis in the birthing tent. I focused on crystals and breathed flowered incense and listened to *Abbey Road* and yelled at Greg and Allie and Perle. But it hurt so much that after a few hours I decided I'd had enough, and would it be too late, please, to change my mind about this whole dumb idea? Really, it was a big mistake and I was late for an appointment and if they would all get out of the fucking way, honestly, I had to leave right then—and another searing contraction had me writhing on my back, on the purple satin pillows, screaming and crying and breathing and finally screaming and pushing.

I NAMED HIM OTIS RAY, AFTER MY THREE FAVORITE SINGERS. It was love at first sight.

He was a week old, sleeping in my arms on the first quiet night since I brought him home. Greg was looking through our pile of CDs, hoping to find something that would set just the right mood.

"Aha! How long has it been since you've heard this one?" He slipped *Sam and Dave's Greatest Hits* into the CD player.

As the opening guitar lick filled the room, the baby's eyes popped open, looking around excitedly for the familiar sound.

"He recognized it from the womb," I said. "That's amazing!"

"Looks like we got a little soul man here after all, huh?" Greg smiled, folding us both into his big, strong arms.

SO I LURCHED INTO MOTHERHOOD WITH NO QUALIFI-cations whatsoever, mystified by the staggering number of products that began appearing in my life. The baby's care and feeding gave Allie and Aunt Perle a whole new arena in which to argue: cloth diapers (Perle) vs. the convenience of disposables (Allie);

handy little presoaked wipes (Allie) vs. a slice cut off the aloe plant on the kitchen windowsill and rubbed on the sore little bottom (Perle); garlic oil dripped into the ear (Perle) vs. infant Tylenol (Allie). There were baby seats, snugglies, strollers, blankets, rattles, and teddy bears. There were cute little plastic dishes, changing tables, bathing contraptions, and a secret baby swing that we hid from Perle, who didn't believe in such things, keeping it in Allie's bedroom closet in case of emergency. It wasn't unusual for a Dewdrop Inn customer, entering our roadhouse for a night of morally questionable fun, to get his table wiped with a *Winnie the Pooh* receiving blanket, or to discover that she'd just sat down on a pacifier. Otis Ray, all eight and a half pounds of him, just rolled on in and took over our lives.

He loved it best when I sang to him, so I began making up little rhymes and songs to get him through the difficult transitions of baby life. Burping songs, sleeping songs, smiling songs, and pooping songs—they were spontaneous and ridiculous and unrecorded, and I loved them the best of all the songs I'd ever written. But no matter what, "Soul Man" remained our special song.

And when I wasn't singing (or even when I was), I was nursing. Wow, could that baby eat!

"Hey, Allie, I have something to show you," I said impulsively one afternoon as Otis Ray was going down for his nap.

"Hmmm?" she asked sleepily.

I opened the drawer of my bedside table and handed her the little stack of letters I'd found going through my box of stuff when I first got home. Now that she'd reconnected with Artie, I thought she might enjoy having them. It had just been a question of finding the right time, and I thought the mellowness of the afternoon offered the proper mood; maybe she wouldn't mind so much that I'd read her private papers.

"Oh!" she gasped, looking at the first letter. "I remember writing this on the way home, to my friend Carla. She must have sent it back to me later on—all about the 1959 Newport Folk Festival, where I met Artie. My God, was it really thirty-five years ago?"

"Tell me more about it," I pleaded.

"It was an amazing time, really. I was almost seventeen, and I talked my parents into letting me go by myself. Perle was off at Bennington by then, writing bad poetry and inventing the civil rights movement, if you ask *her*. My mom thought folk music was a wholesome hobby, so I took a Greyhound bus from New York, dumped my stuff at some nice lady's rooming house, and went out looking for adventure. It couldn't have been more than five minutes later that a battered VW bug pulled up beside me, and a guy leaned out and asked if I wanted a ride. You have to realize I was kind of a late bloomer and had hardly ever dated before. I mean, a little bit, and there was this one guy I liked on the wrestling team, but he never paid much attention to me unless no one was looking—I guess I was considered a little weird in high school. But this guy at Newport—he was older, about twenty, and really cool, with shaggy hair and faded jeans and the cutest crooked bad-boy smile you ever saw. There was a guitar case in the backseat, so I figured he was okay. Of course, that was Artie. Thinking back, he was a kid, too, but he was so worldly— had been everywhere and done everything and met everyone— compared to me. So the short version is, we ended up spending the weekend together.

"I woke up the first morning in Artie's sleeping bag, in a parking lot overgrown with weeds, feeling like a woman of the world. I didn't have to care about Charlie the Wrestler anymore, or any of the other clumsy, beer-soaked high-school boys. I was a woman who could wake up next to a man and toss her hair and accept a bouquet of parking-lot weeds like the Queen of Sheba. See, here's the picture—he asked someone to take it that morning, with my camera. He really did pick me a bouquet of weeds, and to this day, they are the most romantic, the most beautiful 'flowers' I have ever seen, and that sleeping bag in the parking lot might as well have been the honeymoon suite at the Ritz."

"It sounds pretty romantic, all right. What happened after that?"

"It wasn't just the romance of meeting Artie, though of course that was amazing. It was the whole thing: the incredible music, being on my own for the first time, seeing that there was a bigger world out there. The second night, we went to the festival, and saw what I think was the first big performance by Joan Baez, coming out onstage to sing with Bob Gibson. She made me shiver, her voice was so good, and I remember feeling excited and inspired and jealous all at the same time. But back in Artie's sleeping bag, I woke up in the middle of the night with the very clear thought that if I didn't leave right that minute I would never finish high school. And I left right then, and later sent him that letter with no return address. I was so self-absorbed and melodramatic, it never occurred to me that he might have feelings, too. Plus, realistically, there was no way I could have explained him."

"But you kept running into each other," I prompted.

"Yes, we did," she answered. "You know a lot of that story already. Fate kept putting him in my path, and I kept getting close, then running away. I got very good at doing that, even though I adored him. I was just so scared of getting hurt. Now it's confusing—getting to know Artie the man is wonderful, but it's wiping out the corner of my heart I'd always saved for Artie the bad boy. Part of me has always loved him, but this is all happening too fast."

The absurdity of that statement, considering it had taken thirty-five years for him to achieve boyfriend status, was lost in the intensity of her feelings. But one thing was seeming more possible—that Artie Blond could be my father.

This was not an entirely unwelcome thought at that point in time, as my beloved dad, Johnny Pixlie, was acting like a full-tilt idiot. He wanted Allie to sell the Dewdrop Inn so that he could liquidate his half. Naturally, Allie desperately wanted to keep the place and was trying to raise the money to buy him out, but she obstinately refused offers of help from Artie because that would be "too complicated." Perle, after infinitely weighing all the pros and cons of accepting her inheritance from Samantha Eustace, had decided to go with it—being able to help Allie buy the club was a huge incentive. But a distant Eustace relative had surfaced to contest the will, and it would be a while before there was any money in the bank. We all hoped that Dad would come to his senses and find another way to work out his finances.

I stayed pretty close to home, except for a quick trip to Nashville that fall to present the Newcomer of the Year Patsy. I was the first presenter ever to walk out onstage with a baby on her hip. Ever-voracious little Otis Ray didn't really understand about live TV and started lunging for my boobs right in the middle of my speech, to the great delight of the audience, and the consternation of the Patsy committee.

The winner, Lindsay Hardaway, gushed prettily and thanked the Lord and her mama, "in that order." Her song, "Baby, She Can't Have You," had pleasant country-pop lyrics:

She's got her house and her car and her kids
And she's got a love that's true
She's got it all, baby, but she can't have you

Back to family values once again, and you could almost hear all of Nashville breathing a sigh of relief.

Cindi-Lu Bender had to relinquish her legend crown that year, to Reba McEntire. On tour in Europe, she offered her congratulations via satellite hookup. Calvin Klein, on hand as a presenter for Best Costume Design in a Music Video, was gracious when I asked him for an autograph to bring home to Richie.

I noticed that Mildred Martin was no longer working in the Ryman Auditorium gift shop. A sign in the window announced that she would be there in a few weeks, though, signing copies of her new book, *Patsy and Me*. The young girl who had replaced her behind the counter announced breathlessly that the movie rights had already been optioned.

So I left Nashville again, this time for hungry midnight howling, exhaustion, insecurity, sore nipples—did I say exhaustion?—worry, and joy. His little hand clasped around mine, his greedy gulps while nursing, soul brother screams, auburn ringlets, and the best smile in the universe were what I lived for. The guys in the band had called him Oats from the day I brought him home, and Oats he stayed. And I cheerfully put my career on hold for a while, to let Oats run my life.

Part Three
1995–1996

Chapter
19

A WEEK AFTER OATS'S FIRST BIRTHDAY, RAINBOW gave birth to Sunshine, my new sister and my baby's aunt. Rainbow had been calling frequently, to fill me in on her love life with my dad, and I'd begun to like her a little, in spite of myself. "Johnsey" was a handful, but she was standing by her man, certain that he'd come around in time. She sent proud photos, and I packed up some of our nicer baby hand-me-downs to send back. Most notable was Allie's reaction—she barely noticed. Without her husband's opinions to worry about, and with the incentive to make enough money to buy him out, she had come into her own as a creative venue owner. The Dewdrop Inn offered nonstop daily community-centered activities in addition to music every night, and she was too busy to care much about Johnny Pixlie's new baby.

Early each morning our day began with "Zydecoerobics" class. This basically consisted of a bunch of women dancing around to a *Bayou Hot Sauce* compilation CD while waving five-pound weights. It was extremely popular. She also started "Gab Group" for teenagers, where high-school girls gathered once a week, fragrant and eager, to discuss their reproductive systems and relationship problems with a trained sex educator. The added bonus was that all the girls fell in love with Oats and offered to baby-sit. Allie hired one of the girls to host poetry slams, and welcomed any nonprofit group that needed a place to meet; there was even an AA meeting on Sunday mornings. Allie's rationale was that it would be easier for members to remain sober if they learned how to walk into bars without drinking, so why not have the meetings in a bar? She even hosted some meetings for the SNAGs, who decided they forgave my insensitivity because of my past as a battered wife.

Artie's music career had picked up as a result of the publicity surrounding Harlan Harris's folk music documentary, and he started performing his cow song again at folk festivals and political benefits. When he wasn't traveling, he found a lot of creative reasons to hang out with Allie and to help out at the Dewdrop. Allie remained confused but enchanted by her old sweetheart, and though there was still tension between Hoagy and Artie, they put a lid on it for her sake.

Things with Greg and me were even more complex. Thanks to Zydecoerobics and Perle's attack-mode nutrition, I was in better shape than I'd ever been in my life. And as my body became more babe-like, Greg became less interested.

"I'm so sorry, honey," he'd say, when my trim new figure failed to arouse him.

The only way I could turn him on was by wearing a T-shirt stuffed with a pillow that made me look pregnant. I did it every once in a while to please him, but honestly, it felt pretty stupid. He even took Aunt Perle's cure, saying he needed it for a friend (which in a way was true): ingesting ground-up animal testicles. When that didn't work, he started making up excuses to hang around the Bhalahdis' birthing classes, where he flirted outrageously with the moms-to-be. Harvey called Perle to complain, and then Greg and I had another talk in which we agreed to just be friends. It was a talk we'd had a hundred times by then, well scripted and predictable, and at the end he moved back into his old room, right next to mine. Whatever sadness—more like numbness—I felt was countered by the fact that now I had more space for baby stuff.

MIRACULOUSLY, I STARTED RECEIVING MONEY FROM MY radio airplay and CD sales. The Unicorn folks, delighted with our sales figures, were impatient for a second CD. They paid for some of the equipment, and we upgraded Lee's home setup to a twenty-four-track state-of-the-art ADAT studio. I was also emerging from my sweet baby cocoon and began writing and recording again.

Oats sang all the time. He listened to just about anything that wasn't especially produced for babies—that stuff drove him crazy. I spent all day with him and worked on the CD after he went to sleep. I wasn't getting much sleep myself.

One early summer evening, Hoagy found me dozing in front of the TV, while Oats sat squirming in my lap, bored with the video we'd been watching together.

"Hey, young lady, how long has it been since you've been out of the house?"

"I don't know, the baby—"

"The baby's happy and healthy," Hoagy reminded me. "You look pale and tired. You need to get out, and I've got just the ticket."

Hoagy had scored great seats and backstage passes for a concert at the Konocti Harbor Amphitheater, where Patty Loveless was performing with Lorrie Morgan and Carlene Carter. Allie offered to baby-sit and Artie was available to sub on guitar, so off we went.

We got there early enough to flash our VIP passes and attend a pre-show reception sponsored by a vodka manufacturer. I remembered that during my year as a touring musician, the backstage reception was what passed for my only social life outside the band. The buffet table with its ever-present cold cuts and cheese cubes; the weak drinks in plastic glasses; the paunchy, gray-haired, ponytailed record company executives—all men— smelling better than we did; the air-kissing and ass-pinching and cell-phone ranting; and satin tour jackets and bolo ties made me sick with nostalgia. Hoagy steered me to the bar and placed a Bloody Mary in my hand. I gulped it down in two sips, and he got me another one. Then he spotted Carlene's bass player, the pal who'd given him the tickets, and went off to say hello. I found a quiet corner and watched the backstage antics for a while before deciding how much I wanted to participate.

"Hey," said a smooth male voice in my ear, "you owe me a pair of boots." I turned around.

"Bobby Lee Crenshaw! What are you doing here?"

"I'm in Patty's touring band now. She's a lot nicer to work with than you-know-who."

"This is such a surprise," I stammered. "I don't know what to say."

"I've been looking all over for you," he whispered.

SEX FIRST AND TALKING LATER—IT SOMETIMES JUST HAPPENS that way. There were many unanswered questions, but it wasn't until we were in bed together in his hotel room after the show that either one of us asked. In the soft light of the muted TV, sweaty and tangled in the sheets, our hastily discarded clothes in piles on the floor, we caught up.

I told him all about the day I got fired, and about the Dewdrop Inn and my continuing adventures as a country-western star. But I didn't know what to say about the baby. It would be impossible and wrong, now that we'd found each other again, not to tell him about his beautiful son. But I couldn't figure out how to bring up the subject. I needed to know what had happened to him, and why there was a strange woman in a hotel room in Japan calling herself his wife, and why he hadn't tried to find me.

He had tried to find me.

After I got fired from Cindi-Lu's band that day in Nashville, Bobby Lee asked management for my contact information. They told him it was against company policy and refused, until he made such a huge scene, threatening to quit the tour, call the press, and bash Cal's head in, that they finally relented and gave him two phone numbers. One was to Aunt Perle's loft in New York. Perle, however, was at the Dewdrop, and the building contractor renovating her loft answered the phone and said no one by that name lived there. The other was a 707 area code in Lake County, where he kept getting an annoyed-sounding guy who finally asked him to stop calling. He left Cindi-Lu's tour to take the gig with Randy Newman, and when his ex-girlfriend called and said she missed him, he decided to give it one more try with her.

Then came the Patsy show, where I'd thrown up on his boots. He'd hoped to talk to me afterward, but there was a midnight flight and the girlfriend was meeting him in Tokyo; when she arrived and told him she was pregnant, they got married. He wanted to do the right thing.

"I have a one-year-old daughter. She's beautiful and sweet. Here, I have some pictures. Would you like to see?" And he reached down in the general direction of his pants, on the floor.

"No! No offense, honey, but there's nothing I'd like to see less right now," I pleaded. "I want to think that if I'd known you were still married, I wouldn't have jumped into bed with you tonight, but I'm not sure that's true. Please, let's keep this separate, kind of our own little alternate universe, okay?"

"God, Sarah Jean, I've thought about you so many times. And Sha—"

"I mean it, Bobby Lee. I don't want to see her photo and I don't want to know her name. I really, really don't."

"Right. Well, when my ex-girlfriend told me she was pregnant and you weren't anywhere to be found, I decided to face up to my responsibilities."

"Does facing up to your responsibilities include screwing around on the road?"

"I don't do that."

"You're doing it right now, buddy, with me."

"I see your point. It's supposed to be 'Don't ask, don't tell' when I'm on the road. And we've had our share of troubles lately, gone so far as to talk about separating. But I doubt she'd like knowing I'm in bed with someone I've been crazy about for years. I feel just the opposite, like why bother if I'm not even going to remember the person's name the next day? I'd rather be getting a good night's sleep, or practicing guitar." I thought I saw tears in the corners of his eyes.

"Why didn't you ask the girls where to find me, Amy and Kath? They had my number. Why didn't you call my record company?"

"I tried your record company. Every time I called there was a different person working there. I sent a letter and got a form letter back, thanking me for my support and offering a membership to your fan club. I even signed up, hoping they might think to send you a list of the members."

"Are you kidding? They never even told me I had a fan club."

"I asked Amy and Kathleen, too. And they confirmed that you were in Lake County, not New York. It never occurred to me to compare phone numbers with them. But I also thought I overheard them talking about how you'd met someone, a drummer? So when some weirdo kept answering the phone and saying he was your boyfriend, I just figured it was true and I'd better back off."

"I don't get that—I didn't even have a boyfriend."

"It doesn't matter now that I've found you again." Bobby Lee hugged me hard. "It scares me how happy I am to see you," he whispered. "I don't want to leave or let you go. I wish we could just stop this night, let the earth stand still for about three or four years, and stay in bed making up for lost time. How would you feel about having a very long affair with a married man?"

"Probably not very good, actually," I answered. "But we have tonight. And it's a relief to know what really happened. I thought you didn't care, and I'm so glad to know you did. And I'm happy to know you have a daughter you love. I guess it makes you seem more complete."

"I feel that way sometimes, too. But can I tell you a secret? The whole time she was pregnant—this is probably going to sound weird to you—I kept thinking she was going to have a boy. I imagined this little red-haired boy who sang all the time, and I was sure I was thinking about my son. I love my daughter so much, but sometimes I still think about the other one, the little fantasy boy. Shit, I've never told anyone about this before. I don't know why I'm telling you now. Is that ridiculous or what?"

"Not as ridiculous as you think," I answered softly. "You see, I tried to find you, too. But when I called and the woman who answered the phone said she was your wife, I just assumed that you'd been married all along and had lied to me. So that's why I didn't try harder to find you, to tell you—" I couldn't say it. I started to cry.

"To tell me what? I just told you my most embarrassing secret."

"I'm not sure how to tell you mine."

"No fair. Really, you can tell me anything." And Bobby Lee got it out of me at last, with that promise and a kiss. I closed my eyes, took a deep breath, and told him about his son.

"He's just the way you described," I said. "Your son—our son. His name is Otis Ray Pixlie. He has auburn ringlets and he sings all the time and his first birthday was May 7. He loves Sam and Dave and Wilson Pickett. He likes noodles with butter," I told him, sobbing into his shoulder.

Bobby Lee was way too quiet for way too long.

"So, what should we do about this?" I asked finally, carefully.

"I need to see him," he said.

We talked for a long time about whether there was any way in the world this all might work out without hurting people, and couldn't think of a thing. I told him about my family, about my on-and-off and ever-changing relationship with Greg, about Aunt Perle, Allie, Artie and Hoagy—

"Oh my God! Hoagy!" I said. "He brought me tonight. I forgot all about him."

In a panic, I collected my clothes from various parts of the room and dressed quickly. I gave Bobby Lee my phone number and a good-bye kiss, a promise to talk—really talk—soon, and left him standing there, crying in the middle of the room.

Hoagy sat calm and alone at the Konocti Harbor bar, sipping a Scotch while the bartender made "Mmmm-hmmm, time to close" noises. He looked up and smiled.

"Hey, girl, you ready? Let's go home."

In the car on the way back, I told Hoagy everything. He was sympathetic and listened quietly until I finished, only once interrupting to remark that Bobby Lee must have had one hell of a fertile month there.

"Here's what I want to know," he said when I finished my story. "Obviously that asshole Cal Hooper gave some guy's number to Bobby Lee on purpose, to keep him from finding you. But who was it? Greg gets a lot of calls. Do you think it was him? And if so, what connects him to Cal that we don't know about?"

It was a really good question.

BOBBY LEE AND I SAT AT AN OUTDOOR TABLE AT TNT, a lakeside Mexican restaurant, talking and crying and crying and talking while Oats cheerfully slammed his fist into a basket of tortilla chips. We were trying to figure out a way to make everything all right.

"Do you need anything? Do you need money?" Bobby Lee asked. "I hate to think of you needing anything for him."

"No, sweetie, we're fine. I have a nice life here, and so does Oats. There's some money from my songs, and the club is doing better these days. We have more baby-sitters than we can use. I have a feeling your home team needs your money more than we do. I mean, if things were different . . . but they're not," I ended lamely, provoking new tears.

For now, we agreed, we would keep the fact that he was the baby's father a secret. He was welcome to visit as often as he wanted to, as long as he maintained the identity of "family friend"—just one more crazy musician uncle—until he decided what to do about his troubled marriage and we figured out how we were all going to fit into one another's lives.

Before we left he held Oats close, smelling his hair, memorizing the feel of him in his arms. I gave Bobby Lee some photos to take with him, and we made plans to talk soon, to try to figure out what our next step should be. He gave Oats a present, a pair of soft leather hand-tooled Western boots. They were a little too big, so Oats wore them on his hands after he climbed back into his car seat. Then he sang all the way home, along with a Wilson Pickett tape he loved, "Muftane Saw-wy."

THOUGH OATS WAS WELL PAST ONE AND EATING EVERYTHING that wasn't nailed down, he took full advantage of Aunt Perle's "nursing on demand" philosophy—I was still nursing him in the evenings, and though I had some secret fears that this practice might raise some eyebrows if it was still going on when he hit high school, I loved our bedtime ritual, including Allie softly strumming her guitar as he fell asleep in my arms. It was also my only guaranteed chance to connect with Allie during the day, and sometimes a girl just needs to talk to her mama. This was definitely the case the evening after my meeting with Bobby Lee Crenshaw.

Oats had drifted off to sleep, and I set him down gently on the bed next to me.

"Oats met his real daddy today," I told her.

"Do tell," she answered warily, staring down at her own fingers on the guitar's neck.

So I did.

"When do you think I should tell him?" I asked her.

"That's a tough one," she answered. "I guess not yet. I guess you'll know when the time is right. A lot depends on Bobby Lee, of course, and how much he plans to stick around. Otis Ray has the right to know, when he's ready." She looked uncomfortable as she patted the baby's hair. I decided to bite the bullet and ask her the question that had been on my mind for over a year.

"When were you planning on telling me, Allie?"

"What do you mean?"

"That Artie Blond is my father?"

"What are you talking about?" she asked, startled.

"The timing works out just right for it to be true. Dad got really upset when I mentioned that you were seeing him again. And I have Artie Blond's eyebrows."

"Oh, honey," she moaned.

"This isn't inspiring a lot of confidence, Allie. You're supposed to say, 'No way, it's not even a remote possibility.'"

"What if Artie was your biological father? What difference would that make?"

"I don't know. It's just something that I have a right to know, that's all."

She got the dreamy look in her eye that always meant trouble, or at least a long story.

"Do you remember when you were five and we went to visit Grandma on Long Island?" she asked.

"A little—just bits and pieces."

"One night the whole family went out to a fancy dinner at a seafood restaurant. It was Grandpa's favorite place to celebrate any special occasion. You were an early reader, you know, and by the time you were five, you could read anything, but you didn't always interpret correctly. Anyway, there was a big red neon sign above the front door of the restaurant. Do you remember what it said?"

Suddenly I remembered clearly. Driving up to the restaurant, feeling starched petticoats scratching against my legs, stuffed in the backseat of the Ford sedan between a perfumed great-aunt and a fur-coated grandma, hardly able to breathe, I saw the sign:

STEAK AND LOBSTER, DANCING NITELY.

There was going to be a show! I couldn't wait to see that steak and lobster dance.

We had cocktails, and I barely tasted my Shirley Temple. Then appetizers and dinner were served. All I could think about was the treat to come. The lobster, dressed as a flamenco dancer, would come out clicking her castanet claws. I couldn't imagine how they were going to pull this off, but I couldn't wait to see. I sat through dessert, coffee, and lingering good-byes, thinking, Any minute!

And when it seemed like exactly the right time for the fabulous show to begin—we left. Just walked right out of there, got into the car, and drove back to Grandma's house.

"You cried and cried," Allie remembered. "We couldn't figure out what you were upset about and you didn't seem able to explain. I was trying to make a good impression on the East Coast relatives, and you weren't helping, and I just got annoyed. But Johnny took you in his arms and rocked and sang to you until he calmed you down enough to tell him what was wrong. The next day he went out and bought some felt and glue and glitter and string, and made a couple of puppets. Then, whenever he was home at bedtime, he performed the *Steak and Lobster Dancing Nitely Puppet Ballet* for you—remember? That was one of the reasons we moved up here and eventually bought the Dewdrop Inn. Johnny thought it would be fun for you to see people 'dancing nitely' if it couldn't be a steak and a lobster. The only way to work that out would be to play in our own club, and live over the store. It took a while, but we made it happen."

"So what you're trying to say is, no matter who my father is, Johnny was my dad?"

"Well, he was."

"But that doesn't answer my question."

"If I tell you a secret, do you promise not to breathe a word to anyone?" Allie asked.

"You mean Artie really *is* my father?" I was stunned.

"No, no, sweetheart."

"Then you're saying you're not sure?" I asked, on the verge of tears.

"Sarah Jean, shut up and listen for a minute, will you? The secret is *when* Artie and I made love for the first time—not fooling around or making out but actual intercourse, the kind that can make babies. Can you guess when that happened?"

"That's what I'm saying. You were sixteen and you met him in Newport—"

"No, honey, we did a lot that weekend—*everything but,* as they say. But the first time we had actual sexual intercourse was— it's a little embarrassing to admit this—a couple of weeks ago."

"What?"

"You better not tell anyone else—it'd be bad for my image, and Artie's, too. As a young woman of the sixties, I was supposed to be sexually liberated. But really I was a pretty good girl. Remember when I told you I left his sleeping bag in the middle of the night because I was afraid of what might happen if I stayed? I was afraid because I didn't have any birth control! And the other times, I won't say we didn't fool around *a lot,* even once or twice after I was married to Johnny. But something always made me stop before it got to that point."

"But what about the Summer of Love? What about all the guys in Nashville who say they adore you?"

"Why do you think I joined the Peace Corps, sweetie? I was terrified of all that stuff." She laughed. "And I was hugely pregnant with you—you were born during the Summer of Love. I wasn't in the mood to be fooling around, believe me."

"But what about now? You and Artie have been hanging out for a really long time. . . ."

"Birth control again," she answered. "I wanted to wait till I was sure I was through menopause."

"Sheesh, you've just single-handedly destroyed all my illusions about free love in the sixties," I whined.

"I'm sorry, Sarah Jean. But believe me, there's no doubt about who was your father."

Stretched out on my bed, we were quiet for a minute, looking at my snoring baby. She put down her guitar and stood up to go.

"Some days I miss Dad a lot, Allie."

"I know, sweetie," she sighed. "Some days I do, too."

Chapter
20

MY SECOND FULL-LENGTH CD, *CHEATS ON ONE*, was released that fall with enormous fanfare and excellent reviews. Once again, a Harlan Harris–directed video of the title song went into heavy rotation on TNN and CTV, closely followed by "SWF, 34," which I ended up singing as a duet with Clint Black. They even edited in some home-video clips from Lloyd's wedding. "Credit Card Christmas" was scheduled for a December release as a single, with another video in the works. There was strong radio play, and my female fans didn't let me down, keeping request lines lit up as always. Everything was great—except sales.

For some reason, according to the Unicorn brass, product just wasn't moving as expected. Steve, the latest in the revolving-door succession of marketing VPs, had a frank talk with me about my "soft SoundScans," explaining that since SoundScan results are used to compile sales reports and *Billboard* chart listings, and to assess the label's promotional commitments, this was not a good thing. He ignored my joke about soft SoundScans being worse than flabby thighs, begging me to go on tour to support the

CD. But I didn't feel ready to leave Otis Ray or willing to drag him on a grueling road trip. We compromised with the agreement that I'd play a few shows close to home and make myself available for radio phone interviews. Then a band canceled and the El Rancho Resort amphitheater needed an opening act for a huge sold-out country music show, part of their "Sunday Sunset" series, and Steve called with the exciting news that he'd just booked me to open for Cindi-Lu Bender.

"Sorry, I can't," I told him.

"What do you mean, you can't? Did you forget to tell us about a previous engagement? You said that date was clear," he said tensely.

"There's history there. She hates me."

"Oh, come on, she probably doesn't even remember you. We need this, Sarah Jean. A lot of people here are working hard for this CD. Don't be a diva."

"El Rancho is bad luck for me. Last time I played there I got picketed and there was a riot. They'll never want me back."

"Are you kidding?" Steve chuckled, knowing somehow that he had me. "After all the publicity they got? They're dying to have you back. They're only hoping they'll get picketed again."

Against my better judgment, I let him talk me into it.

AMY AND KATHLEEN HAD BEEN ON TOUR WITH CINDI-LU Bender for over three years. They were getting very tired of her by the time the Magnolia Heart bus rolled into town.

The amphitheater was filled to capacity. Every room to be had for miles around was booked, and adoring fans had been partying all weekend. I was holed up in Kath's room, visiting with my two pals before the show. Kathleen sat cross-legged on the floor, sewing spangles onto her stage outfit, while Amy made tea on her little portable hot plate. I lounged on the bed, trying to relax with an Ume Boshe plum stuck in my navel. Aunt Perle had insisted that this was the perfect solution for jittery nerves, even though the Bhalahdis used it as a seasickness cure. But, as Perle said with her usual convoluted logic, the Bhalahdis never went anywhere, so how would they know?

My friends had some great stories about life on the road.

"Remember what a pussy hound Victor-the-Roadie always was?" Kathleen asked. "Well, one night he went off with a little cutie as usual, only it turned out that was the night his wife went into labor. Her sister finally reached Buddy at, like, three in the morning, and he was trying to convince her that Victor was just out taking a walk while Jake tried frantically to find him."

"You'll love this one," Amy chimed in. "There was this time we were playing at Summerfest and our wardrobe trunk got mixed up with a band from California. But it wasn't just any old regular band—this was Those Darn Accordions. They ended up with a bunch of our gear and we ended up with three crinolines apiece, sparkle sunglasses, and big hair wigs."

"Whoa, what did you do?" I asked.

"We didn't know what to do. There wasn't any time to make the switch, so we just wore their stuff onstage."

"How did Cindi-Lu react?" I could just picture it.

"That was the weirdest part," Kathleen said. "She didn't react. I'm not sure she even noticed."

"You're so brave to do this show," Amy sighed.

"Hey," I told her, "brave has nothing to do with it. I was coerced by my label. I'll be fine as long as I don't run into the happy newlyweds."

"Well, that's not likely to happen unless you stick around after your set," Kathleen reminded me. "You know how they are—they'll show up at the very last minute acting all cute and kissy-face."

"Oh, barf me!" Amy said as she handed me my cup of tea. "Mr. and Mrs. Christian Values. Those two are all over the radio talking about monogamy. Meanwhile, he can't keep his stupid little thing in his pants. She's totally oblivious. It's a highly dysfunctional situation."

"Yeah, those two put the 'fun' back in dysfunctional, all right." Kathleen giggled.

"Gee, and I assumed they were just two crazy kids in love," I said, pretending to look sincere.

"You know," said Kathleen, "the sad thing is I think she really does believe in her marriage. She has no idea what's going on with Cal. And don't you think it's weird that she's out on tour supporting the same album for over three years now? No new material, no new product, she's just going out over and over again with the same show to the same venues, like a broken record. That's not how people usually do it, is it? We haven't learned any new songs in ages. It's the exact same show as when you left."

"I think she's too out of it to learn anything new. I'll bet you anything he's keeping her sedated," Amy added. "You know, it's all about money. They've been buying real estate all over Tennessee, and I heard they made a bid on one of the major distributors."

"Really?" I asked.

"They figure they can grab even more of the market, I guess.

It's not like they need it—she really is a legend, and she sells like crazy. But apparently they've had a minority share for a while, and they're trying to maneuver things around so they have control. Then there's her gift shop and all the other merchandising. Our little country girl is very big business these days."

"And the new redhead?"

"Aw, there've been about four of them since you left," Kathleen sighed. "Cal rolls in with the schnapps-and-blow-job welcome wagon and they don't stick around long. Besides, no one ever gets quite the right vocal blend. We three really were magic."

"Hey," I asked shyly, "what would you say about trying that vocal blend one more time? Come on out and sing a couple of songs with me."

They looked at each other uneasily.

"We can't," Amy said. "We already—presumptuously— thought of that, but it's been expressly forbidden."

"Well, double shit."

"I'm sorry," Kathleen said as she got up and slipped on her spangled top, turning to see herself in the hotel-room mirror. "But wait. We brought you a present—actually, eight presents. Big Lou, the glamorous accordion princess from the other band, was really nice and gave us these. We have one for each of your guys, too. Now you can all drink beer and sing at the same time." She handed me eight plastic beer mugs with battery-operated microphones built into the handles, the best Summerfest souvenir I'd ever seen. They were so amazing they almost made up for the fact that my friends couldn't join me onstage.

I tried to hide my disappointment and headed backstage. I'd never have asked them to jeopardize their livelihood, but still . . .

THE DEWDROP DRIFTERS RARELY GOT A CHANCE TO PLAY TO a sold-out amphitheater crowd, and backstage spirits were high. Once again, I felt as if my invitation to the party had been lost in the mail. I tuned up quietly, letting Richie pile makeup on my face and enjoying the guys' high spirits. We'd had a good sound check, with just enough glitches not to tweak Allie's superstitio-meter, and since we'd been running the set at the Dewdrop for a week, everyone was confident. Then the houselights dimmed and the stage manager appeared to lead us to our places with his little flashlight. This ritual always cheers me up, and I followed him onstage with a smile.

I was hit with a collage of sensual impressions on my way to the stage. The crisp smell of the lake at dusk combined with a nearby barbecue; the soft, wet sweetness of Otis Ray's lips as I kissed him, secure in Perle's arms, for good luck; the twinkling smiles of Amy and Kath in the wings; the surprised chuckle in my throat as I realized that an overly conscientious roadie had discovered my bag of microphone beer mugs in the dressing room and, thinking they were props, placed one next to each microphone and amplifier onstage. I heard soft fabric rustling and a tinkling bell, and noticed that the entire Bhalahdi community occupied the first two rows. Harvey, Desi, Molly, and the rest all wore long purple tunics and white Beatle boots; the tinkling sound came from Molly's elaborate Mary Quant earrings as she turned her head toward the stage. The Bhalahdis rarely ventured outside their commune as a group, especially to hear music, and the fact that they'd come out to hear my show was high praise indeed. I felt flattered and loved.

Hoagy counted off "Hell on Heels" and I sidled up to the microphone to sing the first line. The monitor mix was clear and the band was tight. I soon drifted into that otherworldly feel-good performance zone, and it took me a couple of minutes to notice the shouts of the crowd.

My first thought when a big guy started yelling was that it was unusual for a man to be so appreciative, seeing as how most of my fans were women. Then when the rest joined in, I decided they were starting another riot. I just kept singing because I didn't know what else to do.

"Turn her up!" sounded to me like "Bummer fuck!" from my vantage point onstage. It wasn't till the stage manager ran out to check my mic that I realized what had happened. The house PA was dead and no one could figure out why.

As roadies scrambled to make adjustments, we had a quick conference. The big main speakers were mysteriously dysfunctional, but the monitors worked fine, as did the back-line amps, which were connected to a different power source. I knelt down and shoved my monitor around to face the audience.

"All right, everybody, we have some technical difficulties, but we're going on with the show. You all ready for that?"

"Yeah!" they screamed.

"Now, we'll sing and play as loud as we can through our amps and monitors, but you won't be hearing anything through the big speakers. So come on down, get as close as you can, and—"

The whole place went dark.

"Okay, gang, I guess we're packing it in," yelled Hoagy.

"No, wait!" I remembered the souvenir microphone beer mug at everyone's place. "Watch me, and do what I do."

There was still a little light in the sky, and I picked up my beer mug and flipped the switch.

"All right, everyone, can you hear me?"

"Yeah!"

"Like I said, we're having some technical difficulties. They're trying to fix stuff, but it might be a while. What do you say? Should we pack it in or go on with the show?"

My voice sounded surprisingly clear and loud, amplified by the cheap microphone in the plastic cup handle.

"On with the show!" they screamed.

"Then come on down. Get as close to the stage as you can. I'll need some help here. Y'all are gonna sing along, right?"

"Yeah!" the crowd roared.

"Then let's boogie!"

Out of the corner of my eye I saw Harvey light a candle and lead the Bhalahdis in a silent prayer. Hoagy used his beer mug to mic his acoustic guitar. Lloyd produced a dobro, and Lee found the battery-operated pig-nose amp in his gear and plugged his bass in. Greg pulled out brushes, and Allie and I sang our hearts raw into the beer mugs. It shouldn't have worked but it did. A thousand people gathered close around and heard us sing, and they sang along. As the sun disappeared behind the foothills, I realized they could see us, too; every sound tech, roadie, and security guard in the place had turned on his little flashlight and aimed it at the stage. Together the tiny lights were powerful enough to keep us visible in the growing darkness.

We ended with "Heartaches for a Guy," of course. But the crowd wasn't going to let us go—they were standing on their seats, screaming for an encore. I signaled to Aunt Perle and she brought Otis Ray to me. Holding him tight on my hip with one arm, and my beer mug in the other, I dedicated the last song to him.

Greg pounded out the familiar drum intro to "Be My Baby," the old Ronettes hit. With my hands full of beer mug and baby and my eyes glued to Otis Ray's smile, I almost dropped him when we got to the chorus and I heard gorgeous angel-choir harmony. Kathleen and Amy had tiptoed onstage and stood with Allie, right beside me, singing backup.

"What are you doing?" I mouthed the words during the solo. "You'll get fired."

Their sparkling eyes told me they didn't give a flying fuck.

NO ONE EVER FIGURED OUT WHAT EXACTLY HAPPENED TO the power, but predictably enough, the lights and sound were fixed by the time Cindi-Lu took the stage. Her set was the usual, minus two backup singers.

The fact that we'd pulled the show off with plastic microphone beer mugs and roadie flashlights seemed nothing short of miraculous. The darn things just weren't powerful enough when we tried them again at the Dewdrop, and everyone had a different theory. Whether due to thermals (Lloyd's theory), endorphins (Perle's theory), or divine intervention (Harvey's theory), it was a moment we could never replicate. But there was no doubt that going through with the show that night earned me my stripes as a trouper, as far as Lake County was concerned. Whatever ambivalence or jealousy my neighbors had felt about my success evaporated for good. It was fun, and a little scary, to be the town hero.

KATHLEEN AND AMY CAMPED OUT AT THE DEWDROP FOR A few days before heading home, relieved to be off the endless tour, realizing they'd been looking for a reason to call it quits. The paychecks had been nice and they'd seen the world from inside an old, broken tour bus, but neither one of them would have trouble finding work in Nashville. In a way, all those years on the road with Cindi-Lu had earned them hero stripes, too.

We did a lot of trio singing and they gushed over Oats, assuming, as many people did, that Greg was his father. This was fine with Greg, but deep down it was becoming less okay with me since my reunion with Bobby Lee. I'd been ambivalent over the whole situation, anyway: resentful of Greg when he quietly allowed people to assume he was Oats's dad; appreciative of his help and friendship; nostalgic for the intensity of being lovers. Greg had adjusted to our current status as friends with no apparent regret or complexity, and I resented that a little, too. Then there was the nagging suspicion that he might have been in cahoots with Cal, conspiring to keep Bobby Lee from finding me. Was it possible that he had not just wandered into the Dewdrop because of an ad in the weekly but had been sent by Cal to spy on me? Perhaps—and this was wild, but I couldn't suppress the thought—even the Laundromat incident in which Pete had broken his arm had been no accident.

On good days, I valued Greg's help and friendship and importance to my son; on bad days, I was overcome with suspicions about his motives, fearful that he might have been placed in my home on purpose, to do me harm. But what could I do? There was no supporting evidence, and if I asked him directly and he denied my accusations, it would be embarrassing at best and possibly even dangerous if I was right. There was also the promise I'd made to Bobby Lee to keep our reunion secret, on account of his being married. So I kept a more careful distance between Greg and me than before, watching for signs of sabotage. I never found any. I kept quiet and enjoyed my friends' visit—and none of us ever even mentioned Bobby Lee Crenshaw, though I couldn't stop thinking about him.

AT LEAST I WASN'T THE ONLY ONE WITH A COMPLICATED love life. Artie Blond, who seemed to be running out of lame excuses for visiting, started making noises about moving in. Allie appeared to be madly in love with him, though not eager to relinquish her newfound independence. Pete and Jamee had been carrying on a long-distance love affair, mostly via e-mail, that didn't seem to be going much of anywhere. When she finally wrote to tell him she was seeing someone else, he found solace in the arms of Pat—a lusty, outdoorsy woman who ran the fishing-boat-rental concession at the El Rancho Resort. And Dad and Rainbow: She sent baby pictures and called now and then, and I continued to send Oats's cutest hand-me-downs for Sunshine. Dad spent lots of time on the road, twin fiddling with one country swing band or another, probably having the time of his life with the hefty checks we were sending each month; Allie had managed to work out a payment plan that would soon make her the sole owner of the Dewdrop Inn. I helped out with my royalty income when it was needed.

Lloyd settled down with his new bride and seven thousand pedal steel instrumental LPs and seemed happy, though it was a little hard to tell with Lloyd. We missed his quiet presence in the Dewdrop dorm but saw him every night at the gig. SWF 34 (now MWF 35?) fit right into our extended family—she was a good sport, always willing to jump onstage for a rousing "Beer Barrel Polka" on her accordion, or volunteer her stretch limo for an airport run. Her book, *I Drove 'Em to It: Stories from the Front Seat,* had sold moderately well, but her publisher was not unlike Unicorn Entertainment: revolving-door executives, inadequate information, and mystifying changes in the marketing plans.

I SKIPPED THE PATSY SHOW THAT FALL, TELLING MYSELF IT didn't matter that the Unicorn brass weren't urging me to go. Not long after the release of *Cheats On One*, I'd assumed they would find a way to send me. But with my disappointing initial sales, they were evasive about their plans for promoting the CD. Bobby Lee lived in Nashville, and there was also the fear I might run into him with his wife. He said they were just going through the motions, headed for divorce or at least separation, but he had to make pretenses for the sake of appearances. I assumed a "been there, done that" attitude about the Patsies, though having been hit with both nausea and lactation my previous two go-rounds, I was not in a hurry to find out what bodily function might next trip me up on national TV; it was best to stay away.

Besides, between baby care and obsessing about Bobby Lee, I didn't have a lot of extra time to worry about my fading career. Despite the miracle of the plastic beer mugs and the wonderful— even national—press my El Rancho performance had generated, despite the ever-increasing stacks of fan mail and radio requests, the CD just wasn't selling, and no one could explain that.

Chapter

21

I T TURNED OUT THAT AN AFFAIR WITH A MARRIED MAN was way more okay with me than I ever could have imagined. Bobby Lee and I met whenever we could. He visited Oats at the Dewdrop a few times, and he arranged for me to meet him at various stops on the Patty Loveless tour. I don't know how it is for civilians, but for two road-wise musicians, an affair was easy enough to justify. We were the ones whom society had put in charge of the playground, right? We felt we could make up our own rules, and we did.

I would sit in an airport waiting area or hotel lobby reading the same page of a magazine over and over again, counting the minutes until we'd be together. In two hours, I would think, he'll slowly undress me and touch me here, and here. I'll hold him and smell him and feel all of him there in my arms. In two hours, in one hour, in fifteen minutes, I'll see him—any minute now, there he is. And I'd fly into his arms across the blurred room. The minute we were together, I'd be overcome with a delicious giddiness that turned me into a ditz. I'd lose the plane ticket that was just in my hand. I'd lose my appetite despite the fact that fifteen minutes earlier I'd been ravenous. I was in ecstasy.

We never had more than one night at a time, often not even that much. Sometimes he had a hotel room with the luxuries of privacy, room service, and a late lobby call. Sometimes it was only a couple of hours in an airport rental car, where we acted like teenagers looking for a secluded makeout spot—we got good at finding them, too. A favorite was Tilden Park, close enough to the Oakland airport and large enough to find a private area, a place I could drive to in my own car. The biggest problem turned out to be negotiating Berkeley's complicated recycling regulations when it came to disposal of the condom.

I wasn't about to get caught without one of those again, and kept them in my purse along with the new cell phone I bought so we could have private conversations. I told my family I was being called away for session work, and they pretended to believe me.

OATS WAS AN EARLY TALKER WITH A HUGE VOCABULARY. But shortly after his second birthday, he developed a fascination with numbers and a precocious talent for arithmetic that was truly spooky. Whenever he got upset, he would mutter to himself, counting from one to one hundred as a calming mantra. Give him any list of numbers and he could instantly add them in his head and tell you the total, or, as he put it, the "make-up-to," as in "Four and six and seven and three make up to twenty." Showing off Oats's math prowess became my favorite party game; I amazed friends and neighbors at every opportunity.

"The kid's so good with numbers, why can't he grasp the concept of number one and number two, Allie?" Perle asked one day, as the three of us sorted piles of laundry. "Here, change your grandson's diaper."

"We have the little chair set up and every book there is,"

Allie was making an effort to speak calmly. "I could train him in two days if you'd just let me buy a bag of M&Ms. That's how I trained Sarah Jean."

"And look how it affected her in the long run. It's nothing short of child abuse, feeding M&Ms to a toddler."

"Here, I'll change him." I said, and scooped him up. We headed for the bathroom, singing merrily.

A few hours later, I had a new song:

Where do they go when they have to pee?
  Birds do it in the air; fish do it in the sea
I once knew a monkey who did it in a tree,
  but what's the best peeing place for me?
Where do they go when they have to poop?
  Some do it in the barn; some do it in the coop
I once knew a chicken who did it in her soup,
  and I know where to go when I have to poop
I'm going to a potty right down the hall,
  I'm not gonna stumble, I'm not gonna fall
I'm not a party pooper 'cause I'm on the ball—
  I am a Potty Animal!

BY THE TIME ALL THE LEGAL HASSLES SURROUNDING THE estate of Samantha Eustace were worked out, our urgent financial need had passed, and Aunt Perle was having second thoughts as she prepared for her move to San Francisco. But the papers were signed, and she had made a commitment to transform the Sunset District retreat into a center for holistic healing. Artie Blond was grateful to have a whole new batch of excuses for visits to the Dewdrop, since Allie had been successful at stalling his efforts to move in. He hired a caretaker and worked out a kind of hippie time-share arrangement with Perle that allowed them both plenty of time in Lake County. I maintained a chilly friendship with Greg for the sake of Otis Ray, who adored him as much as everyone else did—I couldn't even raise the subject of my suspicions. We hardly ever spoke about our relationship anymore, though my worst fears gradually subsided, surfacing only in occasional cold-sweat nightmares. He pretended not to know about my affair with Bobby Lee, and I pretended to ignore his occasional one-night stands with women who followed him around at gigs. Frankly, it was easier to keep all our communications focused on the baby.

WHEN THE PATSY AWARDS ROLLED AROUND THE FOLLOWING fall, I assumed I wouldn't go. But three years after our Newcomer appearances, Marvella Claxton received another nomination in the gospel category, Bobby Lee said he would be there with his wife out of town, and they both urged me to come to Nashville for a few days of R&R.

My plan was to sneak into town for a quiet visit with my friends, but then Marvella asked the Patsy committee to help arrange a room for me at her hotel. When they heard I was coming, the producers asked if I'd be willing to sing "Got My Modem Working" as part of the segment promoting their brand-new Web site. My feeling was, Why not? This time there was no budget for bringing the band, but Bobby Lee offered to help me pull a group of sidemen together in Nashville.

"Remember to bring a shitload of your CDs with you," Hoagy advised. "They are like business cards in Nashville. You'll need a lot more than you think."

That sounded fine in theory, but I was almost out of CDs. I'd been gradually going through the few hundred I'd initially bought from Unicorn, using them as gifts, and autographing and donating them to charity auctions. I placed a call to the newest VP at the label, to ask about buying more. I figured that since so little product had been sold, there were bound to be some boxes of returns sitting around in a storeroom that they'd be happy to unload. He said he'd look into it and get back to me. He never did.

On the Friday morning before I left town, Oats and I made a special breakfast for everyone. He did all the counting and measuring, and I poured pancake batter on the griddle. Hoagy, Perle, Greg, and Allie eagerly waited to be served, along with Artie, who had appeared moments before, explaining that a guy was offering a 1948 Gibson J-50 in an online auction for under a grand, and he had to drive up to make sure it was authentic. It was near here—well, actually Oakland, but he'd gone left after the Bay Bridge and somehow missed Oakland, so he'd decided to come on up. Hoagy, who wasn't familiar with online auctions, looked crestfallen.

"Hey, Artie," I asked, "you got any of my CDs I can have to take to Nashville?"

"Couple of copies in the car," he told me, "but not enough to make any difference to you. Say, why don't you try calling your label again? Squeaky wheel gets the grease."

"I've been trying all morning," I said.

"So try again. Do it now, I'll spell you on the pancakes." Artie took over kitchen duty while I dialed the phone.

"Unicorn Entertainment, Valerie speaking."

"Valerie, it's Sarah Jean again. Is he free yet?"

"Sorry, hon, he's still on his conference call."

"Well, would you please tell him—"

"You know," Valerie whispered, "I'm not supposed to say this, but I don't see the point in letting you get all crazy and run up your phone bill. Hon, he's not going to take your call."

"Why not?" I asked. "I just want to buy some copies of my own CD, which I happen to know were returned by the truck-load. What's the problem?"

"That's it exactly. They've been tearing the warehouse apart looking for all those returns. They can't find them anywhere. Whoops, gotta go. You didn't hear this from me, right?" Valerie slammed down the phone before I could get another word in.

Given Unicorn's general flakiness in so many areas, I didn't find it astonishing that they'd misplaced thousands of units of returned product. It was, however, really inconvenient, as I was leaving in two days.

"So where can we find some CDs in a hurry?" Allie asked.

"You know," Perle mused, "I think I saw some at the Wal-Mart over in Clearlake."

"I can't walk into Wal-Mart and buy a ton of my own CDs," I wailed. "How would that look?"

"I'd go pick them up for you," Perle said, "but I have to lead a two-day 'Befriending Your Colon' workshop for Harvey. In fact, I'm late as it is. Got to run, doll." And she blew me a kiss on her way out the door.

"I'd help you out," Hoagy offered, "but I have a session, then a softball game."

"I have the same session, then I have to give the producer's kid a drum lesson," said Greg.

"And I have a meeting with my accountant that promises to be a doozy," Allie added.

"Shit, sweetheart, I still have to check out that guy's guitar. Looks like you're on your own," Artie called out as he ran up the stairs to put his overnight bag in Allie's room.

A phone call verified that there were indeed a lot of my CDs at Wal-Mart. As mortifying as the thought was, it looked like I was going to have to drive there myself and buy out the entire stock. Then I had an idea.

"Heavens, Cupcake," Richie trilled into the phone, "I'll be over in a jiff."

It took about two hours, but the transformation was incredible. With a long black wig, bronze foundation, turquoise jewelry, and a fringed vest, I looked like a dead ringer for Princess Lupiyoma herself. It might seem strange to a Wal-Mart checkout clerk that a young woman from the Pomo reservation appeared to be buying too many copies of one CD, but at least it wouldn't get around town that I was hoarding the last remaining stock of my own product.

"No one will recognize you in a million years, Banana Tush."

"Thank you so much. Come on, Oats, let's get in the car."

"Wait." Richie held up one hand as though he'd forgotten, for a moment, that he wasn't Diana Ross singing "Stop in the Name of Love." "You're bringing the baby?"

"Of course."

"Well, silly girl, let's do a little number on him, too."

"What did you have in mind?"

"Oh, you'll see."

But when Hoagy, stopping in between session and softball, saw what Richie had in mind, he put his foot down. He was just old-fashioned enough, he said, not to want any nephew of his going to Wal-Mart in drag, no matter how tasteful the party dress.

We settled for an old Beatles wig from Allie's costume trunk. By then Richie had been at the Dewdrop dressing us up for over three hours.

"Richie," I asked, "if you had this much time today, why didn't you just offer to go buy the CDs for me?"

"I thought of that, Wigglebuns, but this seemed like way much more fun. I tell you what, let's all go."

WE RETURNED TO THE DEWDROP WITH FIFTY-SEVEN CDS, A vacuum cleaner cover decorated to look like a cow, purple rhinestones for Richie, a value-pack of VHS tapes, a little wooden train for Oats, and an empty wallet. Oats immediately pulled the wheels off the train and tossed it aside in search of fresh amusement, while I wrestled the shrink-wrap off one of the CDs. I hadn't listened to my own album in a while and wondered how it would sound to me after all this time. Richie turned on the CD player and wandered over to get my guitar. He wanted to measure it for a new slipcover.

Like most preschoolers, Oats could be counted on to prefer the packaging over the contents of just about anything. He sat quietly on the floor playing with the plastic CD case, trying to jam it back into the broken shrink-wrap with his chubby fingers.

Hoagy returned from his recording session and scooped the baby up just as I lunged to grab the chokeable shrink-wrap out of his hands.

"It's okay, I'm watching him," Hoagy reassured me. He settled Oats on his lap as he sat down to remove his boots.

Oats proudly waved the CD box and the shrink-wrap in Hoagy's face.

"Your mama's CD, pretty cool."

"Wook! Numbews!" Oats had just noticed his favorite thing in the world, a row of numbers, on the CD's printed bar code. "Dose numbews make up to, um, firty-ate."

"Thirty-eight, huh? Let's see if you're right." Hoagy did the arithmetic in his head. "Yup, thirty-eight. Oats the Wonder Boy does it again."

"And dese numbews make up to fowty."

"Which numbers?" Hoagy asked.

Oats pointed to a second bar code, on a sticker attached to the outside of his precious scrap of shrink-wrap.

"Let me see that. Where did you get this sticker?"

"From dere." Oats pointed to the CD box.

"Sarah Jean?" Hoagy called to me in the kitchen, where I was still putting stuff away. "Sarah Jean, where did this piece of shrink-wrap come from?"

"Right off the CD. I just opened it a minute ago. What's going on?"

"I think your son just solved the mystery of the soft Sound-Scans."

ALLIE'S MEETING ENDED, AND SHE AND ARTIE JOINED US IN time to hear Hoagy explain that the UPC number, or bar code, is what computers use to identify products. The whole SoundScan system is based on these numbers scanned at the cash register at your local retail store. Obviously, there is only supposed to be one UPC code per CD released. The number printed on the little box on my CD artwork was 7 9005-82001-2 4. But the number on the shrink-wrap sticker was 7 11758-00092 0.

"Look," Hoagy said. "The 9005 represents the label, in this case Unicorn. That's their unique ID for the system. The rest are related to a specific album. Someone made a mistake and slapped stickers that belong to a whole other company and a whole other product over your real bar code. You probably sold a lot more CDs than you think, and didn't get credit for them."

Artie took the CD and the shrink-wrap out of Hoagy's hands and looked at them for a minute.

"Maybe it wasn't a mistake," he said quietly.

"Let's think this through," Allie suggested. "Get another shrink-wrapped CD. In fact, get a few of them."

I brought the whole bag of CDs into the room. Just as we feared, each and every one had a "11758" sticker carefully attached to the shrink-wrap, covering the CD's real bar code.

"You're right, Artie. This doesn't look like a mistake to me," Hoagy mused. "But who would do this, and why?"

"Do you think Unicorn is trying to cheat you, honey?" Allie asked.

I thought for a minute before I answered her.

"You know what? I honestly don't think they're smart enough to think of something like this. I mean, I'm sure they are trying to cheat me in all the regular little ways they're supposed to, but this is too creative for Unicorn. They can't even find my returns in the warehouse. Besides, what would be in it for them if their ID isn't on the bar code?"

"Good point," said Allie. "But think about it. Maybe there are no returns. Maybe all the CDs really did sell through—"

"And some other label and artist got credit!" Hoagy shouted. "Then this would have to be happening at the retail level—or wholesale, if there was a middleman. Who distributes Unicorn?"

"Let's look." Artie grabbed another CD out of the bag. "It says right here on the CD, 'Distributed by Crutch Records, North Hollywood, California.' Who else distributes through Crutch, and what's their connection to Sarah Jean?"

I thought I could take a wild guess.

We ransacked the CD racks searching for my old copy of *Magnolia Heart*. I finally found it filed under "Pedal Steel Instrumentals." Lloyd was a great admirer of Buddy, Cindi-Lu's steel player, and must have thought the CD's rightful place was in his section. Heart pounding, I searched for the bar code.

"Fuck if it doesn't match the sticker!" yelled Hoagy. "So Cindi-Lu's been getting all the credit for Sarah Jean's sales. But how can they do that? Crutch is a reputable company that's been around for years. I know people who work there. The only way you could do this is if you were, like, paying someone off on the inside."

Richie, pinning fringed leather on my Stratocaster, shrieked at exactly the same moment I did.

"Little Max!"

Artie raced around in a rage, gathering random stuff and throwing it in the back of his truck.

"Whoa there, buddy. Calm down." Hoagy placed a gentle hand on his arm. "What are you doing?"

"Driving to L.A. to beat the crap out of a little cokehead weasel. You coming?"

"Shit, yeah." Hoagy jumped into the truck and off they went.

Well, at least those two are finally getting along," Allie sighed. "But who's going to play guitar tonight?"

Chapter
22

"**D**ON'T WORRY ABOUT THE BABY, HE'LL BE FINE,"
Allie reassured me at the airport departure gate. She and
Perle would be watching Oats while I was in Nashville.

"I know. Don't forget he likes *The Chinese Siamese Cat* at
bedtime, and he can't go to sleep without the Sam and Dave 'Soul
Man' reissue. Wilson Pickett is fine for the car, though—the *Best
Of* with 'Funky Broadway,'" I reminded them.

"Like we could ever forget. You haven't told us enough
times already?" Perle scolded.

"Oh, wait. I almost forgot." Allie tore through her messy
purse. "Perle and I got you a little present. We cashed in some
frequent-flyer miles and upgraded you to first class."

"We want you to have a relaxing, healthy trip," Perle added.
"For crying out loud, promise you'll stay away from the chicken
fried steak. But look, your flight's boarding; better run or you'll
miss that plane."

I gave Oats one last hug and handed him over to Allie and
Perle. This would be the longest we'd ever been separated, five
whole days. Without the huge bag I always carried containing his

snacks, toys, Kleenex, Handiwipes, kazoos, and soul compilation tapes, I felt as if I were missing an appendage. On the other hand, how liberating to get on a plane holding nothing but my purse and a good book.

I settled into my comfy first-class seat and opened my new book, *Pigs in Heaven*, a precious autographed thank-you gift from the Lake County Family Literacy Program.

"You're a Barbara Kingsolver fan? You've got good taste," exclaimed the woman taking the seat next to me.

She was about my age, a slim woman with long, dark, glossy hair, olive skin, and startling green eyes. Her name was Charlotte. She also had a preschool-aged child—her little girl had a developmental disability that had sparked her interest in special education, and she was returning from a conference on the subject—and it turned out we had similar tastes in books and movies, as well as similar child-rearing philosophies. Before I knew it, we were landing in Nashville and I'd made a new friend. We exchanged phone numbers, agreeing to get together again before I left town.

While I was in Nashville, the plan was for me to keep my eyes and ears open and find out anything I could about Cal and Cindi-Lu's connection to Crutch Records, then compare notes with Artie and Hoagy when they returned from L.A. I had so many things on my mind that I almost forgot to get knots in my stomach in anticipation of meeting up with Bobby Lee Crenshaw. But seeing him cross the lobby made my heart leap in that old familiar way. Holding him, nuzzling his neck, and smelling his special smell made me even dizzier. If he seemed a little edgy and distant, I tried not to notice. Nashville was his hometown, and we had to be more circumspect about our relationship than usual.

"I can't wait for you to hear the band," Bobby Lee said as he opened the car door for me. "We're meeting them at Studio Instrument Rentals, out near the stadium, in a half hour."

Somehow he had called in a bunch of favors and hired the cream of the Nashville sidemen to back me up on my silly blues parody, including the legendary Angel Martinez on bass and Andy Reiss joining Bobby Lee on guitar. It wasn't exactly a stretch for the band to nail the Muddy Waters classic with my new high-tech lyrics.

I tried to swallow my disappointment later when Bobby Lee dropped me off at the hotel without coming in, explaining that his wife had returned to town early, and there were plans for the evening that he couldn't avoid. I didn't want to appear whiney, so I told him not to worry about it. Still, it didn't feel great. I was determined not to sit around in my room on the off chance he could get away later. Besides, I had work to do.

Jimmy Clearwater was my first call. He knew everyone in Nashville and he wasn't singing in the Patsy show this year, so he didn't have to worry about protecting his precious throat. He met me at the Station Inn, wearing his trademark purple scarf. I told him a short version of our SoundScan story.

"I've heard of things like this happening before," he said. "Remember the gal who won Newcomer the year before you?"

"Yeah, I never met her, though. She was off in rehab or something."

"Well, that's what they told everyone, but there's more to the story than that. She was a good friend of mine who had a similar incident occur with her record sales, on a whole other label, of course. She got wind of some shenanigans and tried to go public with the information. Unfortunately, she had a predilection for kinky sex—nothing too weird, just light bondage stuff, but there were some photos of her in nothing but her collar and leash, in a compromising position. She was threatened with the pictures getting published if she didn't back off. Poor kid figured her career in Nashville was over either way, so she packed it in and went home to Mama. Too bad, her voice and those photos were equally gorgeous. They gave her the negatives in return for a promise to 'disappear,' and she felt she didn't have a choice."

"Who do you mean when you say they threatened her?"

"Well, you'll never be able to prove it, because he's very smart about covering his tracks, but there are those around here who have it on good authority that the guy behind all this is—"

Jimmy looked over both his shoulders before scribbling something on a napkin, folding it, and sliding it across the table to me. The napkin said *Cal H.*

"Ca—"

"Shush!" Jimmy scolded me. "You never know who could be listening." And he astonished me by tearing the napkin into little tiny pieces and eating a few of them.

"How can anyone, especially that asshole, be so powerful and scary to you?"

"Don't underestimate him, honey. He's a clever and power-hungry guy who's gotten more outrageous since he married Miss Country Legend. You'll never get anything on him, and you can't beat him. He's got a controlling interest in Crutch Records, through a phony corporate name. Those two little lovebirds are going to own a very big chunk of the Nashville music industry before too long, and no one even realizes it. I've even heard talk of a blacklist of some kind, where they pick people to thwart any way they can. A lot of those folks are Newcomer of the Year Patsy nominees and winners, for some reason."

"How much do you think Cindi-Lu has to do with all this?" I asked.

"Hard to say. I think in the beginning they were definitely in cahoots. Now she seems so out of it, I wonder if maybe he's got her manipulated into doing whatever he wants. She's a good actress, though, that Cindi-Lu. So she could also just be playing the role of the little woman."

"Friends of mine who've worked with her think she's over-medicated."

"That's possible, I guess. I sure wouldn't put it past Cal. She still sings like a motherfucker, though, doesn't she? Amazing."

"Thanks for meeting me, Jimmy."

"Shucks, it's no big deal. I'm happy to help. I always had very special feelings for your mom, you know."

"That's another thing I've always wanted to ask you about— how do you and my mom know each other?"

"I'll tell you the whole story sometime," Jimmy said, "but now isn't it. I'm supposed to meet my girlfriend here, and she's coming through the door right now. Best to tell you about me and Allie another time." He waved to a familiar-looking woman approaching our table: Jamee! She gave each of us a giggly hug, then Jimmy wrapped his purple scarf around his neck and led her out the door.

Over the next two days, I called old friends of Hoagy's and Artie's. They all suspected Cal of any variety of evil maneuvering but said he was too well-protected by layers of bureaucracy to be implicated. There was more talk of a secret list of artists who would be subjected to a kind of corporate blacklisting, but no one had any proof or any real leads.

The night before the awards show, my cell phone rang just as I got back to my room.

"Hi, it's Charlotte, from the plane?"

"Oh, hi! It's great to hear from you."

"Listen, I know it's last minute, but we're having a little dinner party tonight for some musicians who came in for the Patsy show, and I was wondering if you'd like to join us. We'll be at the Sunset Grill at eight o'clock. It'll be a chance for you to meet my husband and some of our crazy friends. You're probably busy, I know, but oh please, just say yes."

A fun dinner with my new pal and a bunch of musicians seemed infinitely more appealing than a night alone waiting for Bobby Lee's call.

"Thanks so much, I'd love to come. I'll see you at eight," I answered cheerfully.

"Oh, goody. That's great. No need to dress up or anything. It's informal."

I ran a bubble bath and selected something nice to wear, thinking how long it had been since I'd dressed to go to a party, and how hard it had been to keep friendships going since having the baby. Except for Kathleen, Amy, and Marvella, whom I hardly ever saw, and swf 34, I had no close women friends. I found the various parenting groups and social events for Lake County toddlers horribly boring, and I suspected Oats did, too. We found it easier to hang around the Dewdrop with people who loved and understood us. It was exciting to find a kindred spirit in Charlotte.

The restaurant was huge, and packed. Looking around the

room, I saw a who's who of Nashville music royalty. It didn't occur to me until I got there that I didn't know Charlotte's last name; I finally found her in the back room, mingling with a large group that included Willie Nelson's drummer, Paul English, along with Rodney Crowell and Hank DeVito. I recognized a couple of musicians from the afternoon's rehearsal, too.

"Oh, I'm so glad you could join us." Charlotte smiled, grabbing my arm. "Look at this great group of people. I can't believe they all came."

I noticed a spectacular-looking woman with long silver hair and an incredible pair of rhinestone-trimmed Western boots.

"Who's that amazing creature?" I asked.

"You've never met K. N. Right? She's written half of Nashville's hits. A little schlocky for my taste, but she certainly knows a hook when she hears one."

"K. N. Right's a woman? I always pictured a cigar-chomping, beer-bellied guy in a Stetson, one of those 'all hat, no cattle' cowboys."

"Hardly," Charlotte laughed. "She's a total glamour-puss. I'll introduce you to her in a minute, but first I'm dying for you to meet my husband. R.C., come over here right this minute and meet my new friend from the airplane," she shouted to a tall man in a cowboy hat, who spun around to greet me with a grin, hand extended. We stood there paralyzed, smiles freezing our faces. He was none other than Bobby Lee Crenshaw.

If Charlotte saw something in the look we exchanged, she chose to ignore it. He was the first to recover.

"Silly Charlotte, Sarah Jean and I are old friends from the Cindi-Lu Bender tour. We've known each other for years. She's the one I'm playing with in the show tomorrow night."

"Oh my God! You're that Sarah Jean? I don't know why that never occurred to me. You just seemed so normal. You look bigger or something, in your video."

"Actually, I was pregnant when we shot the video. I guess I did look different," I stammered.

Charlotte gazed at her husband adoringly and kissed him gently on the cheek. If this marriage was troubled, I had the feeling it was news to her.

"Well, come on everyone. Let's sit down. Sarah Jean, you sit here, between R.C. and me. We intend to monopolize every ounce of your attention."

I'll say.

THE PATSY SHOW HAD BECOME A FAMILIAR CIRCUS OF OLD friends. Hoover and Mouse still reigned as gods of the mixing board. Porter Wagoner winked at me when we passed in the backstage hallway, as though we shared a deep secret, which I guess we did. I met up with Marvella and Elroy, still cozy as ever, in the bar at Roberts Western Wear, down the street. Elroy was relieved not to have to sing this year. We'd be presenting the Songwriter of the Year trophy together, and that was just fine with him.

Once again, Marvella opened the show, this time with her newest gospel hit, "Raise Your Head." She was backed by a local church choir and a full band, even including pedal steel.

Raise your head! Raise your head!
I'm with you, I'm with you, He said
See the stars all around

You don't have to be alone,
  He's standing there right beside you
Raise your head! Raise your head!

And once again, Marvella brought the entire Ryman Auditorium to its feet, shouting and praising the Lord and believing
with all our hearts, if only for those few minutes, that we weren't
alone.

I performed the modem song a little while later, after a very
hokey skit announced the new Web site at www.patsyawards.com.
Warmed up by Marvella and not yet catatonic from hours of
sitting, the crowd jumped in on the call-and-response part and it
went over well. I had decided to put my worries over Bobby Lee,
Charlotte, Cal, Cindi-Lu, and Little Max on hold until after the
show. I knew a lot of things needed to be resolved, but I was in
Nashville with what felt like one last chance to revive my sagging
career, and this performance came first.

I got my modem working, but I can't connect with you
I got my modem working, but I can't connect with you
Your parity is odd, babe, let's try VT-102

I got my modem working, but my baud rate's much too slow
I got my modem working, but my baud rate's much too slow
I'm gonna get a virus if I unzip you anymore

I'm going down to Louisiana, get me some extra RAM
I'm going down to Louisiana, get me some extra RAM
We can interface tonight, if I can find the right command

I got an 800 number, tech support will treat me right
I got an 800 number, tech support will treat me right
I need so much attention, I'm gonna keep 'em up all night

I send you all my e-mail, but you only flame me back
I send you all my e-mail, but you only flame me back
I guess you don't like my equipment,
Maybe I should've bought a Mac

I got my modem working (got my modem working)
I got my modem working (got my modem working)
I got my modem working (got my modem working)
I got my modem working (got my modem working)
I got my modem working, but I can't connect with you

Talk about not connecting—Bobby Lee and I had maintained a very polite and cautious distance since Charlotte's dinner party the night before. We finished our song to delighted applause and ran offstage.

"Hey, Sarah Jean, don't slip away. We've got to talk," he pleaded.

"I know, but not here," I snapped. My voice sounded colder in my own ears than I'd meant it to. "We're in the middle of the show."

"Well, then when? I don't know if I can get away later. I really need to see you."

"Then you'll figure out a way. I'm not having this conversation backstage at the Ryman Auditorium." I started to walk away.

"Sweetheart—" he began.

"I'm sorry," I said, cutting him off. "I have to present in a few minutes. Don't do this to me."

BOBBY LEE KNOCKED ON MY DOOR AROUND MIDNIGHT, AS I was packing to go home. I knew what I had to say to him, but I had trouble finding words. He held me tight and I tried to fill myself up with his smell and the memory of his touch, in between waves of anger over his omissions.

"It's been kind of weird, huh?" he asked.

"Duh."

"I'm sorry, honey. When I realized Charlotte was coming home early, I just freaked. I promise you I won't let anything like that get in the way of us being together again."

"You don't have to promise that."

"Yes, I do. I want to. I can see how hurt you are. I'll make it up to you next time, I swear."

"There's not going to be a next time," I whispered.

"What do you mean?" He sat on the bed, pulling me onto his lap. "We're in love. How can you say that?"

"I love you so much. But I met your wife and I totally adore her. She's lovely and she doesn't know her marriage is in danger, and somehow that makes a difference to me. And you never mentioned your daughter's disability, either. I think that for the first time in my life I might be making a mature decision. I just can't do this anymore."

"What about Oats? He's our son."

"I know, I've been thinking about that. You can see him as much as you want to, of course. You can be one of the guys, a friendly uncle, and I'll help you make that work. But if you want him to know you as his father, you have to tell Charlotte about him. Don't make him carry that secret, it's not fair. Do you understand that?"

"I guess I need a little time to think."

"Take all the time you want. You know where to find us."

"I love you."

"I love you, too."

"Is there anything I can do to make you change your mind?" he asked, stroking my hair. I pulled myself away.

"Right now, I don't think so. Let's see what happens, if anything changes."

"Can I kiss you one last time?"

And it's better if I don't say what that kiss turned into, one last time.

BACK AT THE DEWDROP INN, ALLIE PACED THE
floor, deeply pissed.

"Where are those guys? They called three days ago. They
said they had good news and were on their way home from L.A.
I haven't heard a word since. Meanwhile, I'm stuck without a lead
guitar player."

"There must be someone," I suggested, trying to be helpful.

"Well, yeah," Allie snapped back, "there's that kid who
thinks he's Stevie Ray Vaughn. He's great but he doesn't know
any country songs. There's Paula, who takes lessons from Hoagy.
She's pretty good, but she's more interested in drinking than playing. And then there's Ralph, who works at the music store, always
sticking his hand up someone's skirt—pretty slim pickings, as
pickers go."

"So what are you going to do?"

"How's your guitar playing these days?" I didn't like the
gleam in her eye.

"I can still do the intro to 'Soul Man' pretty well," I answered
tentatively.

"So it's settled. I'll invite all three of them, and we'll play a really long version of 'Soul Man.'"

The front doorbell rang, and she stormed off to find Reverend Walter Little standing in the doorway with a stack of flyers advertising a church social in Clearlake. He wanted to know if it would be all right to put one up on our bulletin board. Allie remembered that he played blues harp, and before he knew what hit him, he'd agreed to join the band that evening, giving his usual reminder that it would be better for his reputation as a dignified man of the cloth if everyone kept their clothes on.

He ended up saving the day for us. Unlike many harmonica virtuosos, Reverend Walter Little was a tasteful player with good stage manners. The guitar players were another story—three wanky show-offs who would have been better off listening than playing. Every once in a while, something made me appreciate the relaxed, good-natured virtuosity of the guys in our house band, and this was one of those times.

We limped through a lackluster first set featuring three bad lead guitars. Then Allie called a quick bandstand huddle during the break.

"Hey, gang, I'm desperate," she whispered. "I'm going to pull out an old improvisational-theater trick, so get your brains and your butts in gear."

She kicked off the next set with an announcement that we would make up a song on the spot, based on audience suggestions. She asked for three words from the crowd.

"Turnips!" yelled a voice in the back. I wasn't sure, but it sounded like Mr. Bagatelle, the produce guy.

"Casket!" from the other side of the room, offered by the town undertaker.

"Tupperware!" shouted Aunt Perle, who had just that afternoon been researching the health hazards of volatile plastic molecules when heated in combination with free radicals.

Even the three amateur guitarists were able to pick up the "I'm a Man" blues riff, and Reverend Walter Little started us off with a long harp solo, while Allie racked her brain to come up with a verse. Under the circumstances she was brilliant:

> *Some folks use waxed paper, some folks use Reynolds Wrap*
> *Some folks use a plastic Baggie, to try to cover up the gap*
> *You can use most anything to keep your goodies from*
> * the air*
> *But nothing works as well as that good old Tupperware*
> *'Cause it's here, take a look at what we got*
> *If you don't try some and buy some,*
> *Don't blame me if your turnips rot*

She gave me the nod to sing the second verse, and I signaled to the Stevie Ray wanna-be to take a solo. By the time he came back around to the one chord, I was ready:

> *I want all you men and women to gather round the*
> * kitchen range*
> *Listen now to what I'm gonna tell you,*
> *Your food storage method's got to change*
> *We don't want no botulism, want to keep our foodstuffs pure*
> *But don't forget to burp the lid to make the seal secure*
> *'Cause it's here, take a look at what we got*
> *If you don't try some and buy some,*
> *Don't blame me if your turnips rot*

Whoa! High fives all the way around, and the other guitar players traded show-off licks while the reverend got it together to sing and brought us home, in more ways than one:

Now you've heard my story, now you've heard my song
Got one more thing I want to tell you,
Won't take me very long
If you like this little product, 'bout which I've been telling you
We'll hold a party in your home;
You can make some money, too
'Cause it's here, and we need it, yes we do
And I hope that when I die, Tupperware makes caskets, too

Sweating and grinning, with the crowd in the palm of her hand, Allie yelled something to Greg and he counted off "Soul Man." For all my months and months of practicing that opening riff, I had never actually performed it in front of people. I was terrified, but what was the worst that could happen? No one was picketing, no one had pulled the plug on the PA. If I blew it, so what? I stomped on my volume pedal and felt transported to the zone as I heard myself blast a perfect lead line into the beer-soaked night. It was heaven. I was playing *lead guitar,* and loving every second, every distorted blistering inch of myself to pieces.

"Sow-Man!" shrieked Oats, running down the stairs and toward the bandstand when he heard the familiar introduction to his favorite song through the floorboards. But he looked puzzled, standing still for a minute staring at the stage, then toddling back upstairs. He returned a few minutes later to sit cross-legged in the middle of the dance floor, clutching his prized "Soul Man" tape. He held it up, comparing the guys on the cover photo with the people onstage. The people weren't right but the song was good, and he couldn't take his eyes off the bandstand.

THE CROWD HAD THINNED OUT AS WE LIMPED THROUGH our last set of blues standards. By one A.M. the place was nearly empty. I was playing the intro to "Soul Man" at top volume for the fifth time that night, when the whole band was startled by a loud crash in the parking lot, followed by a lot of yelling.

"Shhhh, doanwakemup."

"Ohshit! Now lookathat."

"Garbagecan."

"Whoyacallingarbagecan, yasshole?"

"Garbage can, garbage can't. What's the fuckin' difference?"

"You goddapointhere."

Hoagy and Artie, arms draped around each other's shoulders, stumbled into the club kicking the spilled garbage. Hoagy looked at the bandstand, surprised to see me playing his guitar and using his effects box.

"I know you . . . you're um . . . don't tell me," he mumbled. Then he shrugged, apparently unconcerned with the fact that I was screwing around with his settings. Allie walked over to the edge of the stage, to state the obvious.

"You're drunk."

"And yourbeautiful'nyermad."

The few remaining customers, who had been headed for the door, stopped to stay and listen. This was better than anything that had happened onstage all night.

"Cut the crap, guys. I can't believe the two of you just disappeared for days without calling. What was I supposed to do about the band?" Allie was mad.

"Ooh Artie, y'knowwwatwedid?"

"Fuggedup?"

"Yep."

And they both collapsed on the floor, convulsing with laughter, which turned immediately to hiccups.

"I give up, we'll talk in the morning." She unplugged her guitar and marched upstairs.

If I hadn't been flushed with glory over my first public guitar solo, I'm sure I would have followed her. But it occurred to me that this was the perfect opportunity to roll out a new song—hardly anyone was in the club, and although I hadn't given the careful attention I usually lavished on a tune before going public, it really did seem like there was nothing to lose, and the lyrics fit the moment. So I counted off a funky New Orleans beat and motioned to Lee to follow me.

Ain't it hard for your feet to keep up with your head
When you're trying to find your way home
Knowing tomorrow you'll wish you were dead,
Swearing never again to roam
Oh, you're such a liar and a lousier cheater
Though you work on it night after night
You're a hell of a boozer and a hullabaloozer,
But you still can't get it right
Well, I'm calling the bouncer at the bar in my heart and
*   throwing you out the door*

You can cry in your beer but you can't do it here
'Cause I loved you before, now I don't anymore
Your credit's no good, neither are you,
I'm telling the regular crowd we're through
I'm kicking you out of the cocktail lounge of my heart

THE TWO MOST HUNGOVER GENTLEMEN AT OUR BREAKFAST
table had a little explaining to do. And Allie, Pete, Perle, Greg,
and I listened intently as they told their story. They had found
Little Max right away, and getting him to talk was easy—they'd
even tape-recorded the conversation. Little Max was basically a
weak person. It turned out that he'd been in Cal Hooper's employ
for quite some time. His first job had been standing by for Bobby
Lee's phone calls and pretending to be my boyfriend. (When I
heard this, I beamed relief and gratitude across the table at Greg,
who looked utterly confused by my reaction.) This led eventually
to a career in the mailroom at Crutch Records, where he carefully
pasted counterfeit UPC stickers onto shrink-wrapped CDs. He
was lured in with cocaine, the promise of a lucrative record deal,
and access to me. He got the cocaine.

"He's pretty pathetic. I ended up feeling sorry for the guy,"
Artie said as he held an ice pack to his head while Hoagy sipped
on some Alka-Seltzer. "The problem is, he can't help us much. I
mean, let's say we took Cal to court. It would be this one little
cokehead weenie against an army of slick corporate lawyers. We
wouldn't have a chance. Besides, he really doesn't know shit
about the bigger picture."

I reported what Jimmy Clearwater and the others had told
me in Nashville.

"See? It's much larger than you think," Hoagy said, "which is good in a way because if we can get Cal, then we're helping a whole lot of people get what's theirs."

"In another way, though, it makes it harder 'cause he's so well protected," Artie added. "Before we left L.A. we had a meeting with that guy at Unicorn—you know, the VP you don't like? I have to give him credit. He was willing to see us and listen to what we had to say. When we showed him the evidence and played our tape of the Little Max show, he was convinced. You'll be getting a call from him in the next few days, Sarah Jean. He wants to apologize to you in person."

"I'll believe it when I hear it," I sniffed.

"Well, that's what he told us. He also asked if I thought you'd be interested in doing another project with them. I told him to ask you directly."

"Thanks, I'll see what he has to say."

"There's one more thing," Hoagy said. "The big question is how we can get to Cal. He seems to have spies everywhere. Going through regular legal channels won't work. It'd take way too long and he's not worth the time or the money. We figured out, just talking to people around town, that the one area he's vulnerable is his marriage to Cindi-Lu. She's the cash cowgirl."

"I talked to Jimmy Clearwater about that, too," I said. "He thinks she might be putting on a huge act, pretending to be Little Miss Wifey when she's really in on everything. But the girls, Amy and Kath, think she's sedated all the time and doesn't have a clue what Cal is up to. They also think she truly believes he's monogamous, so that would be one way—"

"Now you're talking, sweetheart!" Artie jumped up and started digging through his satchel.

"But how can we—do we know anyone who would . . . you know?" Greg stammered.

"I think we have that little detail taken care of." Both Hoagy and Artie's faces lit up with shit-eating grins.

"Okay, spill." Allie was still trying hard to be annoyed with them but was not succeeding.

"We're heading up Interstate 5 on the way home and pulled off the road just outside of Bakersfield so Artie here could take a pee," Hoagy explained. "This was a couple of days ago, right? We figured as long as we were in Bakersfield, we'd stop in and check on Monica, see how business is at the Boom Boom Room."

"And you were there for three days?"

"Well, we got a little distracted." Hoagy grinned.

"I think you lost your heads. Both of you."

"Wait now," Hoagy said. "Let us finish. There's this dancer there, named Peaches. She does the most amazing thing with her—"

"What he means to say is this," Artie interrupted. "We told Monica the whole story. She thought she might be able to help."

"Come on, guys," Allie yawned. "If you wanted to stay in Bakersfield drooling on Peaches's pair, why don't you just admit it? Why didn't you call?"

"Yeah, we should have called. But Monica had it all planned," Artie explained. "She didn't want to give us the original and she didn't have the right connectors and shit to make a copy. We had to wait till Monday when the electronics place opened to get the transfer done."

"And we had to promise Monica we'd give it to Allie and Perle as soon as we got back. She didn't want us to try to do anything with it."

"What is it you're talking about?" Allie asked. Artie reached into his bag and pulled out a small parcel.

"Pay dirt, Allie. It's Cal Hooper's ass in a fucking sling."

Inside the package we found a VHS tape and note:

Dear Allie, Perle, and Sarah Jean,

This was some night, even for the Boom Boom Room! Please make sure Otis Ray is out of the room when you watch, seeing as I would rather not be responsible for corrupting a toddler. You might want to fast-forward past the first ten minutes, since it's just business as usual for us. Use it in good health and for heaven's sakes, be careful!
Love,
Monica

"Where's the baby?" asked Aunt Perle.

"I've seen this kind of stuff too often," Greg said, taking Otis Ray's hand. "I can check out the important parts later. Come on, Oats, let's go to the park."

"Yes, de pawk!"

The rest of us trooped upstairs to Allie's bedroom, where there was a VCR.

"Fast-forward through the beginning," Allie said, tossing me the remote.

"No!" Artie, Hoagy, and Pete shouted in unison, lunging. Of course, they wanted to watch the whole thing.

The video offered complete documentation of Cal Hooper's bachelor party, from the exotic strip acts to the wild furniture-breaking rampage that ended the festivities, including the part where Cal pulled down his pants, waved himself around, and demanded a blow job. It was not something he would have wanted his bride to see.

"This is disgusting," Perle exclaimed.

"Are you kidding? It's great!" the guys shouted. Allie looked thoughtful.

"What it is is useful," she said slowly. "Now, how do we get his attention?"

THE MAGNOLIA HEART TOUR WAS ON HIATUS AND I WANTED to go to Nashville, find Cal, and show him the video myself, extracting a promise that he'd leave me and all the other Newcomers alone. He would also be required to sell his interest in Crutch Records and give the money to charity. That plan was vetoed as too risky.

"If Cal knows you're in town, and he will, he'll have his guard up. We want to take him by surprise," Artie explained.

"I think three of us should go," Allie suggested. "Perle, Monica, and me—I have a few things to say to that asshole, anyway. And maybe Perle can fix one of her special wheat-grass enemas for him."

"I still don't think that's safe, Allie." Hoagy looked worried.

"Wheat-grass enemas are perfectly safe. You'd be the better for one," Perle protested.

"No, I mean the three of you going unaccompanied. You need someone Cal doesn't know, for protection," Hoagy thought out loud.

"Don't be ridiculous! We can take care of ourselves."

"Ladies, I'm not implying you can't. It's just that we're dealing with a very clever, manipulative, and dangerous person here.

Humor me, okay? Take a gun with you. It doesn't even have to be loaded."

"Where are we going to get a gun?" whined Allie.

"I think I know someone who can get us one," said Pete.

Chapter

24

ALLIE, PERLE, AND MONICA ARRIVED IN NASHVILLE with a state-of-the-art, all-plastic stun gun ("No airport security hassles," the instruction booklet proudly proclaimed) provided by Pete's new girlfriend, Pat, who knew someone who knew someone who knew Major Booty, head of the SMUGs. Since we happened to know the Magnolia Heart tour was short a couple of backup singers, Allie had tracked Cal down through Hoagy and Pete's network of musician friends and made an appointment to see him under the pretense of scheduling an audition.

I've heard each of them tell the story of what happened next so many times that it seems more real to me than if I'd actually been there. They left out none of the juicy details. In fact, if anything, the details have grown juicier with the telling, over time.

Hooper Enterprises occupied an office on the twelfth floor of the United Artists Tower on Seventeenth Avenue. Jimmy Clearwater drove the ladies to their appointment. He proved once again that he had an "in" virtually everywhere in Nashville by proudly flashing the card key that gained access to the building's underground parking garage.

They looked like an odd crew: Perle in her natural hemp drawstring trousers and Reeboks; Allie all done up in Country-sweetheart spangles, eel-skin boots, and a ten-gallon hat; and Monica in a scandalously tight cardigan sweater, animal-print Capri pants, and impossible high-heeled sandals. Jimmy wore his purple velvet scarf. There was the inevitable checking of lipstick, hair, and overall appearance, followed by the inevitable waiting for Allie to fumble around for the suite number. This gave Monica time to readjust her boobs and stick a mysterious parcel inside her purse.

Jimmy Clearwater walked them to the lobby, where he suddenly remembered that he had an urgent appointment elsewhere. They agreed to meet him at the car in half an hour.

Cal Hooper was in the middle of a very busy, very bad day. His secretary was out sick and he'd actually had to do his own errands—pick up lunch and some audio-visual materials he needed for the quarterly financial meeting with the Hooper Entertainment Board of Directors. Jimmy Clearwater had it on good authority that a certain board member, the general manager of Christian Family Values Radio Syndicates, had been making unhappy noises about some of the company's financial dealings, and Cal was not looking forward to the meeting. There was just enough time beforehand to audition the hopeful young singer who would give anything to work with the legendary Cindi-Lu Bender. In fact, though he didn't usually drink before board meetings, he'd been sipping a glass of his favorite peppermint schnapps and most likely daydreaming about what exactly the aspiring backup singer might be willing to give this afternoon, if she turned out to be cute. He couldn't quite hide his disappointment when his three o'clock turned out to be the not-so-young

Allie Pixlie and her entourage. The three women sat on wooden chairs across from his antique rolltop desk.

"All right, ladies, what do you want? Let's make it snappy. I have a meeting in a few minutes."

"We have something we think you'll be interested in seeing," said Allie. "Do you have a VCR?"

He nodded toward a portable unit on his desk. Perle popped in their videotape and fast-forwarded past the first ten minutes. As Cal watched himself on the screen, his breathing grew heavy and sweat appeared on his temples.

"We're going to show this to your wife if you don't meet our demands." Allie was the first to speak.

"And we're going to slip something to the press," added Perle.

"And we're going to sell copies on the Internet," Monica added.

"We are not!" Perle and Allie looked horrified.

"Oh, well, it was just an idea."

"Are you finished?" Cal asked quietly. "Because, quite frankly, my wife won't care. The only thing that bothers me about this tape is the fact that you shot from the left. The right is my good side. Publicity doesn't scare me, either. I've been around long enough to know that the only really bad press is your obituary." He popped the tape out of the video player and swept up a pile of papers and materials from his desk. "Now, if you'll excuse me, I have a board meeting in the conference room. You can show yourselves out." He slammed the door hard as he exited.

"What do we do now?" Perle whispered.

"I think he may be bluffing about the wife," Allie whispered back. "We have to call his bluff, but I need some time to think. Let's regroup in the ladies' room."

"Wait," said Monica as they got up to leave, "get the tape."

Allie picked up the videocassette from Cal's desk. "Holy cow, girls, look at this—*Third Quarter Financials 1996, Hooper Entertainment*. Looks like our buddy took the wrong videotape to his meeting. I think this show might be worth the wait."

They all sat down again.

A few minutes later, a door slammed out in the hall, and heavy footsteps approached the office. Monica held up her manicured fingers for a silent countdown—five, four, three, two, one. Right on schedule, a red-faced Cal burst through the door and threw the VHS tape against the wall.

"So you're still here, you conniving bitches. I guess we have to talk after all."

Allie began searching for the stun gun in her purse.

"I'm glad you see things our way at last," Perle said, just as Cal locked the door and pulled a revolver out of the top drawer of his desk.

No matter how hard they tried later, it was impossible to reconstruct exactly what happened next, but they all agreed they were sure they were going to die. Cal's eyes seemed to glaze over as he backed them against the wall with their hands above their heads. It was clear to everyone that he was not thinking things through, that he was beyond caring about the rational consequences of his actions.

"Where's the stun gun?" Perle whispered to Allie.

"Somewhere in my purse."

"Well, get it out!"

Since she figured she was a dead woman anyway, she continued to dig through her purse, finding a lipstick, five guitar picks, half a candy bar, a pair of earrings, a packet of breath mints, a Stephen King paperback, Advil, Handiwipes, one of Otis Ray's soul tapes, a toy harmonica, a rubber dog bone, a Phillips-head screwdriver, and three sets of keys—but no stun gun. She stopped searching when she finally noticed that Cal had pointed his gun at her head.

Cal found some electrical tape in his desk drawer and used it to tie Perle's, then Allie's, hands together behind their backs. He roughly slapped a piece of tape across each of their mouths, then pushed them into a storage closet and locked the door.

Monica, meanwhile, had moved away from the wall and sat cross-legged on the edge of the desk, filing her nails.

"Hey, Cal," she said in a breathy voice, "good for you for getting rid of those two stick-in-the-mud old maids."

"I'm not falling for that crap, Monica. Get in the closet with your friends."

"All right, Cal, but I was hoping I could give you that private little show you wanted the night of your party, now that we're alone."

She stood up and did one of her spectacular Monica Boom Boom wiggle-stretches and managed to undo a couple of buttons on her cardigan at the same time. The woman was, after all, a pro.

"Come on, Sugar," she cooed. "The girls are locked in the closet. No one will ever know." And somehow more buttons came undone, and she gently draped the sweater around Cal's neck. "You'll let me use your cassette player, won't you, Poopsie?" She began grinding her hips into Cal's as she reached behind her and pulled a tape of "Lonely Little G-String" out of the pocket of her tight Capri pants and popped it into Cal's boom box. Out of another pocket materialized an airline-sized bottle of peppermint schnapps. The sixties stylings of David Rose and His Orchestra, complete with siren sound effects, filled the room. Smiling, dressed now in her Capris and high-heeled sandals and black lace push-up bra, she held the schnapps bottle to Cal's lips and told him to pull down his pants. Miraculously, while still aiming the gun at her head, he pulled his jeans and boxer shorts down as far as his knees. He was panting, eyes glazed over, the gun in one hand and his penis in the other. Monica did a few bump-and-grind dance steps to the music, bravely turning her back to him as she inched her tight pants down to expose the top of the G-string underneath.

"Ooh," she said, lips pursed in a kiss, "baby, would you help me pull my pants down? They are so tight." Cal placed the gun in his shirt pocket and his hands on Monica's hips, tugging her pants down below her splendid rear end. She wiggled away, neatly stepping out of the Capris and dancing around him, now wearing only her G-string, bra, and high-heeled sandals. Cal grabbed his penis again, following her around the room as gracefully as he could with trousers around his ankles, as she continued to dance to music punctuated by muffled cries from the locked closet.

She scooted up onto the desk, where she unfastened and started to take off her bra. Cal lunged for her.

"Now, baby, you know better than that. Stand back and enjoy the show," she teased, pointing toward the wall next to the office door. She slowly removed the bra, arching her back to give him a long, luscious look, deftly pulled the bra behind her, and stretched it as far as she could. Then she let fly a powerful black lace thirty-eight double-D slingshot aimed directly at Cal's left eye.

The impact and the sheer surprise cost him his balance and he pitched over backward, hitting his head hard on the edge of one of the wooden chairs and knocking himself unconscious.

Monica was stepping daintily down from her perch on the desk when she heard someone yelling and banging on the office door. Still carrying her bra and wearing nothing but a G-string and high heels, she walked over to the door and unlocked it.

There in the doorway stood Jimmy Clearwater with Cindi-Lu Bender.

Monica had some trouble establishing credibility with Cindi-Lu, but finally managed to convince her that she personally was not having an affair with Cal. He was, however, up to some stuff that might be construed as worse, which Cindi-Lu should know about. Meanwhile, Cal, trousers wrapped around his ankles, was beginning to stir.

Jimmy Clearwater arriving at just the right moment with Cindi-Lu was a stroke of luck. He had been ambivalent about being seen in public with three broads crazy enough to think they could reason with Cal Hooper. What if word got out? He might never work in Nashville again. On the other hand, if the impossible happened and their plan succeeded, it would be in his interest to have been visibly on their side. Then he realized that he'd never be able to forgive himself if anything serious happened to them while he waited downstairs like a chickenshit. So he called Cindi-Lu on her ultra-private cell-phone number and invited her to surprise Cal for tea. Cindi-Lu, who got very few social invitations of any kind not related to work, had been delighted to accept.

Cal shielded his head from Cindi-Lu's white leather boots as she kicked him, screaming her pretty voice raw while Monica tried to pick the lock on the closet door. Jimmy stood still, mesmerized by the sight of Monica's breasts.

"Sheesh, what's wrong with men, anyway?" she said, exasperated. "They're just tits. Your friends are locked in the fucking closet. Help them get out, you idiot." She stormed off down the hall in search of a promotional T-shirt to wear, to the great delight of every man lucky enough to have an office on the twelfth floor.

Jimmy opened the closet door; Cindi-Lu called the police. By the time Cal came to his senses, he was on his way to the hospital and Allie and Perle were unbound and happy to be alive. They were also furious that they'd missed most of the action, but couldn't stop thanking Monica for saving their lives.

"I'm just glad I happened to be wearing well-constructed undergarments," Monica grinned.

"Always important for a lady," said Allie.

They all went out to celebrate and ended the evening at the Nashville Palace, where Allie knew the bass player and sat in on a couple of tunes. Monica recounted their adventures to anyone who would listen, and Perle spent the evening dancing the two-step with a guy named Bubba. She even broke down and drank a couple of beers.

Jimmy Clearwater drove them to the airport the next morning. He held Allie's hand, looked into her eyes, and told her he'd always had very special feelings for her.

"Have we actually ever met before?" she wanted to know.

AT THE DEWDROP INN WE HAD A LARGE *YOU ROCK* BANNER hanging between the buffalo heads, and a lopsided carrot cake waiting for their arrival. SWF 34 went to pick Perle and Allie up at the airport. Hoagy, Lloyd, Pete, and Greg joined Oats and me to form the welcoming committee at home, along with Artie, who popped in on his way to buy some organic pears (or so he said) at a farm down the road. We ran to the back door when we heard the car pull into the driveway.

They were all lit up.

"What's got into you gals? You look like you're up to no good," Pete teased.

"What do you mean?" asked Perle. "Just because we brought down the evil empire."

"Stared death in the face and laughed," Allie added.

"Danced the two-step in a cowboy bar."

"No shit. Perle danced the two-step?" Hoagy was impressed.

"And," Allie continued, "wrote a damn good song."

"Really? That's great," I said. "Let's hear it."

"No, I mean we wrote a *song*." And they both started giggling.

"What are we missing here?" Greg wanted to know.

"Perle, tell them what happened."

"Well, we were in this bar in Nashville, the Nashville Castle."

"Perle means the Nashville Palace."

"Right," Perle continued. "Anyway, there we were minding our own business with Monica, having a cocktail, when in walked this male creature . . ."

"He was really gorgeous," Allie sighed. "About twenty-two years old, long hair, great butt, adorable face—just, you know, a perfect specimen. Probably in one of the touring bands at the Opry—he had a laminated backstage pass on."

Artie, suddenly interested, wondered which band. We all shot him a "shut up" look.

"So I saw those two, Allie and Monica, check this guy out and roll their eyes at each other like, *Somebody hold me back!* And Monica went into her irresistible flirt routine, right?" Perle continued.

"Yeah, we've all seen that one. Did he flirt back?" Artie asked.

"That's the thing!" They both roared. "He didn't even notice us!"

"It's very lucky," Perle snorted, barely able to breathe, "that this cowboy didn't have Cal Hooper's job, because he would have been immune to her particular charms and we would be dead now."

"Why, was he gay or something?" I didn't quite get it.

"Honey," said Allie. "Due to the mere fact of our age, we were exactly as interesting to him as the wallpaper."

"You have to hear the song," said Perle, more excited than I'd seen her in a long while.

Allie got her Martin off the bandstand and checked the tuning. As always, thanks to Hoagy's quiet ministrations, it was perfect. She strummed a one-five-four progression in the key of G and sang.

Long hair and a laminate, I took one look and that was it
Tight buns in torn jeans, tattoos and an earring
Oh, I wonder if he'd care, if he knew I had underwear
Older than him—better get back to the gym

Husbands and hormones, mood swings and kidney stones
So many years I've played the game,
But when he walked in I forgot my name
I've got my reservations, he's not strong on conversation
But who cares?
Who cares?
Who cares?
I don't care!
Is it love or is it lust, or could it be that I am just
Still the total slut I used to be—perhaps his dad remembers me

"So, what do you think?" Allie asked, beaming.

"Look at her. She doesn't like it. She thinks it's a terrible song," Perle sighed.

"If you don't think it's any good, maybe you could help us fix it up a little."

"Are you kidding? That song doesn't need fixing. I'm just totally jealous that I didn't write it myself. Sing it again," I begged.

This time I added a harmony part.

"You know, Perle, you should learn this part. It's your song, too. I can teach it to you, it's really pretty easy," I offered.

"Oh, honey, I can't sing, you know that."

"Don't believe her," Allie protested. "She had a very nice voice as a child. That one stupid teacher who insisted you had to be a *listener* ruined you for life."

"No, really, I can't sing."

"You know, we used to think that about Sarah Jean. Then one day all of a sudden she was hearing harmonies all over the place, and there was no stopping her. You just need a little inspiration,

Perle. A good easy song to harmonize to, like, oh, I don't know, 'Soul Man.'"

"No, not that one!" Perle exclaimed.

I had an idea.

Down in the basement I found my dusty old portable turntable and, after digging through many boxes, the perfect LP. I brought them upstairs to the kitchen table, placing the needle carefully on the title cut.

When Allie heard the piano intro, she grinned wide and grabbed the nearest spatula. We all danced around the kitchen teaching Aunt Perle to harmonize to Warren Zevon's "Excitable Boy," playing it over and over again. It sounded as wonderful as ever to me.

Chapter
25

UNICORN ENTERTAINMENT WANTED ANOTHER CHANCE. They offered a sweet deal and I thought hard about signing with them again, but ultimately I decided against it. Even though most of the problems weren't really their fault, I had never liked the way they handled things. I gave them permission to re-release my first two CDs and never looked back. Instead, in what must have been a moment of sheer lunacy, I decided it would be fun to start my own record label.

"Greg, I need your help. I have to think of a name for my record company."

"How about Belly Button Records?"

"Cute, but what does it mean?"

He shrugged. "Push-face Productions? Pixlie Entertainment?"

"Boring."

We heard a door slam, and Artie Blond came in, explaining that he was on his way to pick up some goat cheese at the farmers' market.

"What are you guys up to?"

"We're trying to come up with a name," I told him. "I'm starting a record label."

"Ha!" He chuckled. "Don't quit your day job."

Greg and I looked at each other and smiled.

DON'T QUIT YOUR DAY JOB RECORDS SCORED A HIT THE first time out with "Older than Him" by the Cohen Sisters, on a compilation titled *All-Star Jam at the Dewdrop Inn.* It seemed a lot of graying baby-boomer broads could relate to its message of unapologetic lust, and the song became the most requested ever at the Dewdrop, partly because a lot of our regulars assumed it was about Greg. The CD also included a new arrangement of Artie's cow song, "The Tupperware Blues," and Otis Ray "Wild Oats" Pixlie singing "Soul Man." I recorded some other musician friends and special guests, and a couple of "Alice and Artie" duets.

Due to Harlan's documentary and our CD, Artie Blond found a whole new audience for his country blues interpretations, as well as old fans who had never really gone away. His career took off one more time. He was invited to play all over the world at major folk festivals.

"You know I can't go with you," Allie tried to explain when he was leaving to tour.

"But I'll miss you," Artie said. "Hey, I have a great idea— let's get married before I go."

"What?"

"I'm going to be gone awhile. I want to know you'll be here when I get back."

"Where am I going to go? I'll be here."

"Marry me, then."

"Since when are you the marrying kind, Artie? I think I've finally realized that I'm not, either. I like being free to run my business and book my bands and come and go as I please," Allie said softly. "It's not like we're young and raising babies together, you know?"

"But I'll miss you," he whispered, holding her against his chest.

"And how will you miss me any less if we're married and I can't go with you, besides adding an unnecessary layer of obligation? Have a great adventure. Drool on strippers guilt-free. You took care of Jasmine for a long time, and you've been taking care of me, and you deserve to let yourself be a free man for a while. You don't need to be married right now."

"And what about you?"

"Same rules apply. Take it or leave it."

"Do I have a choice?"

"Your choice is not to go."

"I have to go."

"I know, sweetheart. So go and have a wonderful time. And don't forget to come home."

From the doorway, tears rolling down her face, she watched him leave.

And Hoagy, watching from the bandstand, saw another chance to try to get up the nerve to ask her out.

THE MOST SURPRISING THING ABOUT OWNING A SMALL independent record company was how much time I spent sitting on the floor at three in the morning stuffing envelopes. That's when I wasn't collating press kits or whining at some poor swing-shift clerk at Kinko's because the copy machine had run out of toner, or leaving the tenth message in as many days on some radio station music director's voice mail. In other words, it's a life of total nonstop glamour. Everyone pitched in, including Oats, whose number-adding skills turned out to be handy at tax time.

In addition to being the record label's president, secretary, and janitor, I was also its primary recording artist. That meant I couldn't pull the prima donna routine, because I'd just end up having hissy fits at myself. It was a little tricky, shifting back and forth in my dual role as artist and businesswoman. But the good news was, from the record executive point of view, I didn't have to deal with a spoiled brat artist. And from the artist's point of view, I had creative control. The best part of all: There were no meetings.

One afternoon in the summer of '98, Greg and I sat at the big table updating our press list for a Patsy Awards nomination mailing while Allie paid some bills.

"Well, that's it," Allie said. "Signed, sealed, and almost delivered. This is my last payment to Johnny—looks like I just bought myself a nightclub."

"Congratulations." I grinned, squeezing her hand. "How's he doing, anyway?" I hadn't heard from my dad in a while.

"Oh, who knows? Rainbow takes very good care of him. Their daughter is cute. He called me the other night, just to talk. I think maybe someday we'll be able to be friends."

"Hey, speaking of buying clubs, did I mention that my mom is selling hers?" Greg asked. "Harlan Harris got a huge grant to produce a documentary about strippers and offered her a gig as creative consultant. She and my dad are moving to Hollywood next month."

"Does she have a buyer lined up?" Allie, now experienced at buying nightclubs, wanted to know.

"Don't even think it. If anyone is *not* suited to run a strip joint . . ." I sputtered.

"What do you mean?" Allie asked. "I'd be great. We'd have to change the sound system, of course, to accommodate a live band, and redecorate, but . . ."

"Sorry," Greg said. "Mom says Peaches is planning to buy the place along with some of the other girls. My mother did a terrific job with that business. They'll keep a fine tradition going without changing much of anything. But you know what's weird? I thought I'd be happier about it than I actually am. I'm going to miss the old homestead."

"That's the first nice thing I've ever heard you say about the place, Greg," I teased.

"And the first unembarrassed statement you've ever made about Monica and her business, too." Allie looked thoughtful. "What changed?"

"I don't know. Maybe all of you risking your lives in Nashville and hearing about how she saved the day. I used to think of her as a kind of cartoon character, all boobs and wiggle. A strip club can be a weird place to grow up."

"No weirder than a honky-tonk, I bet." Allie winked at me. "Your mom is a smart, resourceful woman, and don't you forget it."

And then a strange thing happened. Under the table Greg's knee brushed against mine, and I felt an electric zap up my spine, right into blush-reflex central. His eye caught mine—he was blushing, too. It was unmistakable. The Crush Bomb had hit us at last.

FTER FULFILLING HER PROMOTIONAL OBLIGATIONS as a Don't Quit Your Day Job recording artist, Aunt Perle completed her move to San Francisco, where she continues to thrive as the proprietress of the Bunny Jasmine Memorial Center for Holistic Healing. She assembles the world's best alternative medicine professionals for workshops and seminars, and also runs a residential nutrition-education program. But she saves one room for Jasmine's longtime weekend guests (as long as they are willing to try her freshly pressed wheat-grass cocktails), many of whom still tell their families that they are going to visit Aunt Sam. Harlan Harris is producing a documentary about the center. He has a lot more clout these days, since winning the Academy Award for *Take It Off!*, his behind-the-scenes film about strippers.

Monica now lives with Stan in the Hollywood Hills. She's become a highly paid consultant to the motion picture and music video industry, teaching actresses how to move. She's talking about teaming up with Peaches and some of the other girls to produce a series of "pornette" videos for women, basically soft-core adult films set in a startlingly realistic facsimile of the

Bloomingdale's shoe department, in which most of the erotic action revolves around shopping and chocolate.

Cal is in a minimum-security prison in Central California. I'm supposed to be getting settlement money from his production company, but I'm not holding my breath. The way the legal system works, it could be a while, and could all eventually end up going to the lawyers, anyway. But if I ever do get paid, I plan to use the cash to offer Jimmy Clearwater the sweetest record deal he's ever had.

Once Cal was out of the picture, many friends in Nashville came out of the woodwork to help and support Cindi-Lu Bender. Still, it took her a while to decide she was ready for rehab. She entered an in-patient recovery program in an undisclosed location, and later ended up staying on as a counselor. The word is that it hasn't been easy, but she's doing well and plans to resume singing and touring with a new manager and a new bus. Kathleen, Amy, and I rehearsed what we would say if she ever gets far enough down her "Amends" list to call us, though it's got to be a long list and it might take years.

The Bhalahdis shifted the focus of their appliance business and added computer maintenance and repair. The Life Goes On Hotline offers spiritual inspiration and tech support twenty-four hours a day. Their voice-mail system plays "Got My Modem Working" for you while you are on hold. Aunt Perle, who always had a soft spot for Little Max, pulled a string or two and got him into their training program when he finally reappeared in Lake County, broke, pathetic, and sorry. He performs at the Friday-night talent roundup and is trying to get a band together to stage *Beatlemania* as a fund-raiser. I'm still keeping my distance.

In its coverage of the last ready-to-wear fashion show, the *New York Times* reported that Calvin Klein's spring line included the "Patsy Collection" in honor of Mothers Day, a sophisticated country-western-influenced style that the reporter attributed to the designer's well-known roots in the music world.

Turns out, I didn't know as much about the record business as I thought I did. Despite the success of "Older than Him," my label has been struggling. But things are starting to turn around. We've added a children's line called "Soul Kid," which features music performed by and for kids: classic soul, country, and rock, as well as some wonderful original stuff. *Potty Animal*—based on the potty-training songs I made up and sang for Otis Ray— looks like our big winner so far. As we say around Don't Quit Your Day Job Records headquarters, a.k.a. my room, the market for this product will never dry up. We found a small, honest Los Angeles distributor that's doing a terrific job for us.

Otis Ray just turned five and we are about to take off on a "Lollipopalooza" tour of state fairs. It's going to be run like those old Motown bus tours, except all the acts are children performing for other children. There's twelve-year-old twins who tap-dance and juggle, a brilliant eight-year-old on keyboards, and Otis Ray, who will play harmonica and sing "Soul Man" and a couple of his other favorites. It'll be my first time on a band bus since the Cindi-Lu Bender tour. This time it's a brand-new Prevost, so I hope we get a toilet that works. One of our stops will be the town where Dad still lives—on and off—with Rainbow, and I'll get to meet Sunshine, my little sister and Oats's auntie. Dad has been calling Allie a lot lately, and I think they're finally finding it easier to be friends. Everyone is on the tour except for Pete,

Lloyd, and SWF 34, who will hold down the fort at the Dewdrop. I'll sing backup with Allie, Hoagy's on guitar—he doesn't know it yet, but I plan to play lead on a couple of tunes—and Greg's on drums. Allie hauled out and updated her old teaching credential, required by law for working with children, so we're even legal. Then when the kids' tour is over, it will be my turn. In my spare time, rare as it is, I've been writing up a storm. I'm almost ready to record my next solo album.

THE NIGHT THE CRUSH BOMB HIT, GREG KNOCKED ON MY door and basically never left. We haven't spent a lot of time trying to define our relationship, and we've been fine, as has our sex life. We feel lucky every morning when we hear Oats running down the hall to pounce on us, ready to start the day. I adore them both. We are a family.

Bobby Lee comes around to see Oats now and then, keeping his promise to act like one of the guys. He could never quite bring himself to 'fess up to Charlotte, and I can't say I totally blame him. In some ways, it is easier now that Greg is back in the picture as leading man. I figure it's Bobby Lee's loss, and if he's too dense to realize that, that's his even bigger loss. I make every effort to be polite and friendly and keep my hurt feelings to myself. And I'm not sure I would do anything different if I were in his shoes. The only thing I find really difficult is when he starts flirting with me.

Because you know what? Just between you and me, whenever I see Bobby Lee Crenshaw, I still get that feeling, like I'm underwater and the top of my head is coming off and my heart is pounding so hard you can hear it across the room. Sometimes I dream I'm standing outside a hotel-room door holding those shoes, and it's all about to begin again. Then I wake up next to Greg and hold on for dear life while he tells me, *Shhh, it's okay, go back to sleep, it was just a dream.*

I stick to my guns with Bobby Lee because there's too much at risk. But there's powerful chemistry going on—I wonder if there will ever be a time when I'll look at him and my heart won't pound. Or maybe our world will change in some tiny way to bring us together now and then, guilt free and safe, in a garden smelling of night-blooming jasmine under the protective care of somebody's Aunt Sam, hurting no one but our own stupid selves.

Or maybe it won't.

I just haven't finished writing that song yet.

ACKNOWLEDGMENTS

Big thanks to Sandra Choron, the best agent in the world, and the whole amazing gang at Chronicle Books: Jay Schaefer, Ben Shaykin, Meg Drislane, Jan Hughes, Sarah McFall Bailey, Alicia Bergin, Steve Mockus, and Nion McEvoy. Robert Foothorap took lovely photos; Compadres Angel Martinez and Sam Barry, both wonderful writers, read every word more than once, and offered expert guidance and nonstop encouragement.

On the home front, my husband, Joe, was indulgent, patient, and knew both versions of "Silver Wings," not to mention a whole lot about our favorite music and musicians, lovingly shared. Our son, Tony, used his comic wit to help me through a couple of sticky plot problems. My parents, Betty and Si Kamen, and their colleague, Dr. Michael Rosenbaum, unearthed many of Aunt Perle's obscure health tips and, along with in-laws Bernice Goldmark and George Goldmark, offered unconditional support.

On location: In Lake County, the Fleishman and Rogers families shared their homes and friends; Cori Rogers—then age twelve—proved to be a surprisingly resourceful research assistant. Shelley and Janay at Tangles provided hair, nail, and Lake County gossip touch-ups. The folks at the Skylark Shores Motel were unfailingly helpful, as was the owner of the Buckhorn Tavern, who went so far as to give me my one and only four-hour bartending gig—tips (all $27) donated to the Lakeport library. In Nashville, I counted on Sheri Malman and guitar ace Andy Reiss to provide the kind of information that only a local would know. Jaime Brockett and Earl Crabb helped me time-travel to the Boston folk scene in the early sixties.

In addition: Cynthia Robins provided fashion advice, including Cindi-Lu's wedding gown—Richie and I both thank her. Lorraine Battle actually tasted a salsa roll-up. Audrey de Chadenedes brought flowers. Artie Blond's lame-excuse committee—Eric Brandt, Liz Winer, Perle Kinney, Alice Cutler, Lisa Steed, Gail Parenteau, and Michael Ross—did a bang-up job. Ruby Blackstock shared colorful memories of her years as a North Beach stripper, as did Patti Wylie, former Playboy Bunny. Thanks go to Kathie Grenell for the pimiento-cheese; Val Steinberg for the ride; Sheila Gordon, coincidentally; Molly Giles and Cecile Moochnek for permission; David Golia for everything; and to Steve Hanselman and the whole gang at HarperSanFrancisco.

On the bandstand: Billy Lee Lewis graciously allowed me to borrow his "Correct Time" business card. My songwriting collaborators offered the lyrics we'd written together (or in some cases, they'd written themselves)—their names appear on the special page of song credits. Big thanks to my bandmates in Train Wreck, the Ray Price Club, the Kath Sisters, the Sweethearts of the Bancroft Lounge, the Coupons, and the Enchanters, for all our musical adventures—to the Rock Bottom Remainders and Steely Dan for the road, and Roger McGuinn for the bus. Here's to Carlos, Nuggett, and Diana at DeMarco's 23 Club in Brisbane, CA . . . and, of course, to my two all-time favorite bandmates, the other Kath Sister and a certain Rhythm Dominatrix, for sweet sweet harmonies and more fun than grown-ups are supposed to be allowed to have.

Don't forget to tip your waitress. Thank you and good night.

SONGS, IN ORDER OF APPEARANCE:

"Heartaches for a Guy," performed by Sarah Jean Pixlie; lyrics by Kathi Kamen Goldmark

"My Baby Used to Hold Me (Now He's Putting Me On Hold)," performed by Sarah Jean Pixlie; lyrics by Kathi Kamen Goldmark

"Take It from Me," performed by Sarah Jean Pixlie; lyrics by Kathi Kamen Goldmark

"Jesus Is My Lawyer Now," performed by Marvella Claxton; lyrics by Kathi Kamen Goldmark and Kathleen Enright

"Magnolia Heart," performed by Cindi-Lu Bender; lyrics by Kathleen Enright

"Put Me on the Guest List (To Your Heart)," performed by Sarah Jean Pixlie; lyrics by Kathi Kamen Goldmark and Kathleen Enright

"I'm a Jet Plane," lyrics by Kathi Kamen Goldmark

"Jack's Got My Front (God's Got My Back)," performed by Sarah Jean Pixlie and Marvella Claxton; lyrics by Kathi Kamen Goldmark and Kathleen Enright

"Excitable Boy," by Warren Zevon and Marinell; performed by Sarah Jean Pixlie and her family, along with the record. Copyright © 1976 Zevon Music & All Nations Music. All rights reserved. Used by permission

"Supermarket Fantasy," performed by Dave and Michelle from Bruno's Market; lyrics by Kathi Kamen Goldmark

"You're Not My Kind of Guy," performed by Monica Boom Boom; lyrics by Kathi Kamen Goldmark and Cynthia Robins

"Billy's Accordion," performed by Sarah Jean Pixlie; lyrics by Kathi Kamen Goldmark

"Credit Card Christmas," performed by Sarah Jean Pixlie, Allie Pixlie, and Hoagy Guitarmichael; lyrics by Kathi Kamen Goldmark, Tony Goldmark, and Sam Barry

"Hell on Heels," performed by Sarah Jean Pixlie; lyrics by Kathi Kamen Goldmark and Joe Goldmark

"Hot Time Chi-Town Talkin' Blues," performed by Artie Blond; lyrics by Linda Dyer

"Cheats on One," performed by Sarah Jean Pixlie; lyrics by Kathi Kamen Goldmark

"SWF, 34," performed by Sarah Jean Pixlie and Hoagy Guitarmichael; lyrics by Kathi Kamen Goldmark and Phil Serrano, based on a personal ad by Theresa James Kamen

"Baby, She Can't Have You," performed by Lindsay Hardaway; lyrics by Kathi Kamen Goldmark

"Potty Animal," performed by Sarah Jean Pixlie and Otis Ray Pixlie; lyrics by Kathi Kamen Goldmark and Gretchen Schields

"Raise Your Head," performed by Marvella Claxton; lyrics by Kathleen Enright

"I Got My Modem Working," performed by Sarah Jean Pixlie; lyrics by Kathi Kamen Goldmark

"Tupperware Blues," performed by Sarah Jean Pixlie, Allie Pixlie, and Reverend Walter Little; lyrics by Dave Barry

"Last Call," performed by Sarah Jean Pixlie; lyrics by Kathleen Enright

"Older Than Him," performed by the Cohen Sisters (Allie and Perle); lyrics by Kathi Kamen Goldmark and Kathleen Enright